SERPENT
of
MOSES

SERPENT *of* MOSES

A NOVEL

DON HOESEL

BETHANYHOUSE
a division of Baker Publishing Group
www.BethanyHouse.com

Published by Bethany House Publishers
11400 Hampshire Avenue South
Bloomington, Minnesota 55438
www.bethanyhouse.com

Bethany House Publishers is a division of
Baker Publishing Group, Grand Rapids, Michigan

Printed in the United States of America

Library of Congress Cataloging-in-Publication Data

Hoesel, Don.
     Serpent of Moses / Don Hoesel.
         p. cm.
     ISBN 978-0-7642-0925-3 (pbk.)
         1. Archaeology teachers—Fiction. 2. Moses (Biblical leader)—Fiction. 3.
     Christian antiquities—Fiction. 4. Relics—Fiction. 5. Secret societies—Fiction.
     I. Title.
     PS3608.O4765S47 2012
     813'.6—dc23   2012004894

Scripture quotations are from the King James Version of the Bible.

This is a work of fiction. Names, characters, incidents, and dialogues are products of
the author's imagination and are not to be construed as real. Any resemblance to actual
events or persons, living or dead, is entirely coincidental.

Cover design by John Hamilton Design

Author is represented by Leslie H. Stobbe

12   13   14   15   16   17   18   7   6   5   4   3   2   1

For Dawn

1

The jeep slowed and pulled off the highway, the suspension struggling to settle the vehicle onto the narrower road that wound a barely discernible path through the hills. The night-vision binoculars in the hands of the Libyan rendered the details of the jeep with perfect clarity despite the fact that it was running with lights out. The absence of headlights suggested the man driving—the only one of the group Boufayed's team had not been able to identify—was a local who knew the terrain surrounding Tripoli well enough to navigate in the dark.

The Libyan watched as the jeep worked its way up a steep hill and then as it disappeared over the edge. Only then did he lower the binoculars and bring a phone to his ear. He said a single word before turning his eyes back down the highway, waiting for the dark SUV that had trailed the jeep from afar. It took almost half a minute before the truck came into sight and, on reaching the turnoff, pulled onto the dirt road and made the same climb as the vehicle that had preceded it. When it too disappeared, Boufayed again raised the phone.

"They are no good to us dead. Remember that," he said to the man who answered, a man who acknowledged the directive and communicated it to the others with him.

As Boufayed ended the call he looked up into the evening sky, searching for any sign of the helicopter, but he could not find it nor hear any sound of its presence.

After he slipped the phone into a pocket he remained at the top of the ridge for another moment, regarding the spot where he had lost sight of the jeep, before turning away and walking down to the waiting car. He slipped into the back of the dark sedan, and the driver started off as soon as the door was closed.

"Do we have any information on the driver yet?" Boufayed asked.

"It just came in," the other man said. "He is a local courier. No apparent foreign connections." The man looked up and caught Boufayed's eyes in the rearview mirror. "It is doubtful he knows anything about his passengers."

Boufayed grunted. "Which means he will be dead as soon as he has taken them where they want to go."

The driver did not answer but returned his eyes to the road, leaving Boufayed to again ponder the presence of the Mossad so near the capital. He thought the Israelis had been foolish to try to send them in by plane—even a small one. They had been spotted before they were ten miles past the border. It spoke of sloppiness and Boufayed was not accustomed to such from the Israelis. Nor was he used to foreign agents ferrying lettered German historians into the country.

When the car reached the highway the driver pulled onto it and aimed for the same road down which their quarry and the tail had disappeared. Boufayed looked at his watch and saw that the current time was within the acceptable engagement window, which meant that things would likely be concluded by the time he arrived.

It took the driver some time to force the sedan onto a road not meant for a vehicle of its type, but soon it was bouncing up the hill, Boufayed bracing himself with a hand on the roof in order to keep from leaving his seat. When they reached the top of the hill, all the Libyan could see was sky until the car shifted to level and then into a decline. And what Boufayed saw with that change in perspective brought a vehement curse uttered quietly enough that it was doubtful the driver heard it pass his lips.

The helicopter he had not been able to spot from the ridge was on the ground, its rotors still spinning. It had come down in the jeep's path, and the SUV had pulled in behind, pinning the Israelis and their passenger between two groups of heavily armed men. Boufayed saw the problem immediately: the helicopter had landed too close. The lack of a buffer zone did all but ensure a fight.

By the time the driver had brought the sedan to a stop within yards of the SUV, the firefight was in full force. Boufayed exited the car in time to see one of the men in the jeep slump forward. It was the driver, who likely only realized that his passengers were anything other than his standard low-profile fares when a military helicopter landed on the road in front of him.

One of the others had jumped from the jeep, strafing the

soldiers pouring out of the helicopter. But he was cut down before he'd traveled more than a few feet. That left the two men who occupied the back seat of the jeep, and Boufayed knew that despite the orders he shouted into the phone, those men would be dead in moments. A lone man stood no chance of stopping what had been loosed.

Even so, Boufayed began to move toward the jeep, his black shoes kicking up dust as he scrambled down the incline and into the line of fire. They had to take the German alive, and he considered that directive important enough to ignore the bullets that filled the air around him. As he ran Boufayed reached beneath his coat and pulled his gun.

It seemed to take a long while for him to cross the empty space between the vehicles, and with each step he waited for the inevitable, for a handful of the many rounds to find the two men who still remained in the back of the jeep. But with each step that saw the foreigners still alive, and with the growing realization among his men that Boufayed had entered the kill zone, the Libyan was beginning to hope that he might secure his prize after all.

He was within steps of the jeep, the reports of gunfire dying off, when he saw the remaining Mossad agent lurch back against the seat. It seemed to happen in slow motion with the blood beginning to flow from the man's chest. Still, the Israeli had not dropped his gun, and even as the Libyan rounds faded, Boufayed held his weapon steady on the foreign soldier. The blood came more quickly now, welling from the man's chest—too much for the wound to be anything but mortal.

With the Israeli dying, Boufayed turned his eyes to the only other survivor: the German, who wore a look that Boufayed could only identify as incredulity. The man's focus appeared to move everywhere yet seemed unable to focus on anything—until Boufayed drew near, and then the German's eyes fell on him. It was only in that moment that the Libyan allowed himself to believe he had captured his prize. He would handle the man's interrogation himself. The German would give up his secrets; he would divulge all that he knew. Boufayed would see to it.

The night air had dropped several degrees since Boufayed stood on the ridgetop watching the jeep pull off the highway, and he felt it for the first time, the crispness on his skin. It improved a mood already enhanced by the success of the mission. As he started across the last few feet separating him from Dr. Felix Hoffstratter, he found himself wearing a smile likely unsuited to the moment.

He did not register the movement right away—a shifting of position by the dying Israeli, a last flailing against the finality of what awaited him. The German himself did not seem to notice, as the man's eyes remained fixed on the approaching Libyan. A second series of movements, though, pulled Boufayed's focus away from his prize. The Mossad agent had pushed himself upright. His shirt was soaked through with blood. Boufayed could see his chest heaving as he fought to draw breath. His face, however, had taken on a look of resolve.

The Israeli looked at Boufayed, and the Libyan thought he saw a hint of a smile touch the man's lips. Then Boufayed saw the gun hand come up. Before he could react, the Israeli twisted in his seat and placed the gun against the German's temple. An instant later, a single shot scattered whatever secrets the man held.

2

After the wall in front of him exploded, Jack had a single moment to consider the one thing more frightening than the fact that people were shooting at him. It was that, if by some chance he happened to get out of the tunnel alive, Esperanza was going to kill him. Then the thought was gone, fractured by the pulverized rock that cut into the skin of his face and neck.

His eyes snapped shut against the rain of debris, causing him to slow involuntarily despite the urgency of his flight. Momentum, though, served to carry him around the curve of the tunnel and out of the immediate line of fire, where he used the flashlight in his shaking hand to find the uneven rock wall that traveled farther into the darkness than the meager light could penetrate.

An hour ago, on the way in, as he picked his way over the sloping terrain, he'd had time to choose his course with care, to ascertain the irregularities of the path and decide where to place each step in order to disperse the pain in his ankle. Now, as he scrambled to keep in front of his pursuers, he felt each step in sharp stabs that ran between ankle and knee. He'd injured the ankle during his journey in, which meant he stood no chance of avoiding further damage with caution thrown to the wind.

Jack stopped for a moment to catch his breath. He could hear voices behind him—closer than he liked—and knew his chances of staying in front of those voices for the mile that separated him from the cave exit were slim. As he started off again, the beam from the flashlight played over the ground, illuminating the multiple pairs of boot prints he'd followed deeper into the tunnel. He'd found himself irritated at the boot prints an hour ago, and not just because their existence signified the presence of other people interested in what he himself had come here for. Rather, his annoyance had come from the fact that they upset the illusion—that they robbed him of the opportunity to convince himself that his were the first feet to pass over this ancient ground in a thousand years. Cultivating that belief, false though it might be, went a long way toward stroking the ego of any respectable archaeologist. In Jack's current predicament, though, he found himself wishing he'd allowed the existence of those prints to dissuade him from entering the cave at all.

He raised the light and shook his head as the far edge of the beam tapered away without finding a wall. That indicated a long stretch of straight tunnel that would expose his back once his pursuers rounded the corner behind him. Forcing more speed into his legs, he sent his mind scrambling for anything that would increase his chances of reaching the open air of Jebel Akhdar, and the only thing that presented itself was the fork in the tunnel that served as the sole split from the main passage he'd followed in. Jack hadn't explored that rabbit hole, as the map now crumpled into a ball in his jacket pocket had kept him on the wider path. Consequently he had no idea where it went or if it provided a way out of the labyrinth that cut through the mountain. But beyond the split Jack's memory provided an image of a quarter mile of ramrod-straight rock that he knew he'd never be able to traverse before they caught him. So the fork was his only chance.

Even as he settled on that goal, he noticed the light behind him was growing stronger, which meant he was about to lose the angle that had provided him some measure of protection from the rounds that had followed him from the treasure room's antechamber. He couldn't run any faster; his breath came in ragged gasps that over time had settled into a rhythm matching the sound of his side bag slapping against his thigh. All he could think to do was to swing his pack around so that it covered the small of his back, then crouch as much as he was able without sacrificing speed. A moment later he heard the advance squad of a renewed volley.

As he cringed against an anticipated hit, and as the bullets struck the rock on either side of him, the small part of his brain that wasn't dedicated to survival picked out a single voice amid the other sounds and, if he wasn't imagining things, it sounded as if the voice's owner was imploring his companions to stop shooting. Unfortunately the command had no effect on whoever held the guns.

In front of Jack, the beam of light bounced along, giving

him just enough information to keep him from running into a wall. And on one of its upward swings he saw, about forty yards ahead, the spot where the tunnel widened to accommodate the second branch. Before he could find any hope in that realization, one of the many bullets that had tracked him for the last half mile nearly found its mark, bisecting the sliver of space between his ribs and right bicep and leaving on the latter a tangible and painful reminder of its passing.

The distraction pulled his attention away from the uneven tunnel floor, and his foot slipped into one of the many depressions that marked its surface, robbing him of balance and sending him hard into the tunnel wall. He recovered quickly, losing only a few seconds, but the incident cautioned him against presuming safety just because he could see his objective. The growing pain in his upper arm suggested that an intact arrival at the second tunnel entrance was far from guaranteed.

With that thought Jack took one last look down the tunnel, fixing the details of it in his mind. He then switched off the flashlight and flooded his way out with darkness. That done, the fleeing archaeologist straightened and poured all of his remaining energy into running faster, bringing his knees up to minimize contact with anything that could trip him up. He stretched out his left hand, finding the tunnel wall and using its light brush against his fingers to keep him centered. But despite that passing solidness there was something almost terrifying in hurtling without reservation into darkness.

Still, he pushed those thoughts aside and ran on, counting his strides. When he reached thirty he suspected he was close. Sure enough, the cold rock disappeared from under his hand.

He brought himself to a halt, feeling a moment's panic at the loss of the one thing that gave him some assurance that he would not run headlong into solid rock. He turned and backtracked the few steps to where the tunnel wall ended, then saw the diffused light from other flashlights coming up the tunnel. He knew it wouldn't take long for that light to find him, although he was thankful that his engineered blackout seemed to have temporarily halted the gunfire.

His own light still doused, Jack stepped to his right, losing sight of the approaching illumination and feeling along the rock until he found the place where it curved into the secondary tunnel. Earlier, on his way to the treasure room, as he'd passed by and briefly shined the light down the smaller passageway, he'd heard a trickle that suggested running water but hadn't seen anything. He heard it again as he started in. If his memory was accurate the tunnel took a sharp right curve several yards in, but he couldn't swear to that. So when he began his advance down the unexplored passage, it was with considerably greater care than he'd shown in exiting the last one.

Hugging the wall, he worked to put distance between himself and his pursuers. He doubted the ruse would provide complete freedom from pursuit, but even if it forced the other party to split up, sending one group toward the exit and another down the branch Jack had chosen, he would consider it a victory.

In the smaller tunnel the silence that normally pervaded the whole of the place beneath the mountain seemed to take on added weight, as if it were a physical thing—silent except for the sound of the water, growing louder now. In less than a minute he'd reached the spot where the corridor began its turn, and in the next few steps the sound of the water increased even more. He fielded an urge to use the flashlight to get a feel for what waited for him, yet he doubted he'd put sufficient distance between himself and the small chamber where the tunnels met for the light to go unnoticed.

Releasing a sigh, Jack started off again and it wasn't long before he noticed a change in the feel of the wall beneath his hand. It took a few seconds for him to realize that the soft, damp skin covering the rock was moss. It was while he was processing that fact that his foot came down in several inches of water that traveled over his shoe, drenching his sock.

He thought a curse, but stifled it before it could pass his lips. Pulling his foot from the water he took a step back and, after weighing the danger of doing so, he chanced the use of the flashlight. With his hand over the lens Jack allowed only a sliver of the beam to escape, just enough to show him what lay ahead.

Taken aback by what he saw, his hand fell away from the front of the flashlight, allowing its full strength to fill the chamber. He stood there motionless, studied the wall that marked the end of the tunnel. To his practiced eye the barrier gave every impression of having been an abandoned project, as if ancient excavators had given up once water started to trickle from the rock lest they loose the trapped reservoir behind it. Over time, though, the water had worked its way through the stone, creating several larger cracks that sent the water down the wall, where it created the stream that pooled at Jack's feet before following a gentle slope that kept the water emptying through a fissure in the ground.

It was an escape route Jack could not take. To make matters worse, the only other way out would now be blocked. It was also possible that they had sent some of their number after him.

Jack stared at the wall for a few more moments, until he heard noises behind him that had nothing to do with running water. Turning away from the wall, he dropped to a knee and swung his pack from his shoulder. Experience had taught him that when fate removed one option, a man had to move quickly to the next one. He unzipped the pack and pulled out the one item in it that lacked any connection to the practice of archaeology.

He held the gun up, bringing it into the light. For most of his professional life he'd never traveled with a gun, and even now he didn't like keeping one near. Esperanza hated it, even if she understood why he sometimes chose to take it along when he traveled. However, he hadn't fired one since Australia.

The sounds of his pursuers grew more pronounced; he knew they would have seen the glow of his light.

Jack moved to his left, putting his shoulder against the rock, and then turned off the flashlight. It took several blinks and a handful of seconds before he could see the approaching illumination displacing the darkness that surrounded him. He raised the gun and waited.

It didn't take long.

When the first of them appeared, stepping clear of the curving wall, Jack sighted on the flashlight in the man's hand. Just as the light began to turn in his direction he started to squeeze off a shot. At the last moment, though, he shifted and put the bullet into the wall a few feet to the side of the shadowy form.

With the time that had passed since the last time he'd fired a gun, Jack almost lost his grip on the weapon. The man he'd shot toward dropped the flashlight in his scramble to get out of the line of fire. Jack smiled in grim satisfaction and settled back to wait for whatever would play out next. He kept the gun raised, but no one else stepped out and he suspected the men who had chased him to this point were debating the merits of making themselves targets for a desperate archaeologist entrenched in a defensible position.

Several minutes passed in that fashion, and every so often Jack thought he heard voices over the sound of the water. However, when the minutes began to stretch out without any activity, he began to grow irritated at the delay. He was about to call out when a voice came from down the tunnel.

"So what happens now?"

The man had an accent—English, Jack thought.

"What happens is that I shoot anyone who steps around that corner," Jack called back, channeling as much confidence as he could.

The immediate response was a chuckle that Jack barely caught.

"Your last shot missed by a considerable margin," the other man said, humor in his voice. "You're either a horrible shot, in which case we might just try our luck and come in after you, or you don't have it in you to kill someone."

"That first one was a warning," Jack answered. "I won't miss a second time."

"Assuming I believe that," the Englishman said, "how do you think you're going to get out of here?"

Jack did not have a ready answer to that question. After

a pause he shrugged and said, "I haven't quite figured that part out yet."

"And while you figure it out, all we have to do is wait. We have the benefit of being able to restock once our supplies run out, so we can simply set up camp here until you starve."

"I'm not so sure about that," Jack said. "Unless you have a pass from the Libyan government, which I'm guessing isn't the case, then you're in the middle of an illegal antiquities operation. Are you really going to wait around and hope the local authorities don't stumble in here while you're waiting for me to die?"

There was no response to his question.

"You know, I didn't even get what I was after," Jack went on. "So, to be honest, I'm not sure why you're concerned with me anyway. The staff is still back there."

Even as he said it, he knew they wouldn't take his word for it. They'd been looking in the wrong place, and the bullets had started flying before they could have gotten a good look at what he was doing. They wouldn't let him go until they assured themselves that he didn't have the artifact.

"I'm sure it is," the Englishman said. "The problem is that I have a few friends with me who are not so trusting."

"Are these the same friends who shoot before making proper introductions?"

"Sadly lacking in social skills," the Englishman conceded. "And that might be why they're discussing where to place the C-4 that will bring the entire cavern down on you."

Jack didn't reply to that. Instead he squatted in the dark, his gun at the ready, wondering if they could possibly have an explosive. He thought the odds were against it. As a general rule, things like C-4 seldom lent themselves to the discipline of archaeology. Too, if they were not content to let him go for fear that he had the artifact, he considered it unlikely they would bury him beneath several tons of rock.

As he considered that, he saw a flash of movement—something flying out from behind the wall and landing on the ground.

"That's so you don't think I'm making up the bit about the C-4," the Englishman shouted. A few seconds later a beam of light emerged from the enemy cover to illuminate it. The object was gray and about the size and shape one would expect C-4 to look like. "There's plenty more where that came from."

Jack had to concede that if it was a bluff, it was a good one—one that left him with few options. Even so, it took almost a full minute before he pushed himself away from the wall, struggled to his feet, and after thumbing the safety in place, tossed the gun a few yards in front of him. The second the weapon left his hand, doubt washed over him and he wondered if he'd just made a terrible mistake. Yet he fought the urge to go after the gun.

"That was the sound of me tossing my gun away," he said.

There was no immediate response, and Jack was about to make the announcement again when a lone figure stepped into view. Even with multiple lights in his face muddling his perspective he could see that the man was enormous. That impression was solidified when three other men joined the larger one, all of them dwarfed by the first. As the parties regarded each other, the previous feeling Jack had entertained—the one that told him he'd made a mistake—returned

22

with a vengeance. While he was already late getting back to Caracas, he suspected his current circumstances would make him a good deal later—if he got there at all.

"I have a friend who's going to be really upset about this," Jack said, adopting a rueful smile.

At that, a man standing to the right of the giant took a step forward. Almost blind, Jack could make out nothing of the man's features, though he suspected it was the Englishman.

"We all have friends who are angered by the choices we make, Dr. Hawthorne," he said.

"You don't understand," Jack said with a headshake. "You've never seen Espy angry."

The Englishman did not respond right away, but Jack could intuit the smile he wore.

"And you haven't met Imolene," the Englishman said.

Then the giant began to move toward Jack, who only in that moment thought to wonder how the Englishman knew his name.

3

As his captors marched Jack back along the route down which he'd fled, he decided that being forced to endure the indignity of retracing his steps bothered him almost as much as the pain of his minor bullet wound. Yet he couldn't blame anyone but himself, as Mukhtar had warned him of these men before Jack left Al Bayda. Four men—three of them European, one Mukhtar had guessed was Egyptian. They'd slipped into and out of the city with a quietness that suggested a desire for secrecy, and when one required certain types of items, such items often had to pass through Mukhtar's hands. And that suggested they were after the same thing Jack was. Even so, Jack had kept on task, intent on being the first to touch the artifact in perhaps a thousand years.

He hadn't realized he'd slowed until the large man—whom the Englishman had called Imolene—placed a hand between Jack's shoulder blades and shoved. Jack tightened his lips against the rough handling but remained quiet. Instead, he focused all his attention on the tunnel ahead, seen now in greater detail with the addition of three more flashlights.

His research told him this cavern slicing through the mountainous part of northeastern Libya had existed since at least the time of Cyrene, and he suspected the ancient Greeks had used it for defense, even as modern Libyans had used it to resist the Italian occupation. By his estimation the tunnel through which he walked was at least two centuries older than the others he'd explored in the area. Whoever built it had taken great pains to hide the entrance. It had been cut into the mountain at an angle so that the shadow falling across the opening gave it the appearance of a much narrower fissure. Hours ago, walking toward it, knowing he was heading in the right direction, he could not find the opening against the brown and gray rock until he was right on top of it. The experience made him wonder if, unlike most secret places surrounded by encroaching civilization, this one might have remained unspoiled.

"This tunnel is older than the others," the Englishman remarked. It was the first thing any of them had said in some time, and Jack was taken aback by how the comment mirrored his own thoughts.

"At least two centuries older," he agreed.

The Englishman walking next to him offered Jack a smile but didn't say anything more. When they'd started out, Jack had asked his name and, failing to receive a response, pressed the man further as to how he knew Jack's. That question had also gone unanswered.

They walked on for another twenty minutes, until Jack began to notice a change in the light. He guessed the darkness in the tunnel had been lightening for some time, but so gradually that he hadn't picked up on it. Up ahead, he could see the place where the tunnel curved to the left, leading to the antechamber he'd been forced from before having the chance to do anything other than have a look around.

At the thought of what lay beyond the curve, Jack's feet began to move faster. Despite the circumstances that occasioned his return to the cavern, he had no more control over his growing excitement than he did his own breathing. It was a feeling tied to a need to uncover the secrets hidden within the chamber regardless of all else. It was what had brought him back to the field after what had happened in Egypt, and what had kept him there following the events in Australia.

Moments later they reached the turn where, just ten yards more, the cavern opened up before them. Jack hadn't realized he'd stopped until Imolene propelled him forward, moving toward a ten-foot drop-off to the cavern floor, where a rope ladder provided by Mukhtar awaited. As Jack waited his turn, the Englishman and another of his associates preceding him down the ladder, he kept a wary eye on Imolene, lest the man find that one final shove was sufficient to get Jack where he wanted him. In this case, though, the giant exercised patience. With the ladder clear, Jack turned and swung his legs over the side.

The cavern was thirty yards across at its widest point, stretching twice that to the back wall. The four battery-powered floodlights his predecessors had wrangled through the darkness barely reached those boundaries and did even less to illuminate the ceiling a hundred feet above them.

When he'd arrived in the cavern the first time, the other

men now in his company had passed through and taken a smaller tunnel into the treasure room, as the original designers had intended. Jack had hoped to use their preoccupation to his advantage by taking what they wanted right out from under their noses. In covert archaeology, however, timing was everything, and Jack's timing hadn't been as perfect as he'd counted on.

"I'm assuming the treasure room was a misdirection," the Englishman said.

Jack didn't reply. Instead, he swung his pack around so he could raise the flap and slip his hand inside. Only when he felt Imolene's huge hand on his shoulder—with enough strength to let Jack know he could crush every bone beneath his fingers—did he look over at the Englishman, who shook his head, his eyes on his enforcer. Jack felt the man's grip ease and so returned his attention to his pack. He pulled out a notebook, flipped it open, studied it for a few moments, and then, without consulting his captors, started off toward the cavern's far wall, which was opposite the exit to the treasure room.

As he neared the corner, the others trailing close behind, his eyes ran along the wall, noting the unnatural smoothing of the surface by ancient tools, the intricate patterns carved into the rock. His first time through, he'd made it no farther before being discovered.

The lights did little to lessen the shadows, forcing him to pluck a flashlight from the hand of one of the Europeans in the party, a man who had not uttered a single syllable since Jack had been forced to join their group. Though the man frowned at losing his light, he remained mute. After looking at the notebook again, Jack began to run the light over the wall. It took him several seconds to find the focal glyph. While that vexed him, it also elicited respect for the ancient puzzle makers who had designed the system, who had set up the false treasure room where the others had wasted their time.

Slipping the notebook back into his pack, he used his free hand to wipe away the centuries of dust that had accumulated on the wall, revealing Semitic text, part of which matched what was written in a scroll he'd pulled from the sarcophagus of the Archbishop Giovanni Visconti in the Milan Cathedral. With a smile of gratitude that the effort to procure that scroll had not been in vain, he ran a finger over the text, his lips moving as he did the calculations. He did them twice just to be sure, and once he was certain of the result, it was all he could do to stop himself from putting the data to use.

Instead, he held back the thing inside of himself that desperately wanted to see his research and labor rewarded and stepped away from the wall, looking toward the Englishman.

"Here's where we decide how we're going to work this so you get what you came for and I get out of here in one piece," Jack said.

The Englishman did not answer right away, but Jack had the impression he'd been awaiting the statement.

"I'm not sure you're in a position to bargain," he said.

"Probably not," Jack acknowledged. "But since the odds are good that you're going to kill me as soon as you have it in your hands, then it's probably my only option."

The other man granted that to Jack with a nod.

"Except that I believe you're overestimating your worth," he said. "Now that we know it's not in the treasure room, and as we would also have possession of your notebook if you were dead, it would only be a matter of time before we found it ourselves."

"Which would at least be a moral victory," Jack said. "If I'm going to die anyway, I'd rather you do some of the work."

The Englishman's lip curled. "But then you would miss the opportunity to see something that no one else has seen in a thousand years."

It was the one thing his captor could have said that stood a chance of enlisting Jack's help, and he did not have a ready response beyond a rekindling of the excitement that had ebbed over the last few minutes. To get as far as he had, to have waded through the research and traveled half the world until he was finally standing in a cave in Libya, and then to be denied the chance to see, to touch the thing he sought, was difficult to swallow.

While he did not respond, he could see that the Englishman could read his thoughts.

"Relax. No one's going to kill you, Dr. Hawthorne. This is about the staff, nothing more."

There was no way to test the truth of that statement, so Jack didn't try. He returned his attention to the wall and located the glyph. Then, using the symbol for its assigned purpose, he counted through the other symbols for the right spot. The one he landed on looked no different than the others, though he would have expected nothing else.

He tapped it once before reaching into his pack and pulling out a small hammer. After a glance at Imolene, to make sure the giant would not snatch the tool from him and use it for some purpose for which it was not intended, he struck the wall, the sound echoing in the chamber. It took a second strike before the hammer went through the thin stone and into the hollow beneath it. A feeling of exultation coursed through him, but he pushed that aside and began to pull away the shattered pieces, revealing a hole less than eight inches across. It took less than a minute to remove the shards, and once he'd cleared the hole he put his hand in, all the while wondering if the men behind him would allow him to do the honors or if they would pull him away now that his usefulness was expended. When no hands closed on him, he decided to reach into the opening.

His hand touched something coarse yet malleable. It took him a moment to recognize it as fabric, but then he felt the solid thing it encased. He tightened his grip and tugged, expecting some resistance but finding none. The thing slid out as if coated in oil—long and slender, wrapped in timeworn linen.

In that moment Jack was alone in the cavern.

He held the artifact up, his eyes bright with the pure joy that came from such a discovery. It was the right size, yet the only way to be sure was to remove the wrappings. That, however, was an honor he would not be allowed.

As he turned away from the wall he felt the hands on him, an arm wrapping around his chest. The Englishman stepped forward and took the artifact from Jack's hands, an apologetic smile his only payment. An instant later the rock wall from which Jack had just pulled the relic came rushing forward, and then all was blackness.

4

When Esperanza entered the store, the violence with which she thrust open the door displayed the anger she'd carried with her from her office and through the streets of Caracas. Even as she let the door swing shut behind her, she reminded herself that none of this was Romero's fault.

Romero, on the other side of the store and with his back to her, did not turn away from his customer to see who had entered. From Esperanza's position, she could just make out the Campeche stele artifact Romero was showing the man, and she guessed the price of the piece hovered in the level most people would call obscene. Romero, though, seldom dealt with anyone unprepared to drop that sort of money. And despite the anger that had brought Esperanza there, she kept close to the door until he completed the transaction.

Her brother—the proprietor of the high-end antiquities shop situated off Bolivar Avenue in the Caracas business district—did just that, with Esperanza picking up only bits and pieces of the conversation but getting the impression the customer was thrilled with the stele and would likely have paid more than what Romero had asked for it. Not long after the handshake and necessary delivery arrangements, the well-dressed gray-haired man was gone, aiming a conspirator's smile at Esperanza as he left. The smile was mirrored by Romero as he turned to watch the man exit through the metal door that would take him down to street level. Only when the door swung shut behind him did Romero turn his attention to his sister, giving her a once-over before crossing the room.

"It's none of my business," he told her.

"He's late," Esperanza said.

"He's always late, Espy."

"Which is exactly my point," she said, her voice rising. She saw her brother frown and offered him an apologetic shrug, to which he responded with a smile.

"When you are in one of these moods I'm used to my customers suddenly remembering other places they need to be, so this is an improvement."

For some reason, she found Romero's remark irritating, and with a flash of her eyes she ignored it and walked over to a display of Saxon pottery, which like everything else in his store was arranged with taste and simplicity, the items charged with selling themselves.

"When was he expected back?" Romero asked.

"Two days ago." Espy's small hand reached for a dish that she knew her brother would only sell with the complete set.

"For Jack, getting back anywhere within three days of when he told you counts as being on time."

Espy looked up from studying the pottery and fixed her

brother with a look she suspected he knew well. It was a look that would have caused others to walk gingerly around the rest of the conversation. But Romero simply sighed. He looked as if he would speak, and Esperanza waited for whatever sage advice he would render, but before a single word left his lips his mouth snapped shut and he shook his head.

"I'm not getting involved," he said after several seconds. "The two of you are adults and should be able to work this out on your own."

Esperanza nodded. "I'm finally doing what I should have done three years ago." At Romero's raised eyebrow, she explained, "I'm done with him strolling in weeks after he says he'll be back, and then disappearing again on a whim. I mean, when you think about it, our relationship right now is just like it was before he left to teach. Nothing's changed."

Even as she said it, she knew her accusation was not entirely true. After all, they'd both returned from Australia markedly different. With all that had happened during the hunt for the bones—an odyssey in which Jack had made her a participant—how could they not have been changed in some profound ways?

She had lapsed into silence, her eyes on the ancient text that covered much of the pottery, a language that, unlike most of Romero's customers, she could read. She'd almost forgotten her brother was in the room until he spoke.

"I can't pretend to understand everything that happened between the two of you when he was working for Reese," he said. "But what I do know is that Jack returned from that job a different person." He paused and added, "And so did you."

Espy turned to face Romero, his words pulling a small

smile from her. "I thought you weren't going to get involved," she reminded him.

"I'm taking a calculated risk that my involvement will get you out of my store sooner than would my silence."

"Touching," she said, turning her back on him and making a pretense of studying the pottery again.

"Where is he?" Romero asked. "I remember something about Europe?"

"His itinerary had him in Milan and then London. He was supposed to be back on Tuesday."

"And when he finally does return?"

"I'm not waiting for that," Espy said.

Romero raised his eyebrow again, except that this time Esperanza could detect a hint of worry in the expression.

"He's out of chances," she said. "And I'm going to make sure he knows that—on my terms."

"Which means?"

"Which means I'm catching a plane this afternoon. I'll be in London by tomorrow morning."

It was one of the few times Esperanza could remember her brother rendered speechless, and she enjoyed watching the progression of thought visible on his face.

"Aside from calling him to find out where he is, which would undoubtedly ruin the effect you're trying to achieve, how will you orchestrate this unhappy rendezvous?"

"Sturdivant," Espy said.

She saw Romero frown and then follow that up with a thoughtful nod. "He's selling to the museum, then?"

"Technically he was supposed to have already done that, but he's three days late for that meeting."

At that, Romero offered a sly smile. "At least you have the comfort of knowing you're not the only one who suffers from Jack's fluid relationship with time."

She responded with a smirk. "I can't wait to see his face when he shows up at the museum."

"*If* he shows up," Romero said. "It's not uncommon for Jack to miss appointments."

Esperanza's head was shaking before Romero finished. "Not when there's money involved," she reminded him. "He might be late but he'll always show."

She knew Romero had to grant her that, and he did with a resigned sigh. She suspected there was a good deal more he wanted to say, but he knew her well enough to realize that none of it would matter.

5

They'd retreated to a small village seventeen kilometers out-side of Al Bayda, and while fires burned in several of the small homes on the fringe of the desert, the night felt as complete as any Martin had ever experienced. He'd traveled enough to know that little could compare to the isolation of a Middle Eastern village, the thought of the desert stretch-ing for hundreds of miles beyond the border. The night here always impressed him with its weight.

But it was something with which he was familiar, and so he could not blame it for his inability to sleep. Instead, he was forced to place that unease where it belonged—on the occasion of a simple plan that had gone awry.

From a purely logistical standpoint he understood that his big mistake had been in letting others—namely Imolene—convince him not to let Hawthorne go. In retrospect, that was exactly what he should have done. He and his team should have come out of the cave with their trophy and allowed Dr.

Hawthorne to go his own way. There'd been no reason to keep him once they'd recovered the artifact. In truth, Martin didn't begrudge Hawthorne the attempt at stealing it out from under their noses. From what he knew about the man, he would have expected nothing less.

But he'd allowed Imolene to talk him into holding Hawthorne, though it was true the Egyptian did not have to twist his arm much. In fact, the moment Martin recognized the man, he'd marveled at the unlikelihood that he'd been dropped in his path. Either way, once he understood who had encroached on their operation, he'd known that there would be no simple cessation of that acquaintance.

For Imolene, it was a matter of leaving no witnesses. He'd reminded Martin who it was that had hired them to liberate the artifact from its thousand-year-old tomb, and what they would expect him to do with a witness who could recount details of the recovery and pick the principals out of a lineup. As far as Martin was concerned, it wasn't that simple, because the man who had been dropped in his path was perhaps the only person on the planet who could supply answers to questions that he himself had been pondering for the last three years.

He knew the rumors—that Australian police had held Dr. Jack Hawthorne on suspicion of murder and theft. How those charges had been dropped, with the American allowed to leave the country. And how the records of all those involved were later sealed.

Hawthorne had been on his radar since then and, as if making up for Martin's failure to track the man down and demand answers, it seemed some cosmic force had initiated the introductions for him.

Once they'd gotten off the mountain, the renowned archaeologist trussed up between the ones named Benton and Phillips,
they'd skirted Al Bayda and driven the jeep directly to the village. They'd left their gear in the cavern, and Martin wondered
if any of it would ever be found. When they'd entered the cavern
he'd felt as if his were the first steps across that ground in many
centuries and he found it easy to believe that another century
might pass before someone else stumbled upon it.

He reached for the glass of wine he'd poured but not
touched. He downed half of it in one draught and then, releasing a deep sigh, rose from the table. The room had one
small window, and he crossed to it and looked out onto the
empty dirt lane that bisected the village. Not a soul moved
out there and he could hear nothing coming from the adjoining room. He suspected he was the only one awake, except
perhaps for Dr. Hawthorne. And if the man was awake he was
no doubt wondering what had happened—how the retrieval
of an ancient artifact had ended with violence and captivity.

Turning his back to the window, Martin let his eyes fall
on the bundle at the foot of the cot. He'd studied it for some
time after retreating to the room, holding it in his hands,
trying his best to make out the text along its slim length and
having only limited success.

He only knew bits and pieces about the artifact, yet that
didn't stop him from appreciating it. The age and mystery
of an item about which even the biblical record had little to
say. He couldn't help wondering if the people for whom he
had procured the artifact knew much more about it than did
he, aside from the fact that it was a part of their history in
a way it could never be for him.

He moved back to the table, picked up the wineglass, and drained it. He'd meant it as a celebratory bottle, one to be shared with the others after successfully taking the artifact, but that was no longer appropriate. He set the glass down and glanced at the bottle, thought of finishing it. Instead, he replaced the cork, doused the lamp on the table, and started to make his way to the cot set against the wall opposite the door, resolving to get at least a few hours of sleep before he had to make a decision in the morning.

He had just settled onto the cot when he heard a knock at the door, which opened even before the sound had finished echoing in the small space. As the dim light produced by the lamp in the adjoining room filtered in, it silhouetted the Egyptian, and despite the fact that Martin seldom felt fear, he sensed something akin to it touch him now.

"Yes?" he said when it seemed Imolene would not move from the threshold.

Yet the silence stretched on after his inquiry, forcing Martin to remain still, to avoid the appearance of unease.

Finally the large Egyptian stepped into the room. With a lighter pulled from his breast pocket he relit the lamp Martin had just extinguished. That accomplished, Imolene turned and closed the door, Martin using that time to rise from the cot and take a step toward the table.

"We must decide what to do with him," Imolene said as the door latch clicked. When he turned back to face Martin he regarded his employer with an expression Martin could not read.

"And we will," Martin answered. He paused and tried to study the Egyptian, but as had been the case since the day the man had joined the team, he remained inscrutable. "The problem is that you don't just get rid of someone like Jack Hawthorne. Killing him will bring us more attention than we want right now. And believe me, the Israelis don't want that kind of attention."

Even at that, the statue that was Imolene did not say anything right away. After a few long moments he took a single step further into the room and asked, "And who is this Hawthorne that we could not put a bullet in him back in the cavern?"

It wasn't the nature of the question that caused Martin's eyes to widen; he'd come to expect cold appraisals from the Egyptian. Rather, it was the content of it that surprised him, because it indicated that Imolene did not understand the importance of the man they held.

"You're kidding," he said, but one look at Imolene told him that wasn't the case. Despite himself, he released a harsh laugh and then took a seat at the table. "What you don't realize is that we're holding one of the most well-known archaeologists of our time."

Imolene did not move, nor did his expression change.

"Over the last three years Jack Hawthorne has done more to further the understanding of a connection between ancient Egyptian and Mayan cultures than anyone in history," Martin said.

At that, Martin saw the other man's face change at last. Imolene might have been a hired gun, but he was an educated one, especially when it came to his own culture.

"He is the one who is said to have been involved in the incident in Australia?" Imolene asked.

Martin nodded. "Nothing much came of it, but whatever happened there, it's credited with taking Hawthorne out of the classroom and back into the field."

Imolene appeared to ponder that, his eyes fixed on the cot Martin had vacated. "I still do not understand how keeping him alive is less dangerous to us than killing him and taking his body out into the desert." The Egyptian shifted his gaze to Martin. "Unless, perhaps, there is some reason why keeping him alive serves us."

The statement gave Martin pause. He wondered if Imolene had discerned whether there was something more at play than a professional interest in Hawthorne.

"I think the Israelis are the ones who have to make that call," Martin said.

It was a perfectly reasonable response, since they were the ones paying the bills, but Imolene still seemed unconvinced. However, rather than question Martin further, the Egyptian turned soundlessly on his heel and left him sitting there alone. After he closed the door and Martin once again extinguished the lamp, the darkness that filled the room held a quality that promised him a fitful night's sleep.

There was little Jack knew for sure, but the one thing he felt most solid about was that he was in a populated area. The smell alone told him that—the odors of cooking, animals, and of commingled humans. But the lack of significant noise told him he was in a village rather than a larger town. A safe house some distance from Al Bayda. Whatever his captors had tied around his face, though, didn't allow him to validate that hypothesis.

He didn't know how long he'd been out but suspected it was less than a few hours, and it would have taken his captors a good portion of that to bring him down off the mountain. He'd been awake for around twenty minutes and had done his best to remain still, to try to get a feel for his surroundings before anyone knew he was conscious. He couldn't be certain but he thought that someone shared the room with him. After coming to, he'd heard movement, the sound of a door opening, the hum of conversation, then what sounded like someone coming back into the room. He hadn't heard anyone leave, and things had been silent for a while now. He thought he'd heard other noises coming from farther away, yet even those sounds had stopped now, leaving a silence that seemed as if it might stretch into forever.

He remained still for several more minutes, which taxed his resolve as the hard floor and awkward position had generated a sharp pain in his side, along with an arm that he knew would go through a severe bout of pins and needles once he was able to extricate it from beneath him. After a while, the fact that he couldn't concentrate on anything but his growing discomfort forced Jack to test the waters.

His first effort involved trying to move his hands, which were pulled behind his back. He raised his eyebrows when he felt what appeared to be a full range of motion; his captors hadn't bound him. The surprise gave way to a sigh, though, when he realized the lack of bonds hinted at a prison secure enough to render secondary measures unnecessary.

He took a breath and tried to push himself up, grimacing

against the pain. His first attempt was unsuccessful, but a second try brought him upright. And while that position was the one that offered him the best chance of escaping, it also sent a wave of pain through his skull. He frowned beneath whatever blocked his vision as the reason for the sudden headache came back to him.

He wondered where the man was who had pushed him into the wall. It was a sobering thought that did much to get him moving. His hands free, he raised them to his head and found the edge of the fabric that blinded him, but it was pulled too tightly for him to work his fingers in. He moved to the back and found the knot and tried to find someplace to loosen it. Several seconds of worrying with it produced nothing aside from accentuating the pain in his side. Irritated, he again moved his hands around to the front, grabbed as much of the fabric as he could with his fingertips and yanked downward with all of his strength, rewarded when he was able to liberate his eyes.

The problem was that all that greeted him was darkness.

With the blindfold resting on his nose, he squinted into the blackness but couldn't see anything. Instead of moving, he stayed where he was, letting his eyes adjust. It seemed like a long time before he could differentiate one shadow from another, disparate shapes that could have been anything. And once he'd decided that the shapes wouldn't resolve any more than they already had, he began to move.

Jack stood on legs that rebelled against the effort, and the pain in his ankle came back with a vengeance. He wobbled a bit but steadied himself with a hand against the wall next to him. The surface under his fingers was rough, likely cement, bits of it crumbling beneath his touch.

He took a few careful steps, mindful of kicking anything, and irritated that his eyes were taking their time adjusting. He walked the length of the wall, skirting what felt like a wooden chair, and when he reached the corner he started down the adjoining wall. While this one offered no obstacles, neither did it provide a door. When he found the third wall he again changed direction, his easy passage thus far causing him to walk faster—which added to the pain when his shin came into contact with something solid.

Peering into the darkness, he could make out a long irregular shape, like a table with several items piled on top. He was starting to walk around it when the table moved. Jack took an involuntary hop away before he registered he'd done so. Consequently he allowed plenty of room for whatever he'd bumped his shin on to resolve into a much taller shadow that looked decidedly man shaped.

A very large man.

After a few moments during which neither Jack nor the apparition made a move, the other man took a step forward. There was something about the way he advanced, the outline of the body coming into sharper focus, that tugged at the archaeologist. But it wasn't until the other man had closed even further that Jack realized his eyes were finally becoming accustomed to the darkness, for he could now clearly see some of the man's features.

It took a few seconds before the familiarity of that face impressed itself upon him, but when it did, Jack released a sigh that was more resignation than anything else.

"That's just great," he said, then braced himself as a massive fist plotted a course for his face.

6

He couldn't help wondering why they hadn't just tied his hands in the first place. It would have saved him a lot of trouble, as well as an additional accumulation of injuries. Provided all of his options were stripped from him, Jack could settle into a good wait, but when left with a chance at extricating himself from a situation he would avail himself of it. Had they bound him securely the first time he would have been content to let things play out. They'd learned their lesson; not only were his hands fastened behind him this time, they'd also wrapped the end of the line around one of the wooden beams that ran the length of the ceiling.

At least they'd not bothered with the blindfold.

The room had lightened as the sun rose, the light finding its way in through the gaps in the lone shuttered window above the cot. He guessed the window looked out on the street because he heard sounds of industry filtering in along with the light. Below the window the cot was empty, though it hadn't been for long. Jack had watched Imolene get up some ten minutes before and exit the room without so much as a glance at his captive. Even in the dim light Jack had been able to get a better look at the man than he'd been afforded up to now. While he couldn't tell for certain if he was Egyptian just by looking at him, as Mukhtar had said, he was definitely of a similar ethnicity. But what really stood out was his size; he seemed larger to Jack now that he'd seen him against the room's furnishings. He was built like Romero, only this man had at least four inches on Jack's solidly built Venezuelan friend.

When the door had opened Jack had tried to see what lay beyond it, but whatever room it opened up to was no more lit than the one he was in. He had the impression it was a thin hallway, with the faint outline of another door directly across from the one Jack's captor had just walked through.

Now that he was alone, Jack felt a little more at ease, as he'd found it difficult to relax with the equivalent of a hungry lion sleeping in a cot mere feet away. However, his newfound solitude also brought some obvious questions to the surface, such as when would these people let him use the bathroom?

Pushing that thought away, he closed his eyes and leaned back against the wall.

Imolene only looked out of place on the street because of his boots. Expensive, and with their newness marred by only the dust of the last few days, they provided a stark contrast to the shabbier footwear of those he passed. By the standards of most African nations Libya was prosperous, much of it as modern as an American suburb. However, the nation could never divest itself entirely of a history that those of the Western world could never understand—a history extending back to the birth of civilization. In such a place, where humans had staked a claim millennia ago and had yet to relinquish it, evidence of that great history was everywhere, including villages like this one, where its residents clung to the old in the shadow of the new.

Though it was early, the streets were filled with people. Imolene drew many eyes and not solely because he was a stranger. The village was large enough to draw visitors from many places and for many reasons. Most would earn little notice. Most, however, were not as large as Imolene.

The Egyptian walked until he found an open café, which he entered and bought a cup of the strong coffee native to the region. Coffee in hand, he walked outside and took a seat at one of the tables lining the weathered brick of the long building of which the café was only one of many establishments. For a while he did nothing but drink his coffee, watching the people who passed, unconcerned that Templeton and the rest might leave without him. When he'd left the house he'd heard nothing from Templeton's room, and in checking on the others he'd found them still sleeping. He would likely be back before they stirred.

As for Hawthorne, Imolene had tied the man's bonds himself. The American would not move until Imolene was instructed to move him. The night before, watching Hawthorne stumble his way around the room had been a bit of amusement for the Egyptian. In retrospect, he should not have done that. Amusing though it had been, there was always a chance that something could have gone wrong, that Hawthorne might have escaped. Yet it had felt good to hit him a second time.

The Egyptian remained at the table, unmoving, until he'd finished the rest of the coffee. Only then did he retrieve his phone from a pocket and dial the number he'd been given.

Imolene brought his employer up to speed on the events of the last twenty-four hours. He gave his report while understanding there was only one detail that really mattered. "We found it" was the Egyptian's subdued acknowledgment of their success.

Part of his lack of emotion, despite the completion of such a difficult quest, was due to the fact that there was something in Imolene that disliked working for the Israelis. While their money was as good as that of others, it would come with a feeling of having betrayed his own. Still, he would do the job he'd been hired to do; he refused to see the reputation he'd taken great pains to cultivate ruined because of ideological differences.

He could hear the pleasure in the other man's voice, and that told Imolene it was the appropriate time to tell him about the part of the expedition that had not gone as planned. When he imparted the news of the captured American the other man fell silent.

"Where have I heard that name?" the Israeli asked, his Arabic passable but heavily accented.

"I am told the man is a well-known archaeologist," Imolene said. "Templeton seems reluctant to deal with him."

Again there was a moment of silence, during which Imolene

knew the other was examining options. The Egyptian understood how much a witness of any kind changed things; how much more so when that witness had a recognizable face. What Imolene suspected would not factor into the decision was the morality of any choice. If the man who had hired him was affiliated with the organization within the Israeli government that Imolene thought he was, then moral equivocation was the norm.

When the silence had stretched to the point at which Imolene was tempted to speak again, he finally received his instructions, delivered in the nonspecific way Imolene had come to expect from this man.

"We cannot afford any complications."

After ending the call he rose and started back to the safe house. The day was already growing hot by the time he reached the house. When he entered he heard nothing. It always amazed him that westerners habitually slept through the best part of the day, missing out on the cool morning breeze, to be replaced before long by hot desert winds. He almost felt bad that none of them would have the opportunity to experience a sunrise again.

Benton and Phillips had pitched their bedrolls in the only other room of the small house, beyond the ones Templeton and Imolene had claimed. It was the living area, where a local family would have gathered for meals and to receive guests. Unlike the two sleeping chambers, no door separated this larger room from the dark hallway. Imolene took a single step into the room and stopped, studying both sleeping men. When he moved again his steps were swift and quiet, and the large knife made no sound when it slid from its sheath.

He opened Benton's throat to the air while the man still dreamed, and was kneeling beside Phillips before the gurgling behind him had ceased. Moments later, Phillips too was dead. Imolene wiped his knife clean on a blanket and then went to finish the rest of his work.

He paused by the two doors that would take him into the remaining sleeping chambers, pondering which to enter first. The only logical choice, though, was Templeton. Hawthorne was bound; he could see Imolene coming yet it wouldn't matter.

The door opened without a sound and the Egyptian spotted the Englishman's rumpled form on the cot, the man so still he looked to be barely breathing. Before he moved, he cast his eyes about for the artifact, spotting it on the floor at the foot of the cot, which seemed to Imolene a slight to the seeming importance of it.

Imolene crossed the room, gratified for the dirt floor that rendered his steps soundless. When he reached the cot he could not see beneath the blanket pulled up over the man's head. He raised the knife, and when he brought it down he did so with sufficient strength to ensure he would not have to strike twice.

He understood that something was amiss before the blade stopped moving. Lightning quick he pulled the knife back and wrenched the blanket away, revealing Templeton's long canvas travel bag. He had but a moment to process that before he saw a hint of movement behind him. Before he could straighten and turn, he felt something strike his head. Then he was falling.

Martin stood looking down on Imolene, who had fallen to his knees, his upper body resting on the cot. The Englishman still held the wine bottle in his hand, instinctively cocked for another blow. But Imolene did not budge. In that respect he was like Martin, who stood rooted to the spot, his heart racing. He knew he needed to get moving, but like the arm frozen with the bottle poised to strike, his legs remained fixed. On some level he knew his fight or flight response was malfunctioning, that he was caught somewhere between the two choices, and this knowledge enabled him to concentrate on slowing his intake of breath.

Seconds later he sprang into action, the bottle dropped onto the cot next to the man who would have killed him. He leaned over Imolene and removed the knife from his hand. For a moment he thought of finishing it; it would make things easier. He moved his hand toward the Egyptian's throat but hesitated, which was enough to tell him he couldn't do it. Pulling the knife back he scooped up his travel bag and then moved to the foot of the bed, where he retrieved the artifact. He straightened and, after a last look at Imolene, left the room.

One of the things Jack had learned over the years was that certain situations served to strip one's needs down to the most basic level. It was a lesson that had served him well at times, helped him to focus on what was truly important. On other occasions, however, it was a much more empirical philosophy, because at the moment the only thing occupying his mind was how much he needed to find a bathroom.

He'd toyed with the idea of calling out, but the thought of causing the large angry man to return and hit him over the head again wasn't appealing. But if no one came back soon he would be left between that and another unenviable choice.

He leaned back against the wall, trying to take his mind off the discomfort. Just as he closed his eyes he heard a noise from somewhere beyond the door. His first thought was that he'd heard a door slam shut. Moments later, when he didn't hear anything else and when no one entered the room to hit him again, he resettled himself. He was just entering that place where he could feel himself beginning to doze when the door slammed open.

Startled, Jack launched himself away from the wall, forgetting the bonds that yanked him back, stretching his arms in a direction they weren't meant to go. With his attention pulled to the door, and to the man who stood there, wild eyes moving around the room, he was able to ignore the pain.

While the man was lit from behind, Jack recognized him as the one from the cavern, the Englishman who had called him by his name. The man who stood before him now, though, was a lot tenser than the one he'd spoken with beneath the earth.

Jack was about to ask him if he would let him use the bathroom when his captor began to rush forward in his direction. His speed and the way he looked back over his shoulder before kneeling in front of his prisoner told Jack that something had happened that had changed the balance of things.

"It looks like you've got a lot on your mind," Jack said, "but I could really use a tour of your facilities."

Even as Jack asked the question, the other man scooted to the side and reached for the ropes binding the archaeologist's hands, his mind clearly somewhere else. But when Jack's question worked its way through his other concerns he glanced up.

"Come again?" he asked.

Jack offered a half smile. "The bathroom," he said.

His captor nodded and gave another tug, yet the bonds would not loosen. Then, with the look of someone just remembering something, he reached into the canvas bag he'd dropped in front of Jack and withdrew a large knife from one of its pockets.

Jack's eyes widened as it passed in front of his face, close enough for him to see the red now drying to brown on the blade.

"On second thought, I can hold it," he said.

The man ignored him and brought the knife around behind Jack, where he began to work on the portion holding the archaeologist to the overhead beam. Jack, who considered this an improvement of sorts to his present circumstances, kept his mouth shut while the man worked, and from the heavy breathing he could hear coming from his new liberator he suspected speed was of the essence. When at last the blade sliced through, the man leaned back and studied his handiwork. With a wry smile at Jack, he stood, took the still-bound man by the arm, and helped him to his feet. That accomplished, he retrieved his bag—which Jack noticed had a longer bundle secured on top of it—and then locked eyes with Jack.

"Shall we?" he said, gesturing toward the door.

"Absolutely," Jack said, although his pleasure at finding himself mobile was tempered by the fact that his hands were still tied and that the Englishman, slight as he was, had a firm grip on his elbow.

When they stepped out into the hallway Jack could see

into the other room and did a double take at what he saw. He was quickly shuffled down the hallway and the image was gone. He turned to look at his companion, asking the question with raised eyebrows.

The Englishman shrugged. "When you do what I do for a living, you learn to sleep in some unusual spots and with one eye open," he offered by way of explanation.

Oddly enough Jack understood exactly what he meant, though the response created another question. "And just what exactly do you do?"

They'd reached the end of the hall, where Jack saw the door leading outside. To the right was an entryway into what looked like a room larger than any he'd yet seen in the house. Instead of ushering Jack out into the Libyan sun, the Englishman directed him into the room.

They didn't spend more than thirty seconds there. Long enough for the Englishman to needlessly feel for pulses. When his captor bent down to do so, the temptation to flee came over Jack, but he resisted the urge, quickly calculating the slim odds of getting past the closed door, much less making a clean escape. The Englishman straightened and blew out a breath. He ran a hand through his disheveled hair, casting a tired eye around the room, then caught Jack's eye as if seeing him for the first time.

"The handle's a bit tricky," he said. "You wouldn't have made it."

"I'll take your word for it."

Once again the Englishman stooped to retrieve his bag and then started for the door, this time without a hand on Jack's arm.

"We should probably step it up a bit," he called over his shoulder. "I don't know how long it'll be before he wakes up."

It took Jack a beat to realize whom the Englishman meant.

"What do you mean 'wakes up'?" he called after him.

"As in gets up off the bed and comes after us and tries to do to us what he did to Benton and Phillips."

Jack, who had begun to follow the Englishman, looked back at who he could only assume were Benton and Phillips. With a small shudder he hurried after the other man.

When he caught up with him, he was reaching for the door handle. Soon the two men were outside. After spending so much time in a darkened room, the sun blinded Jack for several seconds before he was able to blink away the glare. When his vision cleared he saw the jeep toward which they were headed, and with that understanding it occurred to him that he was following a man he didn't know and who had, only minutes ago, been keeping him tied up and subject to beatings by a much bigger man who at any moment might burst from the house for another round of the same.

It was then that he noticed the number of people around him. It was midmorning and the street teemed with bodies, an undulating sea of humans following no noticeable traffic pattern. And not one of them paid the two foreigners a bit of attention, despite the fact that one of them had his hands bound behind him. Yet Jack had spent enough time in this part of the world to understand that this apparent obliviousness was nothing of the sort. Most of these people saw precisely what was happening, noticed every detail, but not once would they allow themselves to look in his direction.

Jack's feet slowed as they neared the jeep. The Englishman, demonstrating yet again an uncanny ability to intuit Jack's thoughts, had already grabbed the knot about Jack's wrists. He'd also slung his travel bag over a shoulder, his free hand now holding the knife. He positioned it under Jack's ribs. When Jack turned his head, the Englishman offered an apologetic smile.

Reaching the jeep, the Englishman used the point of the knife to urge Jack into the front passenger seat, where he used the dangling ends of the rope to secure his captive in position. That done he set the bag, longer bundle still secured on top, in the back. As he slid into the driver's seat, Jack noticed he wore a satisfied smile. Neither man spoke as the Englishman turned the key, put his hand on the gearshift. Then, after glancing at his unwilling passenger, he leaned toward Jack, reached past him, and pulled the seat belt across. The buckle slid in with a click.

Righting himself in his seat, the Englishman aimed another smile at Jack.

"Can't be too careful," he said.

"No, I suppose not," Jack agreed.

When the Englishman put the car in gear, Jack asked a question that he just had to have an answer to. "What's your name?"

The man glanced at Jack, then returned his eyes to the road, carefully navigating the street's foot traffic. He removed a hand from the wheel long enough to retrieve a pair of sunglasses from the center console. Only after he'd put them on did he respond with, "Martin Templeton."

The name meant nothing to Jack, but as the jeep picked up speed along the dirt road, finding what seemed to be every rut, something beyond the identity of his polite captor started to surpass it in urgency. As if to emphasize his new area of focus, one of the jeep's tires dipped into a hole deep enough to separate Jack from his seat. When he landed, and after a groan that pulled the Englishman's eyes away from the road, Jack gave him a pained smile.

"About that bathroom?"

7

When the plane touched down at Heathrow, Esperanza, in the aisle seat, barely noticed. It wasn't until the one sitting next to her—a businessman who had given up trying to establish a rapport within an hour of their flight leaving Caracas—indicated a desire to slip by her that she realized they'd landed. Somewhere over the ocean the lunacy of what she was doing had struck her and she'd spent much of the flight bouncing between passion and calculation. She'd come to the conclusion that she preferred the former state, even as she understood that the best decisions generally came while in the grip of the latter.

She wasn't sure which one had brought her from South America to Europe, but she suspected it was some combination of the two—a need to act tempered by solid reasoning behind those acts. When she and Jack had renewed their relationship, when he'd brought her on as a linguist in the treasure hunt that had almost killed them both, it was the passion that carried her through that time. Even then, though, there were hints of the burgeoning maturity that now caused her to consider things with an eye focused past the immediate. And that, to her, was the problem as far as Jack was concerned; he lived in the immediate. Despite what they had gone through together, that was something that had not changed. And the reason she was in London, pulling her carryon from the overhead bin, was she was no longer content with the status quo.

Once in the terminal, she took a few moments to get her bearings before heading for the car-rental area. Fifteen minutes later, she was traveling east on the M4. It had been years since her last visit to London, so as she drove deeper into the city she viewed everything through the eyes of a tourist, filling the time between Heathrow and Apsley House by taking in the feel of the bustling city.

When she'd deplaned, she'd intended to check into her hotel before heading to the museum, but somewhere between baggage claim and sliding the key into the rental's ignition, the order of those events had changed.

She'd never met Sturdivant in person. In fact, the day before had been the first time she'd ever spoken with him. Before that, all of her knowledge had come from secondhand accounts of others' dealings with him, namely Jack and Romero—whose professions had them running in similar circles. She'd found him pleasant enough in a stuffy sort of way, and as he was the curator for several of London's museums, she wouldn't have expected anything else.

The M4 transitioned to the A4, and before long Hyde Park opened up on her left. While Sturdivant executed his role for a variety of museums, he spent most of his time at

Apsley House, and within minutes Esperanza was bringing the car to a stop in front of the sixteenth-century structure. On most other occasions she would have enjoyed studying the building as well as the extensive collection of artwork and cultural icons it contained, but the purpose of her visit excluded such casual enjoyment.

Once inside, she located the administrative wing in short order, and Sturdivant's office not long after that. The director was inside, an open file on his desk and a phone to his ear. Esperanza could not get a feel for the height of the man sitting behind the large desk, though she suspected he was quite tall—the height accentuated by a rail-thin physique. He looked up when Esperanza appeared in the doorway, but she might as well have been invisible for the way his eyes seemed to pass right through her. Then they were back on the desk, moving over the open file.

Esperanza took the lack of acknowledgment as tacit approval to enter and she did just that, stepping in and claiming a seat across from his desk. When he looked up again, she engaged her best smile, the one she knew was manipulative but that seldom failed to get her what she wanted. The problem, which she sensed immediately, was that Milo Sturdivant had no use for her charms. Still, the fact that she had invaded his personal space prompted him to finish his call, although he did not look at his guest again until he had gathered the contents of the file, meticulously replaced them, and slipped the file into a desk drawer.

"Can I help you?" he asked her, looking over his glasses and using a voice that let Esperanza know he would have rather done anything else.

"I'm Dr. Esperanza Habilla," she answered, determined to ignore his demeanor. "We spoke on the phone yesterday."

Sturdivant did not answer right away, but he did meet Esperanza's eyes for the first time.

"You're Romero Habilla's sister, aren't you?" he asked after a time, and she couldn't tell by the tone if confirming the relationship would help or hinder her efforts.

"I am," she admitted.

The museum director pursed his lips and nodded.

"I've purchased a few things from him," he said. "His items are generally a bit higher priced than I believe is warranted, but I've found him to be fair."

"He'll be happy to hear that," Esperanza said, pleased to have found some common ground but also beginning to believe that the man only dipped into his emotional well when perusing a painting by a dead master or an artifact from a vanished civilization—a theory granted weight by the speed with which he moved on to other matters.

"What can I do for you, Dr. Habilla?"

"As I said, we spoke yesterday—"

"You asked me about Jack Hawthorne."

"The last time I spoke with him, he said he was planning to pay you a visit."

"We had a meeting set for three days ago, and while I'm used to Dr. Hawthorne arriving in his own good time, he's testing the limits of my patience."

"Believe me, I understand," she said.

"While I've allocated money for what he said he would be able to procure, I can't hold on to it indefinitely. In fact, there's an extraordinary display of Celtic weaponry I would love to have here in Apsley House and I'm considering redirecting the money meant for Dr. Hawthorne."

"What is he supposed to be bringing you?" Esperanza asked, but Sturdivant's head was shaking before she finished the question.

"I'm sorry. I'm afraid I can't reveal that," he said, although Esperanza doubted he was sorry at all. Still, she offered a smile meant to convey understanding. "To be perfectly frank, Dr. Habilla, the only reason I haven't yet reallocated the money is because of Dr. Hawthorne's reputation. But that reputation does not entitle him to operate as if Apsley House is his personal trading post."

"I'm sure that's not how he looks at it," she said, even as she suspected that was exactly how Jack viewed it. Esperanza saw Sturdivant's eyebrows come together in thought.

"Forgive me, Dr. Habilla, but I'm still unclear about the reason for this visit."

"It's simple really. Jack is going to show up in London soon with an artifact that he wants to sell you, and I want to be here when he arrives at Apsley House to make the exchange."

If her explanation did nothing else, it served to change the way Sturdivant looked at her. Rather than an entirely dismissive expression, the new one also contained a hint of puzzlement and a dash of worry.

"Why?"

"Because I have something very important I want to say to him," she explained, using the voice that would have made most any man willing to accept something purely nonsensical. However, as she had already ascertained, Milo Sturdivant was not most men.

"And this something can't be said over the phone?"

"Sadly, no," Esperanza said, feeling the first hints of irritation—annoyance that grew as Sturdivant did not follow the Venezuelan's response with one of his own. Instead, he leaned back in his chair and regarded her as one would a puzzle. After several seconds, he leaned forward and placed his elbows on the desk, making a steeple of his fingers.

"Just so I'm clear," he said. "You flew here from Venezuela to track down a man you could just call—a man who, to be honest, may not show at all?"

Esperanza could not begrudge the man his questions. After all, hadn't she asked some of the same ones during her long flight? However, hearing those questions come from a man who had spent the last several minutes robbing her of many of the tools she customarily used to get what she wanted brought the irritation to genuine anger and in less time than was normally the case.

After letting the director's question hang there for a moment, she too leaned into the desk, closing the distance between them. "I'm here because I'm going to say some things to an absentee archaeologist that just might make his ears bleed," she answered, her accent thick with frustration.

She waited a beat to make sure she had Sturdivant's attention. Seeing that she did, she continued, "I swear to you, if he shows up here and you don't call me to let me know, I will show up at your office door again. And I promise you that that visit will not go as swimmingly as this one has."

She'd said every word with a calmness that would have been appropriate for a discussion of traffic patterns around Hyde Park, yet there was no mistaking the genuine threat in each syllable. She suspected that Milo Sturdivant knew she wasn't bluffing.

Which was why he did something for the first time in her presence: he smiled.

"I can certainly do that," he said, the barest hint of apology in his tone. "As soon as I hear from Dr. Hawthorne—*if* I hear from him—I will call you and let you know."

In that instant, the menace that had taken over Esperanza's whole being vanished, replaced by the smile with which she'd entered the room.

"That would be wonderful," she said, sliding her card across the desk. Then, to further reward his acquiescence, she rose and started for the door. She had just reached it when a thought struck her. "By the way, how much are you set to pay Jack for whatever it is he's bringing to you?"

When Milo Sturdivant provided the answer, Esperanza felt everything shift. Less than sixty seconds later she was in the hallway calling Jack.

The Egyptian resisted the urge to run a hand over the back of his head, as he had a number of times since waking. He knew the wound had clotted and his hand would not return blood, which meant that, for now at least, it was not a concern.

He'd pulled what he could from the pockets of Benton and Phillips, which wasn't much, but he had a tidy sum of his own—enough to track Martin Templeton to the ends of the earth if need be.

The heat had cleared the streets of most of its traffic, which allowed Imolene to make good progress toward the area of town with the few shops that offered him a chance of renting a car that would take him to Al Bayda.

The dirt road ran into a stone wall twenty yards ahead, with an adjoining road following the length of the wall in both directions. He took the path leading to the left and followed the cut-through until it emptied into a busier thoroughfare. Here, the Egyptian stopped to collect himself and to readjust the heavy pack slung over his shoulder.

He could see all three of the businesses on his list and selected one based on the fact that it was the only one with a car parked out front. Resettling his pack, he started toward the store, pausing when he reached the car—a Yugo that seemed held together by rust. Grunting, he gave some thought as to how he would fit his large frame into it. In the end he decided that necessity outweighed comfort.

The interior of the shop was dark and smelled vaguely of garlic. The Egyptian took a position behind another man who had arrived before him and exchanged a look with the proprietor, a middle-aged Libyan with thinning hair and a faded but vicious-looking scar that began below his right ear and traveled down his neck, disappearing beneath his shirt.

"I only have the one vehicle," the man said to the other customer.

"That car will not get me to Tiblisi," the customer said.

"It's a good car," the owner said. "It will take you across the desert and back if you let it."

"Is the Yugo the only car you have available?" the Egyptian asked, leaning past his competition.

"It's the only car," the shopkeeper said. "The first car I've had in two weeks."

He assumed an apologetic smile before dismissing Imolene.

The first customer had pulled a billfold out of his pocket and peeled off several dinars, placing them down on the counter.

"You can have the car for two hundred," the owner said. He gestured at the sixty dinars the man had offered. "This will not even fill the tank of the next car that comes."

Imolene understood the intricacies of this process but lacked the patience to deal with it this day. He leaned forward again.

"Is there anywhere else to get a car in town?" he asked.

This time the man did not even look in his direction.

"This is the only car," he said.

Imolene returned a thoughtful nod and then turned to his fellow customer.

"Excuse me," he said, placing his massive hand on the man's shoulder. When the man turned, it was obvious that he had not taken a good look at his competition for the vehicle because his expression was pure irritation. It wasn't until the much shorter man was forced to look up into Imolene's cold eyes that his face changed.

"I need the car," Imolene said. It was not a request as much as it was a simple fact.

"I already told you," the merchant interjected. "I only have the one car."

Despite the merchant's protest, the Libyan customer appeared uncertain. Imolene took a half step forward, invading the other man's space and pointedly ignoring the merchant.

He leaned down so that his face was a scant few inches from that of the other man.

"I require the car and, consequently, I am going to leave with it. You may either allow me to do so or I will break each of the bones that I can reasonably assume you would use in the course of driving." He allowed the threat to settle in before smiling and adding, "And I imagine the average person uses a great many bones in the process of piloting a manual Yugo with no power steering."

Once he'd made the threat, he did not pull back but kept his face close. He could smell the odor of the man, the sweat of days. He watched a bead of sweat develop on the Libyan's forehead and start a trail down the side of his face. Beneath this inspection the man finally caved. Without a word, or a look at the merchant, he swept his money from the counter and hurried to the door, giving Imolene a wide berth. Once he was gone, Imolene turned to the merchant, his calm expression unchanged.

His original customer gone, the proprietor appeared to weigh his options and returned the Egyptian's look with a shrug of his shoulders.

"Okay, we have one car," he said. "It is out front. Perhaps you've seen it?"

8

Despite the distance between them, Esperanza felt as if Romero were in the room with her. She could almost see him sitting at his desk, the thoughtful look on his face. It was an image that gave her comfort as she considered the ramifications of Jack not having answered his phone.

Romero had also tried to reach him, but as Esperanza knew it would, it went to voice mail. Then he'd called Sturdivant, who had repeated what he'd told Esperanza, while she stood in his office and listened to the telling for the second time.

On one hand, Esperanza felt silly for even entertaining the thought that something was wrong. Few people were better travelers than Jack. The man knew how to take care of himself, and with a history demonstrating that missing an appointment by a few days was a common occurrence, there was little reason to suspect anything but willful irresponsibility.

Except for the money.

Espy still had a difficult time imagining Jack pocketing

a quarter of a million dollars. She was reasonably certain that nothing Jack had ever recovered—excepting some items from the Egyptian digs and those had gone to the Egyptian government—had commanded such a price.

And if she knew anything about Jack, it was that he had a heightened sense of punctuality where money was concerned. For a quarter of a million he would have been in London a day early.

"Regardless of what happened to you and Jack, what he does for a living is not usually dangerous," Romero said, as if listening to her thoughts.

"You'd be surprised how many people don't like him," she said. "They're scattered around the world."

"Actually I'm not surprised." Romero chuckled. "I was there when a number of those impressions were formed."

Esperanza knew that, of course, but Romero had played the honest businessman for so long that she sometimes forgot about his days spent gallivanting around the globe. The exchange pulled a smile from her, although it faded almost immediately.

It wasn't lost on her that she had come to London for the sole purpose of ending things with Jack, yet now the anger that had fueled her flight was transitioning into something else. She wouldn't call it worry—not yet—but it was something close, despite that Romero was right—there were few real threats to someone in Jack's profession.

"Reese is dead," Romero said, again knowing where she had gone.

At that, Esperanza released a sigh. "I know. I also know that it's been three years, and if anyone was going to come after me or Jack for what happened, they probably would have done it by now."

All of them had looked over their shoulders for a long while, even after the billionaire had succumbed to the cancer he'd hoped to cure with the bones. After all, a man as powerful as Gordon Reese could have paid any amount to have the ones who had ruined his chance at an extended life killed—and such a directive could well have extended past the duration of that life. There came a time, though, when one had to stop living in fear, and Espy had chosen that path some time ago.

Still, she knew that Reese was not the only player in those events.

"If they'd wanted you dead, they would have done it when you were in Australia," Romero said.

She knew this, but entertaining the thought that the secret organization that had protected Elisha's bones for millennia was somehow involved in Jack's disappearance played into her need for closure. In her estimation, these people who had played Jack against Reese were an open question, and she disliked not having answers. Even so, Romero was right again. They could have killed her and Jack, as well as anyone else who had helped the pair, at any time and yet had not done so.

"You know how he gets," Romero said. "He likely began what he thought would be a simple expedition and it has become something more involved."

"And so he turns off his phone?"

"Or he's someplace with no cell reception."

Esperanza grunted and leaned against the wall.

Romero did not say anything else right away, and Espy knew he was thinking.

"What is the name of Jack's friend at the university?" he asked. "The one that worked for their government."

"Duckett. Jim Duckett."

"And he has a way of procuring manifests for plane flights?"

Esperanza's eyebrows rose, but a frown replaced that expression in short order. "Except that we don't know what flight he was on." She paused and then added, "If he was even on one. For all we know, he was driving somewhere."

Romero grunted an acknowledgment of that possibility but then asked, "What other choice do we have?"

Esperanza's silence told both of them the answer to that.

———

Jim Duckett leaned back from the table and released a contented sigh. He didn't know what it was about the pancakes produced by the grill staff in the student union, but even after years of weekly consumption, and a pancake count he couldn't hope to recollect, they remained the pinnacle of perfection. Over the years, as the grill staff had turned over time and again without a fluctuation in pancake quality, he'd even stooped to bribing the cooks for their secrets, only to discover an undergraduate staff that was either as clueless as he was or who had formed a thin, buttermilk line of silence.

The meal finished, he reached for his breast pocket, his hand running over the two cigars he'd placed there when he left home that morning. However, before he could pull one out, his hand fell away. As habitual as the pancake consumption, the reflexive action of reaching for a cigar at the conclusion of a good meal remained something he could not shake.

As he leaned away from the table, he glanced around the student hangout. Evanston was, comparatively speaking, a small college, which meant that he often saw the same faces around him as he ate. Today, the place was near empty. The slowness of the place matched his own energy level, which had dropped precipitously over the last few months.

While downplaying it, he'd also made a few attempts to analyze it and the only thing he was able to come up with could be summed up in a single word: *boredom*. But the analysis did not venture much beyond that. He liked his job—and the perks that came with it—and couldn't think of doing anything else. He suspected that it was just a phase and that it would pass. After all, one did not leave a position with the CIA for idyllic Ellen, NC, and the slower life of teaching at a small liberal arts college without occasionally recalling those more adventurous days with fondness.

Rather than allow himself to contemplate that further, he slid from the booth and reached for his tray—an action that still felt uncomfortable, even after three years. It had always pleased him to leave the tray on the table, knowing that Jack would take care of it along with his own. Like the reach for the cigar, busing his own tray had taken some getting used to.

As he headed for the trash can, he reflected on the fact that the time of year could have something to do with his mood. It was December, and the winter break was fast approaching—and the same time period three years ago had seen Jack Hawthorne teach his last class at Evanston.

On one hand, he was happy that the events that transpired

had pushed his friend from teaching and back into the career he was meant to pursue. On the other hand, he had to take care of his own tray.

The air outside was crisp, and he contemplated lighting up a cigar on his way to his next class, but Evanston was not a large campus and the cigars he carried deserved a long enjoyment. He released a sigh and had just shifted his thoughts to his class when his phone rang.

"Duckey?" a woman with an accent said when he answered.

"With an accent like that, I can be whoever you want me to be," he replied.

The fact that his statement was met with a laugh rather than indignation told him the voice belonged to the woman he thought it did.

"Jack wasn't lying about you," Esperanza said, and Duckey could feel the genuine warmth coming through the phone.

"That's a shame," he said. "In my experience, a good lie or two makes things a lot more interesting."

That was followed by another laugh, and without ever meeting her, Duckey thought he was beginning to understand what it was about her that had made Jack swing by Caracas and pick her up three years ago. Because if Duckey knew anything about Esperanza and Jack's shared history, it was that making that side trip—even though it had improved Jack's chances of success in securing the biggest payday he'd ever imagined—was fraught with more danger than anything he'd faced during his pre-teaching profession.

"By the way, only my friends call me Duckey."

In most other people that statement would have generated a pause. In this woman, though, it did nothing but fuel her mirth.

"Then I guess we'd better decide to get chummier than we already are," she said. "Because that's all I ever heard Jack call you, and I really don't think I could bring myself to call you Jim."

After a morning spent teaching the same classes he'd taught for years, followed by eating the same meal—however delectable—in the same place he'd always eaten it, this unexpected repartee was something he did not want to relinquish. However, the trade he'd practiced before assuming his present role forced him to analyze the various elements of the conversation—including the probable prompts for it—and despite his wishes, he found himself growing serious.

"What's wrong, Espy?" he asked, also using the nickname made familiar by their shared friend.

Without so much as a pause she told him, and Duckey didn't interrupt with a single question while she did so. In his experience, most good intel was generated by spontaneity. Duckey had risen through the ranks by letting his informants spill their guts and only asking clarifying questions when such were absolutely necessary.

Consequently, it wasn't until Esperanza ran out of steam that the dean of the Humanities Department at Evanston University, who had long reached his destination but who remained standing on the walkway in front of it, said a word.

"And what makes you think that Jack not checking in is anything more than Jack being Jack?" he asked, unaware that his question echoed the one posed by Esperanza's brother.

In truth, he didn't need to hear the answer to the question. The simple fact that a woman who knew his friend well—likely better than Duckey knew him—was concerned, made him concerned. Nonetheless, he knew Jack. He knew that regardless of the personal and professional growth the archaeologist might have gone through over the last few years, somewhere inside existed the man who eschewed responsibility and commitment.

Duckey did not know where Espy was calling from but he pictured her on some street in Caracas. If he concentrated, he thought he could hear the sounds of traffic moving by her. She waited a long time before answering.

"Sometimes a person just knows something," she said and the conviction in her voice swayed Duckey more than most other things might have.

"Okay," he said with a nod she could not see. "What do you need me to do?"

When she told him, he couldn't help feeling a measure of disappointment. Perhaps it was that he'd spent a portion of his morning bemoaning the static nature of his existence, and that this call from Esperanza Habilla signified something that might break the monotony. But discovering that he was only needed in order to procure and skim through flight manifests disappointed him.

Still, there was something about being asked to do a task— even a simple one—by a faraway woman with a foreign accent that had him quickly agreeing to help.

After ending the call moments later, he felt a return to the habits that had served him well for so long. And as he mounted the steps to the building where his students waited, he divested himself of everything but the facts. For analyzing facts was something he was good at.

9

Despite everything Jack had gone through over the last couple of days, a few stood out. One of them involved the different levels of feeling one could experience in one's wrists. Since leaving the safe house in Libya, his hands had not been absent the rope that bound them. Early on, he'd convinced his captor to at least adjust the bonds so his hands were in front of him. Jack believed the main reason for Martin Templeton's cooperation was so he wouldn't have to help the archaeologist do all the things people had to do in order to navigate through the day. He suspected the first bathroom break was the tipping point.

Yet even with his hands in a more comfortable place, they were still bound with coarse rope. Jack had used the new position as an opportunity—or a series of small opportunities—to try and break the bonds. But he'd come to realize that, while Templeton didn't appear to be the killer the Egyptian was, the man could tie a fantastic knot.

As Jack stared into the complete darkness, he contemplated the events of the past few days and was surprised to find himself feeling calm. In fact, the night was actually quite pleasant. They were camping without a tent, exposed to the elements, but the weather was such that they didn't need to fear either rain or the cold. The end of Jack's rope wound around the front seat of the jeep, with Templeton sending another rope around the vehicle's front tire. Both lines had been tied in such a way that Jack could not reach the end of either with any hope of untying them. Yet Templeton had laid out a sleeping bag for Jack and had taken great pains to make sure his captive was comfortable.

And so, once again, Jack did what he was good at: he settled in and waited.

Nothing he'd experienced thus far could equal the events from a few years ago. After running through that gauntlet, he suspected there was little that could unsettle him. It helped of course that what he and Espy had gone through had clarified much for him—had helped him weigh things of true importance against things that were less so. He hated to reduce things to the metaphysical, but there it was.

Thinking about Esperanza served to distract him, to pull his thoughts from his present surroundings. He wondered what, if anything, she'd done when he failed to check in. He was, by his count, at least three days past the time when he should have concluded his business in London and then caught a plane back to Caracas. He couldn't help the slight smile he wore at the thought that his multiple past failures at keeping a schedule could now come back to haunt him. Knowing Esperanza as he did, he thought there was just as much chance that she'd wash her hands of him completely as there was that she'd search for him. In truth, were he in her position, Jack thought it unlikely he'd search for himself.

Even as he thought these things, he found the smile still rooted.

"What has you in such good spirits?" Templeton asked.

His captor had rolled out his bag ten feet from Jack, a few feet past where Jack's bonds would have let him advance.

"Just thinking about someone," Jack said.

He saw Templeton nod. The man was on his back, hands laced behind his head, watching the stars as if they were poised to reveal some valuable truth to him. The Englishman didn't say anything right away, and Jack, who had ceased asking questions that wouldn't be answered, settled back and waited—either for sleep or a continuance of the conversation. After several moments, Templeton revealed his desire to extend the exchange.

"Who is she?"

"What makes you think she's a she?" Jack said.

"Because when a man is tied to a jeep on the edge of an African desert, I doubt very much that he would be thinking about anything else."

While Jack had to concede the point, he wasn't about to give the Englishman more information than the man had shown himself willing to return.

"Help me out here, Martin," Jack said. "Why are you doing this to me? I mean, if you want to hear me say I'm sorry for trying to snatch the artifact right out from under you, then I'll say it. I was wrong for trying to take it."

He tried to gauge if his words had any effect on Templeton, but the man's expression had not changed.

"I don't get it," he said after a while. "You have what you want, and from what I can tell, the large man you knocked unconscious isn't following you. So why do you need me?"

"I studied archaeology at Oxford," Templeton said quietly.

"I taught a few classes there," Jack remarked.

"I know. Right before Egypt—before your brother died."

A few years ago that kind of statement would have done a number on Jack's psyche. It was yet another testament to the strength granted by experience, as well as by the God Jack was now firmly convinced had orchestrated it all.

"Why am I here, Martin?"

The question was answered by silence, and after waiting for the Englishman to break it, Jack closed his eyes. He had just started to surrender to sleep when Templeton finally spoke.

"What happened in Australia?" he asked.

Jack couldn't process the question right away, but it wasn't because it was entirely unexpected. Rather, the query startled him because it felt as if Templeton was intruding on a dream Jack hadn't shared with anyone. It was like the Englishman had invaded his thoughts.

"I've been in Australia on several occasions," Jack said. "It's a great country. Have you ever been to Bondi?"

Templeton smiled. "Three years ago you were teaching at Evanston University. A month later you're arrested in Australia after a double murder." Templeton took his eyes off the stars long enough to catch Jack's eye. "Then all the charges are dropped and you're gallivanting around the globe as if nothing happened."

Jack absorbed that and, after a time, grunted an admission to the general accuracy of Templeton's recounting of events.

"I wouldn't say *gallivanting.*"

Templeton shrugged.

"Suddenly you were in a cave in Libya trying to steal something from me," he said. "Call it whatever you want."

"Fair enough," Jack said.

"Do you know that the Australian government has a Freedom of Information Department that's a lot like the American one?"

"No, I didn't know that."

"Yes, well, they do. And do you know what I found when I submitted a request for the records involving your case?"

"That they were going to charge you an enormous processing fee?"

"That no such records exist." Templeton let that hang there a moment before continuing. "It didn't matter that I could show them news articles that talked about the killings. Or pictures of you in handcuffs. As far as the Australian government was concerned, you were never there."

"Has it ever occurred to you that maybe they're just bad at keeping records? Besides, why should you care about what I do with my spare time?"

Jack was growing used to the long pauses in his conversations with the Englishman, but there was something different about the one that followed his question. He could sense the iciness coming from Templeton's direction, could feel that he'd said something that had changed the man's mood as if flipping a switch. And he could tell that the new emotional state was not one he wanted Templeton to act on.

"Let's just say that I've always been intrigued by puzzles," Templeton answered.

And with that, he closed his eyes and didn't speak again.

Imolene had to give the shopkeeper credit. The Yugo had lasted far longer than he would have thought possible, carrying him well past Al Bayda and toward Tripoli. He'd chosen to retain the vehicle when, in stopping in Al Bayda to check in with those who knew most of what went on in the city, he'd learned that two men matching Templeton's and Hawthorne's description had passed through there, ostensibly aiming toward the capital. And so Imolene had decided to hang on to the Yugo rather than use up precious time in finding a different vehicle. He was also lower on funds than he liked, and until he caught up to his quarry, he had to make his money stretch.

In Tripoli, the tracking had become much more difficult. It took Imolene some time to conclude it was because the pair had not stopped within the city. That was the only explanation he could come up with that would explain their absence from any of the places Templeton may have gone to procure supplies, or from the notice of those charged with monitoring the city's ingress and egress of outsiders.

He had not gone all in on the idea. In a city as large as Tripoli, Imolene thought it possible that Templeton and Hawthorne had arrived two days ago and not left, that they'd holed up somewhere. But something had told the Egyptian that was not the case, and when he'd followed that belief he was rewarded to learn about a brief stop in a village thirty kilometers outside the capital by men who could only have been his quarry. Interestingly, a local merchant had told Imolene that one of the men seemed bound and unable to get out of the jeep they'd driven into the village. This told Imolene that whatever Templeton's objective, it in some way involved Jack Hawthorne, and that the American was not entirely sold on his role.

It also told Imolene that Templeton and Hawthorne could be caught. He thought it unlikely that they could retain their lead when one man had to act as the other's jailer.

The difficulty was in tracking them. If they remained in Libya, they would be hard enough to locate. But with both Egypt and Tunisia bordering the country, both relatively simple boundaries to cross, Imolene had a good deal more ground to cover. Of only one thing was he certain. As long as Templeton insisted on dragging the American around, they would not be able to leave the region.

Were Imolene faced with such a choice, the decision would have been obvious. He would have killed the American and left his body in the desert. He wondered why Templeton did not do the same. Or if he lacked the steel to kill a man, he could have found someplace to secure his prisoner while he made his escape. He did, after all, have the prize he'd come for, and unless Imolene caught up with him and took it, the Englishman could make a great deal of money from the artifact. A great deal, if he could gauge such a thing from the Israelis' interest in it.

His arrangement with the Israelis was something else he had to consider, especially if he didn't succeed in retrieving the artifact. This had been only his second job for them—the first a more sordid affair that had paid quite well. And so when this opportunity had come along, he'd jumped at it. If he failed in this one, he doubted there would be another.

The Yugo hit a deep rut in the road, and Imolene mouthed a curse when his head hit the ceiling for what seemed the hundredth time. He moved his knee so he could downshift and navigated a turn around a line of boulders that seemed out of place in the middle of nowhere. The next village was a little over forty kilometers ahead, and as the next concentration of civilization was almost a hundred past that, he guessed that Templeton would have stopped at the nearer one.

If he was traveling this way. And if he was even in the country.

Imolene grunted and pushed those thoughts away. He was seldom wrong when it came to finding someone he wanted to find. And he very much wanted to find Martin Templeton.

10

As Duckey set his phone on the seventeenth-century desk with the Boston-manufacture imprint that he had the luck to acquire from a little old lady at a garage sale in Des Moines, he pondered the advances in technology that made the procurement of multiple flight manifests a thing accomplished with a single phone call, rather than the arduous labor it had been when he was cutting his teeth at Langley. On one hand, he understood that the ability to do something like that signified a level of technological sophistication rightly lauded. On the other, well, it just seemed too easy.

Even just three years earlier, when he'd performed a similar service for Jack, the technology had not been as advanced as it was now. He'd had to make two phone calls and one fax. And even then he'd not felt as if he'd really accomplished anything. After all was done, he'd come to understand the importance of the role he'd played, but he hadn't felt the fulfillment he thought one was supposed to feel. No wonder, then, that he felt less so as he pushed away from the desk and took a draw from a cigar he'd been nursing since dinner. He would get the manifests within the hour and, if one of them had Jack's name on it, he'd call Esperanza with the news. Until then, there wasn't a great deal for him to do.

His office adjoined the family room and from it he could hear that his wife had settled down to watch the evening news. Duckey removed the cigar from his mouth and ground it in an ashtray. When he entered the family room, Stephanie was curled up on the sofa, book in hand. She didn't look up as he crossed the room and settled down next to her. A few moments passed before she placed a bookmark between the pages and set the book on the end table. As soon as her eyes moved to his, Duckey saw the sly smile in them—the one meant to inform him that she knew something was going on.

Duckey could muster only a weak smile in his defense.

"So are you going to tell me what's got you so excited?" she asked, to which Duckey only returned a feigned puzzled look.

"Don't give me that," she said. "You've been bouncing off the walls since dinner."

Duckey, who thought he had a pretty good handle on the events of the evening, none of which had him engaged in any sort of bouncing, nonetheless understood what his wife meant. Except that, by his reckoning, the energy she referred to had been building for quite a while, and the reason it was so noticeable tonight was because it had a focus. Even if that focus wasn't a very exciting one.

"I've just been doing a small favor for a friend," he said.

Stephanie took that in and parsed it. "My guess is it's the sort of favor that requires a call or two to Langley?"

"Just one call," he said. "And not even a long one."

The question of how his wife would respond to his acknowledgment of having done "spy work," as she called it, was an open question. After what had happened three years ago, when Duckey had been forced to call in more than a few favors, both during and after Jack's jaunt around the globe, she'd let him know that she was not willing to spend her days wondering when someone her husband had ticked off would show up at their door. That had been one of the reasons Duckey had quit the Company to begin with.

"It was just a phone call," he said.

"Just a phone call," Stephanie repeated. "Well, who's the friend?"

"Esperanza Habilla. Jack's friend."

"Can I assume that Esperanza calling means that Jack's in some kind of trouble?"

Despite the fact that the former Evanston University archaeology professor had once turned their lives upside down, Duckey knew that Stephanie was fond of him.

"I really don't know," Duckey said and then proceeded to tell his wife what he knew, which wasn't much. When he'd finished, Stephanie pursed her lips and nodded.

"How long until you get your lists from Langley?" she asked.

"Any time now."

Stephanie nodded, drumming her fingers, and Duckey saw the same look on her face that he saw when his lawyer wife was thinking through a difficult legal concept. When she emerged from this processing she fixed her husband with a smile. "So what does your gut tell you?"

He snorted at the question. "My gut's expanded way too much over the years to be trustworthy."

"More of you to love," she said, reaching across the couch and taking his hand.

Duckey gave it a squeeze but then he grew serious.

"I really don't know if he's in trouble," he said. "But Esperanza thinks he is. And from everything I've heard about the woman, I'm willing to throw in with her."

There was a long pause before Stephanie finally said, "Do what you can to help." Then, at Duckey's questioning look, she added, "You won't be any good until you get this out of your system."

Duckey laughed, then frowned as what his wife had said sunk in. "Wait a minute. Good at what?"

Stephanie was saved from answering when the phone Duckey had left in his office started to ring.

At some point during the night, Jack thought they had crossed into Tunisia. Going by his knowledge of the region, he knew they could not keep driving west without crossing the border at some point. The only question was whether his captor meant to continue through the narrow southern tip of the country or run straight through to Algeria. He had no way of answering that question without a way to intuit Martin Templeton's end game. Because regardless of how calm Templeton appeared outwardly, there had to be some kind of plan in mind.

What Jack could not figure out was how he fit into all

of it. He understood that Templeton might hold a grudge for Jack's attempt to steal the artifact out from under him, but he didn't think that had much to do with being dragged across northern Africa against his will. After all, Jack hadn't succeeded and the prize was tucked into the back of the jeep with Templeton's supplies. The fact that Templeton still had him secured in the jeep's passenger seat told Jack there was something else going on.

For the hundredth time since Templeton had awakened him that morning and they'd started off again, Jack's thoughts went to the long, slim bundle wedged between two bags in the space behind his and Templeton's seats. Because of the way the ropes held him, he could only catch a glimpse of the bundle by turning his head, but doing so hurt his neck and so he contented himself with knowing it was back there.

Oddly enough, neither he nor Templeton had mentioned it. At first, Jack's confinement in the village outside Al Bayda, followed by their flight from the murderous Egyptian, had stymied conversation. Now, though, it was almost all that occupied Jack's thoughts—even more so than what might happen to him.

"I have to give credit where it's due, Dr. Hawthorne," Templeton said, breaking a silence an hour old. "You finding the Nehushtan is a good deal more impressive than my accomplishment. Would you care to tell me how you did it? Professional to professional?"

Momentarily taken aback that Templeton seemed to have intuited his thoughts, Jack didn't answer right away. Instead, he returned his eyes to the poor excuse for a road over which the Englishman guided the jeep.

"I don't make a habit of telling trade secrets to people who tie me up and drag me all over the desert and don't even bother to let me shower once," Jack returned.

Templeton *tsk*ed and shook his head. "Here I am trying to make nice and you're hung up on the travel arrangements."

"Since we both wound up in the same place, I can only assume we got there the same way," Jack said, but Templeton's head was shaking before Jack had finished.

"You're the intrepid explorer who had to figure it out for himself," Templeton said. "I had considerable help."

Jack's brow furrowed. His current circumstances were strange enough, but with each word the Englishman said, Jack could not help but make comparisons to the last time he chose to seek out a biblical relic. The way Templeton made veiled allusions, as well as the knowing smile he aimed at Jack—it all seemed too familiar.

"Whose help?"

"Let's just say that someone did most of the footwork before I was brought on board," he said. "My employer simply told me where to go and what to look for."

Even knowing that Gordon Reese was dead, Jack could barely suppress a shudder when Templeton referred to his employer. However, he recognized the irrationality of that reaction and chose to focus on the fact that his captor was actually giving him information he might be able to use.

"So you're some sort of mercenary archaeologist, then," Jack said, understanding it would be taken as a barb and smiling when he saw it work in that fashion. "Let someone else do the work and then sweep in and take all the credit?"

"'I have only seen farther because I have stood on the

shoulders of giants,'" Templeton quoted, and Jack could not disagree with that.

"What do you plan to do with it?"

"I really don't know."

That answer didn't surprise Jack. After all, the Englishman didn't seem to know what to do with Jack either.

They rode in silence for a while, the desert passing beneath and around them, until Jack, giving in to the temptation to turn and look at the artifact, asked, "Do you have any idea what it is you have back there?"

Martin shrugged. "I'm sure I don't know its history—its significance—as well as you, but yes, I know what it is."

Jack nodded, comforted at least that the man knew enough to appreciate it.

"I wasn't under the impression that you've done much work with biblical relics," Templeton said. "And even those who have generally neglect this one."

"Let's just say that, despite what might appear on my résumé, I've looked for a relic or two in my day," Jack said. Then with a wry smile he closed his eyes and didn't elaborate.

11

"Do you have any idea how hard it is to find one person on a flight manifest from a region with more flights per day than any other part of the world when you don't even know what airline he's traveling on?"

"I'm going with not very hard," Esperanza said.

Her response was met with silence, and she imagined Jack's friend nursing a feeling of righteous indignation.

"Well, you're right," Duckey said after a pause. "But that's only because I know people."

"Which is why I called you," Espy said.

"Your lost archaeologist boarded a KLM flight in Milan on December fourteenth."

"Which was a few days before he was supposed to meet Sturdivant in London," Espy said.

"But this bird wasn't going to London," Duckey said. "For some reason, our friend purchased a one-way ticket to Tripoli."

Espy's brow furrowed. "Jack went to Libya?"

"After a brief stop in Amsterdam, where Jack had a stroop-waffel and a bourbon in the terminal." Duckey paused and then added, "I don't think much of the combination myself, but then I've never had a stroopwaffel."

"You're good," Espy conceded.

"That's what I've been trying to tell you."

"Let me think a minute. . . . We know that Jack had something he was going to sell to Sturdivant for a lot of money. And the Jack we know wouldn't pass up on the chance at a score that big. So why would he decide to change his plans and go to Libya?"

"I can't answer that," Duckey said. "But I do think you're presuming too much. You're assuming that Jack had in his possession whatever he was going to sell in London."

"You're right," Espy said, stretching the words as she mulled over what Duckey was saying. Then she shook her head, as if ridding herself of Duckey's attempt to make things more difficult than they already were. "But he told Sturdivant—"

"The point is that we can't presume," Duckey interrupted. Yet despite the pointed nature of his words, his voice was kind. "Unless I'm mistaken, he didn't say that he had what Sturdivant wanted. All he said was that he was going to bring something to him."

"Okay, let's assume that Jack didn't have in his possession the item he was going to sell to Sturdivant. How does that affect how we look for him?"

She asked the question more as a means of focusing their efforts than as any sort of minimization of her mistake, which was exactly how Duckey took it.

"It means that we have a few more variables to consider than we might otherwise have had," he said. "Was Jack trying to procure whatever he was going to sell to the buyer in London, or did he get distracted by something else?"

"And any single variable you add makes everything that follows a whole lot more complicated."

"Right."

"Okay. So where does that leave us?"

"As near as I can tell, it leaves us with two places to investigate: Milan and Libya." Without waiting for a response, he went on, "First, we could figure out what happened in Milan to make Jack buy that plane ticket. Whether that was a new lead in whatever he went to Italy for or something else entirely—we don't know at this point."

"And second?" Espy asked.

"Second would be to figure out what happened to Jack when he touched down in Tripoli. Because aside from his buying lunch in the terminal and then renting a car, his credit card is cold."

Esperanza absorbed that and immediately began sifting through the data they had, along with the options Duckey had laid out. And what she kept running into was the large number of variables they had to consider, as well as actions they could take.

"I'm not sure where to start," she said.

"You're presuming again," Duckey said.

"Am I?"

"You're presuming we have to start anywhere." He paused as if to make certain that she was on the same page. "After all, we can't forget who we're dealing with. This is a man who locked himself in his apartment every winter break at the university and didn't talk to a single soul for a month. The way I see it, now that he's not tied to the fine institution I still draw a paycheck from, I think he's just substituted the world for his apartment."

"So you don't think there's anything wrong."

"I have no idea if anything's wrong," Duckey answered. "All we know is that Jack went to Libya and now he's not answering his phone."

Esperanza didn't know what to say to that. She'd already pondered the possibility that she was worrying over nothing. Now one of Jack's closest friends and a former CIA agent was intimating the same thing.

Duckey continued. "I'll level with you, Espy. Knowing what I know about Jack, if I still worked at Langley and this came across my desk, I wouldn't do a thing. Because the odds would suggest that the missing person would show up on his own."

Espy sensed a *but* coming.

"But what I know about you—and Jack's told me a lot—tells me that your hunch carries a lot of weight."

Espy digested the compliment, then said, "Which means?"

"Which means you should work the Milan angle."

"The Milan angle?"

"Listen," he said. "You're much better equipped than I am to handle all that highbrow stuff that goes on in a city like Milan. Obviously Jack would have been dealing with people who know a thing or two about ancient artifacts. That's something I'm unprepared to dive into."

Espy nodded, accepting his reasoning. Then something struck her. "You said the Milan angle. Usually you don't say something like that unless there's another angle that also needs investigating."

"I'll take Tripoli."

"Excuse me?"

"I figure that's more my kind of town."

Esperanza could almost see Duckey's shrug through the phone.

"I'm pretty good at finding a needle in a haystack," Duckey said.

Espy had never met Jim Duckett in person, but she'd heard Jack speak of the man on many occasions. While she wouldn't have called the feeling Jack held for the man reverence, it was something close. But she also knew that Duckey was retired— that his days of working in the field were well behind him.

"I'm not sitting this one out," he said, understanding where her thoughts were headed. "Libya's my kind of place. If Jack's there, I'm the one who stands the best chance of finding him."

Again, Espy had to rely on what she'd learned of the man during her association with Jack. He was ex-CIA, hard-headed, and loyal to a fault. She knew that her chances of talking Duckey out of stepping into the fray were next to none.

"Thank you" was all she could think to say.

"Think nothing of it," Duckey said.

12

Jack was awake for five minutes before he moved, despite the feeling that an ant was crawling up his pant leg. He mustered every ounce of determination that he had to ignore it, trying to concentrate his attention on the world around him.

He thought dawn was still an hour off and he could hear Templeton's light snoring from somewhere off to his right. After waiting to be certain that the man was indeed asleep, Jack tested the bonds around his hands. He'd convinced the Englishman to untie him the previous evening so that, under Templeton's watchful eye, he could wash off with a rag and a bowl of water. When Templeton had bound him again, having Jack make the first loop around his wrists while the Englishman kept a gun leveled on him, Jack had been sure to keep his wrist curved. Now, as he worried at the coarse rope, he straightened his hand and felt the rope slacken. It wasn't much, but beyond the few minutes given him to bathe, his range of motion was better than it had been since he'd first been tied up in the safe house. Even so, it took him several minutes to slip one of the loops past his hand. But once he'd accomplished that, the ropes were off in less than a minute.

That done, he listened for any change in Templeton's breathing. Still sound asleep. As quietly as he could, he pushed himself up to a sitting position, stifling the groan that threatened to announce his collection of pulled muscles. Templeton had wrapped a rope around Jack's legs, the other end secured to the jeep. Even with having the full use of his hands, it took Jack longer to loosen these, and during the process he kept expecting Templeton to awaken and end his flight attempt. But Jack heard no break in the man's steady breathing.

A few minutes later he'd freed himself and gotten his feet underneath him, ignoring the pins and needles as the blood rushed back to his feet. Though the sun wasn't up yet, it was hot, and Jack was sweating as he put a hand on the jeep and rose along its side.

A part of him wanted to see if he could overpower Templeton while the man slept, but he knew the man had bedded down with the gun and Jack wanted to avoid the prospect of getting shot if at all possible. And in lieu of turning the tables on his captor, there was only one other option.

He leaned into the cab. No keys in the ignition. With that means of exit unavailable, he turned away from the vehicle but then thought better of it before he'd completed his first step. Instead, he reached into the back of the jeep and pulled out a duffel bag holding the rest of their bottled water. He had no idea where he was, other than that they were somewhere in Tunisia. Before they'd bedded down for the night, all he'd seen in any direction was desert. He suspected the three water bottles in the bag wouldn't take him far, yet in a situation like the one he was in, it did no good to pine for what he didn't have.

There was, however, one additional item in the jeep. With the duffel bag removed, Jack could see the entire length of the bundled artifact, its length such that it could not rest even on the floorboards but at an angle, rising behind Jack's seat, where it almost reached the window. Without a moment's consideration, Jack removed the serpent staff from its resting place. There was no way Jack was going to leave without it.

By the time he started off into the desert, he could see a thin line of light touching the place where sand and sky met. He kept to the road, knowing his only chance of getting away was to put as much distance as he could between himself and Templeton before the man discovered he was gone. Heading into the desert—where travel would have been more difficult—would only have slowed him down. He remembered seeing some break in the sameness of the landscape a few miles back as he'd watched beyond the jeep's windows. It had looked as if a thin strip of land perhaps a mile off the road suddenly came to an end, while the rocky terrain on both sides of it continued on. Jack imagined that he'd seen some sort of small cliff face, perhaps overlooking a gully.

Jack pushed himself to cover as much ground as possible before full light, but days of restricted movement had left him sore and made his escape more difficult. Still, he thought he'd covered about a mile in less than fifteen minutes, and in another mile or so he would leave the road and cut an angle for the drop-off. If he guessed wrong, he might miss it completely and then all Templeton would have to do would be to drive around in the daylight until he saw Jack's form standing out against the eternal gray flatness.

He shifted the staff from where it had been resting on his right shoulder to his left. When one first picked it up, it didn't seem that heavy, but carrying it for a distance with already sore muscles made it seem heavier with each step.

Legend had it the staff had been formed almost entirely of brass, yet he suspected there was also some gold mixed in, which would have accounted for much of its weight. He'd been deprived of the opportunity to examine it and so he could not verify that. He would have liked the chance to stop and unwrap it, just to get a peek at it. After reading the story in the book of Numbers, he had his own ideas about what it looked like and wanted to see if he was even close. He suspected he was. After all, there were few people in the world better equipped to look past a brief mention of a biblical item to the existing technology, materials, and methods the ancients would have used to craft such a thing. Consequently, while his visual picture might not have been accurate, he was confident he knew what it would not look like.

He thought he'd crossed another mile. Keeping his misgivings in check, he left the road, which essentially was nothing more than a well-traveled path through the desert. Even with the approaching sunrise, it was still quite dark. He realized then that while on the road, he stood a much better chance of avoiding an injury. Off the road he would have to exercise greater care. As if validating that, Jack's foot settled into a hole in the ground before he'd taken more than a dozen steps.

As luck would have it, the foot in question was attached to the ankle Jack had already injured, which made the pain a good deal worse than it otherwise would have been. Before he could catch himself, he was stumbling and had to drop the staff in order to keep from coming down hard on the desert rock. He sat on the ground for several moments, massaging his ankle, but knew he had to get right back up and keep moving. He had to reach a hiding spot if he stood any chance of getting away from Templeton.

With a groan he pushed himself to his feet, dusted off his pants, and stooped down to retrieve the fallen staff. As he balanced the staff on one shoulder and resettled the duffel bag over the other, he glanced up into the lightening sky.

He thought back on how he'd spent a good portion of his life denying the faith his parents had taught him, although over the last few years he'd begun to believe. And yet he wondered why it seemed that God had it in for him. True, he was no saint and probably never would be. But he hadn't expected the kind of obstacles that God seemed intent on throwing his way.

"Is this because I haven't married Espy yet?" he asked.

The question was met with silence, and so Jack shook his head and started off again.

Off the road, time passed in a different fashion. Jack had a hard time determining how many minutes had passed or how much distance he'd covered. Periodically he turned to look back at the way he'd come, looking for the road, for a jeep on it, but he could see nothing—despite that the sun had risen enough to grant him a clear field of vision.

By this time, Martin Templeton would know that he was gone. The only thing in Jack's favor was that the Englishman would not know which direction Jack had taken. On foot, the last village they'd passed would have taken Jack far too long to reach—longer than his meager water supply would have made possible. A logical man, then, would have proceeded on foot in the direction they were heading, hoping for cover along the way. Even if Templeton decided to backtrack, what were the odds that he would find the spot where Jack left the road, let alone the one patch of land in the desert for which Jack was aiming? True, Jack had kept his angle narrow, believing that the cliff face—if that's what it was—was no more than a mile or so from the road, which meant Templeton could maybe spot him if he was looking in the right place at the right time. So Jack took periodic glances in that direction. If he saw the jeep, his plan was to drop to the ground, trusting in the vision-obscuring properties of the desert to cause Martin's eyes to flit over him.

Although it wasn't intensely hot yet, not in terms of the temperatures common to the desert, still, Jack's thirst forced him to stop and sling the bag holding the water bottles from his shoulder. Kneeling down, he fished a bottle from the bag and downed half of it before replacing the cap and returning the bottle to its canvas cocoon. Then he started on his way again.

It seemed as if he walked for a long time. Long enough that he'd begun to suspect he'd missed the inland promontory and had crossed into some spot in the desert where he would not see a change in terrain until the environment shifted—until the barrenness gave way to the steppes to the north or the coastal plain to the east. By rights, he would be dead long before reaching either locale. But he reminded himself that he'd been in similar situations and had come out on the other side. He just preferred not to do it again if he didn't have to.

As if in answer to that thought, he began to notice a slim line of darkness—a break in the terrain—ahead. Focusing on it, he pushed himself, switching the staff from shoulder to shoulder as necessary. Before long, the break in the terrain resolved itself into what Jack thought it was: a low cliff that provided a hedge against an aggregate of sand. Beyond that the desert stretched unbroken as far as he could see. In spite of his growing excitement, he stopped and took another drink before continuing on.

It took almost an hour before he reached it. Up close, it looked smaller than he'd expected. Leading up to it, the constancy of sand and rock meant that the only way one would notice it from the front was because of the ribbon of darker rock that topped it. Approaching from the side, Jack could see that it was a sheer cliff, dropping down about ten feet into a hollow bordered by rock. The closest approximation Jack could make was that it resembled a dead-end road that terminated beneath a bridge. It seemed a perfect place in which to hide, and he hurried toward it, reaching the near edge of it several minutes later. Once there, he traversed the line of the rock that extended past it before finding a place where he could slide down into a depression.

He backtracked until he could put a hand on the rock wall that extended some four feet above him. The sun was rising from the other side, which sent a shaft of shade for a good distance beyond Jack. In fact, Jack could stay in that spot until noon without feeling the first of the sun's rays fall on him. He removed the staff from his shoulder and leaned it against the rock, then reached for a water bottle and took a drink, well aware that he had to conserve his resources if he hoped to last more than a few days.

After that, he settled down to wait.

Setting his back against the rock, he lowered himself to the ground, resolved to remain there until night came again and he could head back to the road and work his way toward the village. He had a few hours to think about shelter—how he might use the few items in his possession to create a barrier between him and the scorching sun.

How long he sat there he didn't know, but at some point it occurred to him that he still hadn't taken a good look at the thing responsible for his current predicament. The Nehushtan leaned against the rock just a foot away, the rotting cloth of centuries charcoal gray in the muted sunlight.

He reached for it, pulling it down across his lap, and began to free it from its bindings. In Jack's estimation, the cloth itself was ancient, perhaps two thousand years old, maybe older. In fact, the fabric, by itself, would have commanded a great deal at auction. Yet, once the last of the cloth strips were undone he tossed them to the side, breaking every rule of antiquities preservation he knew.

Freed now from its bindings, the Nehushtan appeared both more and less than he'd expected. There was a sense of reverence, to be sure, as a thing crafted by a civilization long dead. However, there was also the letdown one felt from imagining something a certain way, only to find that the reality did not match the expectation.

The artifact was less than five feet in length. Jack's practiced eye could see that, at some point, someone had chopped at least a foot from the staff. His initial thought was that the wood that made up the staff itself was oak. The passage of more than a millennium had rendered the surface dark and mottled. Jack ran a hand along it, taking in its age. He then let his eyes move to the serpent. Perhaps not surprisingly it looked much like he had expected it would. One of the things he'd learned during his years excavating ancient items was that a good many of the important ones had wrought significant influence on the world prior to their own passing into obscurity. The brass serpent—the metal darkened with the passage of centuries—that coiled about the staff had been reproduced countless times in various forms, from the Rod of Asclepius to Ningishita to the mythologies of more cultures than Jack could recollect.

Jack's eyes moved over the surface, over the intricately carved scales that covered its form, to the face, the eyes set in anger, the tongue flitting in contempt. As when he'd pulled it from the wall in Libya, he felt much the same sense of accomplishment—an awe of the age and beauty of the artifact. If all he took away from the moment was this feeling, it would have been worth it.

He studied it for a while longer, taking in every detail, and when he was satisfied he reached for the aged cloth and carefully wrapped it. Then, after placing the artifact on the ground beside him, he settled in to wait.

13

Despite the bumpy flight and the airline food, Duckey had to admit it felt good to be in the field again, even in an unofficial capacity. During his last few years with the Company, he'd spent his days in an office keeping tabs on the foot soldiers who did the real work. So when he'd boarded the plane in Charlotte, he experienced a slight fear that he wouldn't know what to do when he arrived in Tripoli.

But it was like riding a bike. As soon as he'd entered the terminal in the Libyan capital, he felt the familiar tingle down his spine as his eyes took in everything and everybody. The big difference was that on this special op, he didn't have the considerable resources of the United States government.

Walking through the terminal, his carryon in hand, another difference occurred to him. In the past he would have had a well-defined mission with a specific set of objectives. This time his only goal was to find Jack, and he was on his own in that task.

He worked his way through the airport, dodging bodies and luggage carts. Because of ongoing construction, all traffic through TIA came through the one terminal, which made navigating its length a challenge. But part of what Duckey had enjoyed about his old profession was that he got to rub elbows with all different sorts of people. It was something he'd missed at Evanston, and something for which he envied Jack.

From the information he'd gathered so far, Jack's trail ended in this airport, his last visible transaction the rental of a car. Prior to that, he'd gone up to the fourth floor to the terminal's only restaurant for lunch. Duckey thought of stopping by the restaurant but decided it would serve no purpose. With the number of people who cycled through the establishment, the possibility that anyone would remember a lone American was minuscule. That left the Alamo counter.

"Can I help you?" the man behind the counter, after giving Duckey a once-over, asked in heavily accented English.

"I have a reservation," Duckey said. "Under the name Duckett."

The Alamo employee punched a few buttons on his computer and after reviewing the information gave a slight nod.

"We have your car available, sir," he said. "Would you like to purchase insurance?"

Duckey declined and handed over his credit card. "Do you get a lot of Americans coming through here?"

"A good number," the other man—Farag, according to his name tag—said without looking up.

"Enough that it would be hard to remember someone who came through, oh, about a week ago?"

This time, Farag did look up, a gesture that coincided with the sound of the printer coming to life. Duckey thought him no older than twenty, a local who, though young, had been in the job long enough to have been exposed to a great many different types of people and cultures. Consequently, even though his English was only passable, he understood that Duckey was not simply making conversation.

"It would be very difficult for me to remember someone who came to my counter a week ago," Farag said, his eyes narrowing.

"I can appreciate that," Duckey said. "But I have a friend who rented a car from you last Thursday. An American, about ten years younger than me, dark hair, a little rumpled. Does that ring a bell?"

Farag gave a slow headshake. "As I said, sir. Too many people come through here for me to remember most of them."

Duckey nodded. "His name's Jack Hawthorne. He rented a Ford Taurus."

At the mention of Jack's name, he saw Farag's eyes light up.

"Hawthorne," he said. "Like the writer."

"Exactly. Like the writer."

"I only remember because of *The Red Letter*," Farag said.

It took Duckey a moment to realize what Farag was referring to, and when it came to him he decided not to correct the Libyan's substitution of *red* for *scarlet*, worried that might put the brakes on their developing rapport.

"I asked him if he was related to the writer," Farag said, obviously pleased that he could recall the man Duckey was inquiring after.

"That's great," Duckey said. "Now we're getting somewhere." He sensed the growing impatience of the man who had taken a place in line behind him and chanced a quick glance, his eyes widening on seeing the line had grown by several more people. "Do you remember him saying anything about where he was going?"

Farag frowned as if giving the question some thought, then shook his head.

"Do you know if he returned the car? Here or somewhere else?"

Another headshake, yet this one was slower in coming, as if Farag was realizing he shouldn't be providing information about one customer's transaction to another customer.

"I'm sorry," he said. "I am not authorized to give you that information."

Duckey tried his best smile. "I know you're not supposed to, although I was hoping you'd make an exception. Jack's a good friend of mine, but no one's heard from him in a while. To be honest, I'm kind of worried."

He could see right away that Farag wasn't biting.

"If you are such good friends, I would think that he would call you if he wanted to talk with you."

Duckey had a hard time retaining his smile against growing exasperation. As his expression changed to something more akin to a grimace, he reached into his pocket and pulled out a twenty-dinar note, which he slid across the counter.

"I could really use that information," he said quietly. Behind him, he could hear a rising grumbling and he saw Farag look past him to a line that kept growing.

The Libyan opened his mouth and Duckey could almost see the denial forming on his lips, but then the man sighed, glanced down at the currency on the desk. He briefly met Duckey's eyes before reaching for the money and slipping it into his pocket. Then he turned his attention back to the computer.

"Jack Hawthorne rented a Ford Taurus on Thursday the fifteenth," Farag said. "He was supposed to return the car on Saturday the seventeenth."

Duckey watched as a frown crossed the Libyan's face. He hit a key, then another. After a few moments, he looked up at the American.

"The police called us on Monday to report that the car had been parked on a street in Al Bayda for three days. It has since been returned to us." He offered Duckey an apologetic shrug. "I'm sorry. I did not work that day and so knew nothing about it."

"Al Bayda?" Duckey asked.

"It is a city about a thousand kilometers to the east," Farag said. "Your friend would have been better served flying into La Abraq." He paused and added, "As you should have as well."

He reached for a folded map on the desk and handed it to Duckey, along with the keys to a car the American was no longer sure he wanted. Farag then motioned for the next customer.

From a northeast window on the twenty-second floor of the Al-Fateh Tower, Amadou Boufayed looked out over the Mediterranean, watching the small boats cut lines along the beach. From his height, Boufayed could see the shallow water stretch out beyond the beach for half a mile, the greenish-blue ribbon of land extending beneath it until, all at once, it gave way to the dark blue water of the open sea. Of all the things Boufayed appreciated about his office, the view it afforded him was chief among them, especially in the afternoon when the sun sent waves of color over the water. Of course, the view from one of the larger windows in the floors above was better, in the offices occupied by the undersecretary and those close to him. But he believed he would inherit one of those offices at some point and so was content to enjoy what he had in the interim.

He'd been pleased that the provisional government had recognized the need to maintain many of the agencies that had served the previous head of state so well. That pragmatism had served to preserve the Liaison Office of the Revolutionary Committees, despite what those in the West might have referred to as the agency's draconian policies. It also meant that Boufayed had been allowed to keep his office.

He stood at the window for another minute before he heard a knock at his door, followed by the sound of it opening. When he turned away from the window, it was to see a member of his team waiting, a folder in his hands. After the loss of the German and his Israeli escorts, those around Boufayed had taken care around him, lest one of them find themselves a focal point for his irritation. Boufayed could see that thought on the face of the man in front of him, but while that past failure still bothered him, the disappointment had ebbed to the point that those who reported to him no longer had to fear a scathing rebuke or additional paper work levied out of spite.

Boufayed gestured for the folder. Once it was in his hands, he wordlessly scanned the contents. It took him only a few moments to review the documents, along with the photo that accompanied them. After he'd finished, he looked up and, with a raised eyebrow, invited Bady to fill in the gaps.

"From what we have been able to ascertain, he is CIA," the other man said. "Our records indicate that he's been retired for several years. He is here alone, and from what we have been able to determine, he has no established itinerary. Or a return flight scheduled."

Boufayed considered the information, wondering what the presence of an ostensibly retired CIA agent in Tripoli could mean. The arrival of an agent in-country was not an uncommon occurrence, as evidenced by the Israelis three weeks before. Yet most took great pains not to be recognized as such while still in the airport. Indeed, according to the rules by which these games were played, foreign intelligence agencies possessed a fair amount of knowledge regarding which of their agents had been compromised and which could still work in a country with a certain level of anonymity. This Jim Duckett did not fit the latter category.

"I assume you've had him followed," Boufayed said.

"I have," the man confirmed. "He rented a car but, strangely, did not take it. Instead, he purchased a ticket for La Abraq. We have someone on the flight."

Boufayed frowned. The change in travel plans smelled of misdirection. It told him that whoever Jim Duckett was, he bore watching.

"I want to know every place he goes once he reaches La Abraq, and every person he talks to."

"Of course," his underling said, nodding at Boufayed and then leaving to carry out his orders.

14

"I still do not understand why it made more sense for us to come here than it did to sit in my office and make phone calls," Romero grumbled.

Espy had stopped listening to his complaints, although she didn't begrudge him the need to voice them. All she'd done was to purchase a plane ticket that would take her from London to Milan. Romero, though, had been forced to reschedule a number of meetings that would have made him a great deal of money. Allowing him to air his grievances was the least she could do; otherwise he would have bottled them up only to see them come out at an inopportune time. However, after several hours of this, her patience was wearing thin. And she would have made the trip without him, for despite all his grousing it had been his decision to meet her in Italy.

"I've tried to tell you," she said. "You can't do something like this on the phone. You have to throw yourself into it, see the face of the person you're talking to, get a feel for the streets."

She gave her brother a sidelong glance as they walked down Via Brera in Milan's city center. While she understood his irritation, there was a part of her that could not understand how anyone could be anything other than invigorated by the chance to walk through a city like Milan—a quintessentially European city with more to see and do than any one person could hope for. No matter where she looked, there was something new to see as they dodged cars racing down the narrow streets between tall, closely spaced buildings with ground-floor shops and apartments above, each with a balcony jutting out into space. Art shops were everywhere, and in those areas not already beset with parked cars and lines of motorbikes she saw outdoor markets that, had she had her way, she would have spent hours exploring.

She understood that she was a more experienced traveler than most and that a city like Milan could be difficult to absorb. Except that the man next to her, the sibling ten years her senior, had spent much of his youth crisscrossing the globe, visiting places she could scarcely imagine. Ironically much of that travel had been done in the company of the man they were in Milan to find. She voiced as much to Romero.

"Why do you think I rarely leave Caracas?" he responded. "In the time I spent traveling with Jack I think I aged twenty years." He shook his head and made a face that suggested he'd remembered something unpleasant. "I have never prayed so fervently as I did on those occasions when we were very far from home and he got that look in his eye." He glanced at Esperanza. "You know the look I mean?"

She nodded and her lip curled into a smile.

"When I saw that look, I stopped and prayed because I knew the day was likely not to end well."

Esperanza didn't say anything, even as her brother's memories elicited a chuckle from him. In her history with Jack, she sometimes forgot that Romero's preceded hers by years and that her brother was as attached to the man—and as vexed by him—as was she.

As she pondered this, they reached Via Fiori Oscuri and, beyond it, the large building that housed Brera Academy. From the outside it didn't look like the venerable institution Espy had pictured, although that was due to the fact that the entire façade was draped in large dingy construction cloth. The building was apparently undergoing some kind of large-scale renovation.

However, once she and Romero passed beneath the archway, they were transported into another world. The massive courtyard had both a look and a feel so markedly different from the city beyond its walls that aside from the traffic noise, Espy could have believed she'd traveled to another place and time. In the center of the courtyard stood the signature piece of the academy: the massive Napoleon that Espy had only seen in photographs.

Glancing at her brother, she saw that the irritation he had carried with him was gone, replaced by the kind of appreciation that only a man educated in the arts could have for such a sculpture.

"And despite the many times I thought I was going to die, it was for times like this that I continued to travel with him," Romero remarked.

They'd come to Brera for one reason and Espy knew how slim that reason was. The Brera Academy was one of the places she'd heard Jack mention—a place in which he had friends. Before they'd come, she'd made a few calls, locating a man whose relationship with the missing archaeologist went back several years. While he'd informed her that he hadn't seen Jack in quite some time, she was hopeful that he would be able to help her shape her list of people and places that deserved her attention.

As if reading her thoughts, Romero said, "Remind me. You said you spoke with this man and that he has not seen Jack, correct?"

Esperanza did not answer her brother immediately. Instead, she started off across the courtyard, toward the entrance.

"We needed a place to start," Espy said when Romero caught up with her. "If it turns out to be a dead end, then we cross it off the list."

Romero let that go without a response, and Esperanza appreciated the gesture. Because more than most cities in the world, Milan was a playground for someone like Jack. Just going through the museums alone would take them a lot more time than she wanted to contemplate.

With a resigned sigh, she entered the building, Romero in tow.

———

There were ways in which Imolene knew he had closed much of the distance between himself and the men he pursued, but most of those ways were ones known only to himself—a feeling the hunter has but cannot explain. Templeton and Hawthorne had crossed into Tunisia, of that he was certain. He was equally certain they would have to head north, because at the point at which they had navigated the border crossing, little existed either west or south but desert. Even moderately equipped, the barren landscape was a formidable adversary. In Imolene's estimation, they would have pointed the jeep in the direction of Raballah. And so he had done the same.

He sent the Chevy truck over the sand and rock as fast as the vehicle would carry him. The Yugo, while having lasted much longer than the Egyptian had anticipated, had threatened to gasp its last a few kilometers east of the border. Anticipating the Yugo's death throes, Imolene had traded it for the truck, although the deal had cost him a hundred dinars.

What also caused Imolene to push the speed of the new vehicle was that he'd spoken again with his employers, and they had expressed extreme displeasure with him when he'd told them of the loss of the artifact. When he'd accepted the job, he was well aware it was not without risk. In some ways, working for the Israelis was more dangerous than performing the same tasks for other neighboring governments—not because those other governments hesitated to punish failure but because they lacked the efficiency of the Israelis to do so. Imolene harbored no doubts about his life being forfeited if he failed to recover what his employers had hired him to retrieve.

For the hundredth time he wondered where Templeton was going. While he carried the American with him, it was difficult—if not impossible—for him to put any real distance between himself and Imolene, whom he would understand to be in pursuit. Whatever reason the Englishman had for keeping Hawthorne alive had to be a compelling one; it was certainly one for which Imolene was thankful.

He reached for the water bottle on the seat next to him and drained it, the lack of air-conditioning in the Chevy a hindrance he could overcome with proper hydration. The desert stretched long before him, yet he had several more bottles of water, which like the urgency simmering below the surface and fueling his pursuit, was more than enough to see him through.

———

There were some skills Duckey supposed he would never lose, regardless of how much time had passed since his retirement from the CIA. Such as the skill of recognizing when he was being watched. On an airplane—even a small domestic flight like the Buraq Air bird that ferried him from Tripoli to La Abraq—it could be difficult to determine when others' eyes were studying him and so Duckey had to rely on his gut. And his gut told him that the man three rows behind him, wearing an expensive suit and pretending to be napping, was a tail.

The big question was *why* someone would want to have him followed. The obvious second question was *who*? For the *why*, Duckey had a guess, and if he was right it meant he wasn't as on top of his game as he thought he was. He should have realized that, regardless of how long it had been since he'd retired, his name would raise a red flag in customs. And with the political unrest that had consumed most of the country just the year before, he suspected the Libyans were being even more careful about whom they allowed to roam freely around their country.

For that, he didn't blame them. With rumors that the CIA had been involved in fomenting much of the unrest, Duckey found himself surprised that they'd allowed him in the country at all. True, his file said he was retired, but the Libyans wouldn't buy that.

Duckey suspected he would be picked up by another tail— maybe more—as soon as he stepped off the plane and hoped he'd be able to spot them as effortlessly as he'd picked up the one sitting not far behind him. Beyond that, he suspected there wasn't much he could do about it—although he couldn't help but wonder what his shadows would make of the investigation Duckey had come to their country to perform. That elicited a smile as Duckey thought of how Jack could vex even the Libyan intelligence establishment.

Thirty minutes later the wheels were on the ground and Duckey grabbed his bag from the overhead compartment and exited. Because the Buraq was a domestic flight, he wasn't held up in customs. Within minutes of landing he stepped out into a comfortable day, the temperature around sixty degrees. As he hailed a cab, he scanned the area for either his original agent or the man's replacement but saw no one who stood out, which didn't necessarily mean anything.

The cab covered the ten kilometers from La Abraq to Al Bayda in good time, despite the heavy traffic, and as the ancient city rose up before him the thought of being followed drifted from his mind.

Duckey's service had taken him to a great many parts of

the world, but he'd spent the bulk of it in eastern Europe, which meant a sprawling north African city still made him feel as if he were a tourist. And in stepping onto the streets of a city like Al Bayda, a visitor often found himself unsure of his footing, unable to get a feel for the ebb and flow of the culture. On one corner he saw a collection of buildings as modern as any he might see in the States—a coffee shop, movie theater, high-end clothing stores. At the next corner he saw a line of rickety market stalls, with merchants offering fruit, linens, even live animals, all within a few blocks of a thriving business district.

They entered Al Bayda on Msah, the main road that bisected the city, the driver slowing as traffic funneled in from Aldayn and Kufra. Duckey's destination was in the modern part of Al Bayda, the part that had been hit hard by the unrest the previous year. The police station had been burned to the ground; he remembered watching on television the protesters dancing and cheering as the fires consumed the symbol of an oppressive regime.

When the cab driver pulled off Msah onto a side street, Duckey looked at the buildings surrounding the car, taking in the enormity of the reconstruction that had brought one of the main administrative parts of the city back from the dead. The cab pulled to a stop in front of a new-looking building, the razed police station restored.

Duckey paid the man and stepped out with his bag, half considering asking the driver to wait but suspecting he would quickly be able to locate a ride in this part of the city. If not, the system of small buses that cut the city into sections would take him wherever he needed to go. He glanced at his watch and hoped he'd have time to do what he needed to given how late in the day it was.

Entering the police station, he stepped into an air-conditioned lobby that included a reception window and a security line. He proceeded to the window.

"Do you speak English?" he asked after he'd gotten the attention of the man behind the glass.

When the clerk raised his eyes, he gave Duckey a once-over, conveying annoyance for what Duckey could only presume was due to his being addressed in a language other than Arabic or Greek. Still, the man managed something like a smile. "Can I help you?"

"I need to speak to someone about a car you towed a week ago," Duckey said.

The clerk said, "Second floor, room 212," then gestured to the security checkpoint.

Duckey made it through the gauntlet unscathed and then, avoiding the elevator at the far end of the lobby, headed for the stairs.

The second floor was no busier than the first, leading Duckey to wonder if the building had another entrance through which the majority of police traffic entered and exited. He found room 212 with little difficulty. The door opened into a waiting room with a bare concrete floor and two walls lined with plastic chairs. After checking in at the counter, Duckey took a seat with six others there before him.

An hour later Duckey was called up to the counter, where a bored-looking young man with an MP3 player and headphones over his ears asked him what he wanted in passable English.

"You towed a car a week ago," Duckey said. "Ford Taurus. An Alamo rental. Can you tell me where you found the car and if you know what might have happened to the person driving it?"

"Was it your car?"

"No, a friend of mine rented it."

The young man shrugged. "Then I cannot help you. Check with the rental company."

Frustrated, Duckey decided to change his tack. "Look. I'm not interested in the car. I'm trying to find my friend."

The Libyan clerk studied Duckey for several seconds before he said, "We tow dozens of cars every week. I can't remember them all."

Duckey knew where this was going. He reached into his pocket and slid his second twenty-dinar note of the day across the counter. The clerk stared at it for what seemed a long while without moving; then with the same gesture and facial expression Duckey had witnessed on the face of the Alamo employee, the man grabbed it and quickly pocketed it.

"Let me see what I can find out," he said.

Fifteen minutes later Duckey stepped out of the building, armed with a street address and the name of a man who might have been the last person to see Jack Hawthorne before he disappeared.

15

Dawn was still hours off when Jack reached the village. In the near darkness, held in check only by a crescent moon hanging in a clear sky, he could see the shapes of the squat, sand-scrubbed structures gathered like slumbering cattle. He stopped at the outskirts of the village, his eyes passing over it, seeing no movement, except for the way the buildings wouldn't hold still. Frowning, he concentrated until his eyes stilled them. He'd finished the water hours ago and it seemed the desert had sucked every bit of moisture from his body. He knew he wasn't thinking clearly as he started off again, looking for the thing he needed, the thing responsible for spawning a fragile community in the middle of nowhere.

He found the well in the village center. Twelve feet across and covered by a wooden cap, half a dozen access doors were evenly spaced around the perimeter. He pulled one open and the recognizable smell of water came rushing out, so sweet he might have shed a tear had he moisture enough to produce one. Taking hold of a rope, its end attached to the well's outer wall, he began drawing the bucket up, feeling the weight of the water that filled it. He gulped down the contents of a full ladle, then a second more slowly, feeling the water work to open his throat. Filling the ladle a third time, he poured some into his cupped hand and washed the dirt from his eyes and face. When he'd finished, he settled on the ground to rest, his back against the cool stone of the well, and let his eyes fall over the silent village.

When he and Templeton had passed it heading west, Jack had seen it as a distant oasis from the main road. What had set it apart, though, was that as they'd progressed farther into Tunisia he'd seen fewer such settlements. If Martin Templeton was smart, he would know that this place offered Jack his only real hope of survival from the elements. That was assuming of course that Jack would not have taken his chances going the other direction, staying near the road and hoping to find another haven farther along. Either choice had its merits, as well as its drawbacks, but Jack was confident his former captor would not ignore the place.

For perhaps the hundredth time, Jack berated himself for taking the artifact from Templeton. In doing so he had assured that the man would try to track him; whereas, had he fled without it, there might have been a chance that the Englishman would have cut his losses and moved on. Yet after thinking on it some more, Jack decided he'd made the right choice, and he was willing to endure hardship if the payoff warranted it. To have left the relic in someone else's hands would have invalidated the struggles of the last few days.

He lost track of how long he sat there, until the thirst that had driven him to the well returned in a less insistent fashion. He pushed himself to his feet and drank more water pulled from the bucket that still rested on the edge of the well, forcing himself to avoid considering how sick he was likely to get by partaking from the bacteria-laden communal resource. As he returned the ladle and began to lower the bucket, he caught sight of movement near a grouping of three small cement buildings that formed part of the village's interior perimeter. He watched as a boy stepped out from the narrow alley between two of the buildings with a large jar in his arms. When he had crossed perhaps half the distance, he raised his eyes and, catching sight of Jack, stopped in his tracks.

Jack smiled at the boy, aware that his passage through the desert had left him looking like something from a child's nightmare. The young Tunisian regarded Jack with the calculating eyes of one with the wherewithal to gauge a potential threat.

While the boy stared, Jack lowered the bucket and closed the access door. The boy then resumed his walk to the well, keeping an eye on Jack as he bent to retrieve the artifact. With less distance between them, the boy had a better look at Jack, who saw the other's eyes widen as he took in his condition. Almost immediately, concern replaced wariness and the boy set his jar on the ground. He circled the well, stopping in front of the American and saying something that, in the first pass, Jack had no hope of understanding. His Arabic, always poor, would improve the longer he spent immersed in it, but trying to interpret it in his current condition was close to impossible. The boy seemed to understand. Rather than saying anything more, he reached for Jack's hand and led him toward the cement buildings.

Before long, Jack found himself inside one of the small three-room homes common to the area. When they'd entered, the child's mother was preparing breakfast and she cast a worried look over the pair. She said something to the boy that Jack couldn't follow, except to note that it sounded like a rebuke. A few moments later, a man emerged from a back room. The older man took one look at Jack and apparently recognized that he needed their help. He motioned for Jack to sit at the little wooden table in the kitchen area. Then he said something to the mother, who responded by placing a bowl of something warm in front of the battered archaeologist. Before that moment, Jack hadn't realized how ravenous he was, and he soon fell to eating while his hosts stood patiently and watched.

As near as Jack could tell, it was almost noon and he'd been alone in the house for nearly an hour, the last of the village elders having left to engage in discussions concerning their visitor.

After the meal—which included tea mixed with honey by the boy's mother to help soothe the irritation in Jack's throat—he'd responded to their questions as best he could, given his limited knowledge of Arabic. He'd mentioned nothing of the artifact but had noticed the man's gaze move to the wrapped staff a number of times. It had been the boy, though, who had walked over to where the staff was propped up against a wall.

As Jack discussed his options with the father, asking about

transportation so he might be taken someplace that had a phone, the Tunisian child removed the cloth from the top half of the staff.

The father's eyes had shifted over Jack's shoulder and then had widened. When he released a gasp, Jack turned to see the boy holding the staff, staring into the gem eyes of the ancient serpent that had looked upon the stricken Israelites. Jack did not need to have a fluent grasp of the language to know that the words the other man spoke intoned a mixture of awe and fear. The Tunisian was out of his chair before Jack could react. He crossed around the table and took the staff from the boy's hands, his own larger hands not touching the wood and metal of the artifact but remaining on the cloth.

By that time, Jack had risen and crossed to the man's side, yet he didn't take the relic away from him. The Tunisian had lifted the Nehushtan and turned it so he could see into the eyes of the serpent. His hands trembled, and for a brief moment Jack thought he might drop it. Finally the man looked away from the snake, a look of deep reverence on his face.

When Jack finally removed the staff from the Tunisian's hands, carefully rewrapping the exposed portion and returning it to its spot against the wall, he could see that his host's opinion of him had undergone a dramatic change. The problem was that he didn't know if the man now regarded him as a hero or a devil.

Two hours later, Jack thought he had that part figured out as a procession of solemn bearded men entered the small home, all of them wanting to see the staff. Although all Jack wanted to do was to steal away with his prize, make it back to

London, and collect a very large sum of money from Sturdivant, he understood he had to allow the show-and-tell—and
not just because of the etiquette involved. He still needed help
from these people and so keeping the artifact from them—a
relic mentioned in their holy books—did little to encourage
generosity, which was something he needed, since Templeton
had divested him of both his wallet and phone.

The visits had ended an hour ago, and Jack had the impression that the men had gone to deliberate. He'd entertained the fear that they were considering keeping the staff
for themselves, but his pragmatic side understood that there
was nothing he could do but relax and wait. Unlike escaping from a single man in the middle of the night, trying to
smuggle the staff out of a village full of people in broad
daylight would be difficult to accomplish. Instead, he settled
into a comfortable chair to nap.

Duckey decided there was a marked difference between
modern Al Bayda—the part that provided a backdrop for the
police station, the legislative plaza, and several businesses—
and the older and more modest part in which he found himself. Khansaa, a sprawling neighborhood in the southwestern
portion of the city, was a conglomerate of old houses, dormant businesses, and streets plagued by potholes and abandoned cars. As he'd driven into the depressed area, ferried
there by an elderly cab driver, Duckey found himself amazed
at the abruptness of the transition. Duckey suspected that
the only reason Jack's derelict rental had raised an eyebrow

had been because, when found, it was parked along the main road that separated Khansaa from Rabaah Adawiyyah—a bustling neighborhood with a university occupancy, lots of green space, and new apartment buildings, all of which warranted a stronger police presence.

Just two streets into Khansaa, with Rabaah Adawiyyah still in sight behind him, the cab pulled over and the driver looked at Duckey in the rearview mirror. Looking out the window, the American saw that they'd arrived at a one-story building that ran the entire length of the block. The brick structure had been divided into a number of different businesses, two of which appeared open: a café and a place that rented motorbikes. The cab was parked in front of the café, which had a large front window, the door next to it standing open to the mild weather. Duckey got out and, asking the man to wait but finding him less than amenable to the request, paid and watched the cab speed off.

When he entered the café, he found himself the only occupant beyond a middle-aged woman standing behind the serving counter. As Duckey paused inside the door, allowing his eyes to grow accustomed to the dim light inside, the woman gave him a piercing look that he barely caught with his compromised vision.

Duckey moved to the counter, the woman looking at him expectantly.

"Do you mind if I ask you a question?" he asked.

Up to this point, English had done the job for him and he hoped it would continue to do so. He couldn't speak Arabic and hadn't spoken Greek since college. The look the woman gave him, though, caused him to believe she hadn't understood a word. He was on the verge of asking the question again in Greek when she spoke in heavily accented English.

"Do you want to eat?" she asked.

Duckey had picked up the cooking smells the moment he walked in, and since he'd left the hotel that morning without having eaten, the temptation to sample the local cuisine was strong but he resisted the urge.

"No, thank you. I'd just like to ask you a few questions if you don't mind."

The problem was that it looked as if she minded quite a bit. He suspected he would find her unwilling to cooperate until he paid for something. Glancing around, he spotted the glass-front cooler filled with soda.

"I'd like a Coke," he said, pointing.

When the woman returned with the drink, he slid a ten-dinar note across the counter and motioned for her to keep all of it. Then, the wheels sufficiently greased, he tried again.

"A week ago, you called the police about a car that had been abandoned right in front of your café. Do you remember?"

The woman nodded.

"Do you remember seeing the man who drove the car? He would have been an American, younger than me."

She did not answer right away. Instead, she fixed Duckey with a look common to those who have suffered beneath a regime in which speaking to the wrong people about the wrong things could get one into trouble.

"Who are you and why do you want to know?"

Duckey, who'd been expecting the question, gave her the same answer he'd given the clerk at the police station, under-

standing that the simple truth worked well in most instances—
except when one was on the CIA payroll.

The woman absorbed his response and then seemed to
resolve some small conflict within herself.

"I saw the car pull up and I saw your friend get out," she
said. As she spoke, her eyes moved to the window as if she
could still see Jack on the sidewalk. "I noticed him because
I didn't have any customers and was hoping he'd come in."

"Did he?"

She shook her head. "No. He walked north down the sidewalk and I didn't see him after that."

"And how long did you wait before you called to report
the car?"

"Two days," she said. "And I only called because the restaurant was busy; the car was taking up space my customers
needed."

Duckey thanked her and then exited the café, heading to
the business adjacent to it. Before even entering, he was already certain he knew one of the three things relevant to
Jack's abandonment of the car: he knew why his friend had
left it. But that still left him trying to find answers to the other
two questions. Where did he go? And once he got there, what
kept him from coming back and reclaiming the Taurus?

The inside of the place was much darker than the café, as
well as a good deal dirtier. Scattered around the floor and
on the sales counter lay cannibalized parts from an untold
number of motorbikes. Besides the bikes parked along the
sidewalk out front, two older models, each with various parts
missing, had been brought inside and leaned against a wall.

Duckey made his way to the counter just as a man in jeans

that appeared to be made more of dirt and grease than the original fabric emerged from a back room.

Before long, he'd exited the establishment with the knowledge that, for some reason, Jack Hawthorne had rented a motorbike for a day and had ridden off on it, leaving behind the rental car. He'd paid in cash, which was why the credit report the ex-CIA agent had pulled had not revealed the transaction.

As Duckey stood on the sidewalk, armed with the new information, hands on hips, he pondered what the last hour had accomplished in terms of actionable information. On the surface, the image of Jack riding off on a bike seemed to leave him no closer to finding Jack. Still, his experience tended to come into play in such a situation. In any intelligence agency, knowledge held more value than anything else—even knowledge that didn't seem important when first acquired. Duckey had served in the field long enough to understand that, at any time, information procured months before and in a different part of the world might be the crucial piece of intel that tied other pieces together.

He hoped too that whatever Esperanza and her brother were discovering in Milan would help them put more of the puzzle together.

———

The black Mercedes had only been parked on Al Faraq for twenty minutes, but in that time the men inside had noticed a significant decrease in the amount of activity on the street. Where on most days the flow of foot, bicycle, and auto traffic would have been constant—the resultant noise of those activities combining to form something like an exuberant chorus—as the car remained there, the flow of bodies and vehicles slowed to a trickle, the song to a whisper.

Boufayed could have chosen a less obvious car from which to watch the American navigate around Al Bayda, but the Mercedes had been the first available, and as the target in this case was a foreigner who would not be as attuned to the city's movements as a local would have been, he'd decided to choose rapid mobilization over invisibility.

The driver, who had not spoken for more than an hour, and whose name Boufayed did not know, kept his eyes on the narrow street down which the American had disappeared fifteen minutes ago, deeper into Khansaa, one of Boufayed's agents following on foot. From where the Mercedes sat, on the street that divided the poorer Al Bayda neighborhood from Rabaah Adawiyyah, Boufayed could see the entrances to the two shops where James Duckett had gone and where another of Boufayed's men had entered afterward to interview the workers.

The American's first stop at the café hadn't been a surprise to the Libyan after interrogating the clerk at the Al Bayda police station, who informed them of Duckett's interest in an abandoned rental car several days prior to his arrival in Tripoli. That revelation had launched another branch of the investigation. They'd run the name Jack Hawthorne and what the system had kicked back was cause for confusion more than anything else. Boufayed wondered what an itinerant archaeologist was doing poking around Al Bayda, and how was he connected to a former CIA agent. That, and if another connection existed. People back in his Tripoli office were working to find a link between Jack Hawthorne and the German killed weeks ago. Both were historians, albeit of different varieties.

As he pondered these things, he saw his man emerge from the rental store and head toward the Mercedes. He crossed the street and slipped into the back seat.

"He told the woman in the restaurant the same thing he told the clerk," the agent said. "Just that this Hawthorne is a friend that he's looking for."

"And the rental shop?" Boufayed asked.

"The owner said that an American rented a motorbike last week but has not returned it. He told the same to the CIA agent."

Boufayed nodded his acknowledgment and then shifted his eyes back to the street where Duckett had disappeared. There was nothing to do but wait until the man tailing him called to say where he would stop next.

16

When he awoke, the light that had entered the home through the lone window in the front room was gone. A lamp burned on a small table in the corner and he could smell the odors of cooking, hear the sounds of people moving around the kitchen. It took him a few moments to realize that he'd been sleeping for hours. Rising, he winced at the tightness in his neck and then walked around the corner and into the kitchen area. The staff was where he'd left it, and he felt an anxiety he hadn't realized he was holding begin to fade—a realization he felt guilty about considering the kindness of his hosts.

Both the man and the woman—Khamel and Nadia, Jack had learned—were in the room and both looked over as he entered, Khamel offering a warm smile and Nadia an expression that he couldn't quite identify, except to know that it was different from the one she'd used on him that morning.

"We were beginning to think you would sleep through the

night," Khamel said, and Jack was grateful that the Arabic was coming back to him.

"I'm sorry for abusing your hospitality," Jack answered. "I hadn't meant to sleep that long."

Khamel waved Jack's apology away.

"A prophet brandishing the staff of Allah can sleep wherever and whenever he wishes," the Tunisian said—a statement that earned the husband a frown from his wife.

Khamel chuckled beneath the glare, which told Jack the man did not believe what he had just said, which meant Jack did not have to disavow the moniker he'd just been granted.

Nadia brought over two cups of tea and motioned for Jack to partake, and so he joined Khamel at the table.

"So you and the others have made a decision, then?"

Khamel's smile faded, but the mirth did not entirely flee his eyes.

"There was some discussion about whether you were a thief who deserves to be killed for carrying a holy item through the desert at night, or a man chosen by God to carry his standard through the wilderness without food or water, with only his hand to protect you."

Jack considered the two extremes and was chagrined to realize he probably fit in the former category. Khamel's smirk told Jack that he agreed.

"You have eaten our bread and drank our tea and so you are ours to protect," Khamel said. "And regardless of your intentions, you do hold the staff of Allah and we must entrust that you have been given it for a reason."

"Do you believe that?" Jack asked before he could stop himself.

At the question, Khamel's face became a thing carved from stone. The look he leveled on the American was one that seemed to take in and measure everything about him, and all Jack could do was to sit beneath the scrutiny. After what seemed a long while, Khamel answered.

"I believe all things happen for a reason," he said. "I believe that very strongly." He let that hang there, perhaps to see if Jack had a response, but when Jack said nothing, Khamel continued, "But I also believe that Allah's plans are such that it does not serve us to ponder their intricacies. Instead, we act on what we know or on what we feel to be true. We make our decisions and we trust that God will take them and make them work within the framework of the story he is writing."

Jack thought that sounded as solid a worldview as he could remember hearing and he was grateful for it.

The two men lapsed into silence as they drank their tea and while Nadia prepared dinner. Only when Jack had drained the cup did Khamel speak again.

"Tell me," he said. "How did you come into possession of it?"

He was looking at the staff and Jack looked over as well. He was certain it hadn't been moved since the last of the elders had left several hours ago. When Jack looked back at Khamel, it was to find that he did not want to answer the question. To the Tunisian, reasonable and educated man that he appeared to be, the Nehushtan was something that validated the deep mysteries of a religion he'd been practicing since boyhood. Because of that, he wanted to preserve for Khamel the image of his God reaching down from the heavens to hand a relic to his chosen infidel rather than to tell him that he had found the staff through research and dumb luck. He was saved from having to make a decision, though, when the front door swung open.

The words that the newcomer said to Khamel were delivered too quickly for Jack to understand, but they had an immediate effect on Khamel, whose face darkened. His host glanced at Jack before responding to the other man. When he did answer, it was at a speed Jack could understand.

"Bring him," he said.

Once the man had gone, Jack waited for Khamel to fill him in, yet the Tunisian seemed content to remain silent and so Jack took his cues from him. Consequently, when the door opened a few minutes later and Martin Templeton was pushed over the threshold, three armed men behind him, Jack had established an equanimity not easily upended.

It took a few moments for Templeton to find him in the room, and when he did, when the Englishman's eyes flitted over him and then shifted back, the one thing Jack noticed was that the other man's face was absent of surprise.

"Well played, Dr. Hawthorne," Templeton said after a moment. "Well played, indeed."

━━━━━

Esperanza was as tired as her brother, but there was no way she would give him the satisfaction of knowing it. Not after her repeated digs at how much he complained about walking through the city, telling him that his years spent selling pricey baubles to tourists had softened him. He'd bristled at that. But as he watched his sister navigating blocks upon blocks of Milan sidewalks without a pause, there was little he could say to refute the insults.

Truth be told, Espy's feet hurt like they hadn't in years and she was used to traversing the streets of Caracas—streets that rivaled those of San Francisco in their steepness. She'd been thankful for the times when the place they wanted to reach was sufficiently separated from the place they were to mandate a bus or cab ride.

They'd been at it for almost six hours, bouncing from one museum to another, as well as checking an art gallery, school, and antiquities dealership, and so far they'd come up with nothing. Their most promising stop had been their first, the evening before, when she and Romero had met with Dr. Joseph Hartman, professor of modern art at Brera. And Espy only considered that stop a success because Hartman at least knew Jack, even if he hadn't seen nor heard from the missing archaeologist in years. At each of the other locations she couldn't find anyone who knew his name, much less could explain why he might have gone missing.

She and Romero had agreed to call it a day and were looking for a place to get something to eat before heading back to the hotel when she decided to check one more place off her list. The sign above the door said *Petrone's Past Fashionables*, and the only reason Espy wanted to stop there was because it was on the same street as their hotel. It was a poor reason to stop and yet she knew that Jack was a creature of spontaneity, which made her wonder if adding a bit of impulsiveness to the hunt for him was worth a try.

When Espy pushed open the door, sending a bell ringing

above her, she fell in love with the place before she'd made it more than two steps in. The place had a charm to it, despite the haphazard arrangement of the merchandise. Before the door closed shut, the proprietor greeted them. He was short, wore dark pants and too large a shirt. He flashed them a smile that showed two missing teeth.

Espy liked him right away.

"How may I help you?" he asked in bad Spanish, likely picking the language from an assessment of the physical characteristics of Espy and her brother.

"You have a fine store," Espy answered in flawless Italian, genuinely impressed by the quality and breadth of the merchandise she could see through all the clutter.

"You have a good eye." His smile widened and he took a moment to run an appraiser's eye over the pair. "You look like a book lover," he said, reverting to Italian. "Can I interest you in a first-edition *I Giochi Numerici*? It has notes from Alberti in the margins."

Esperanza offered a smile and shook her head. "What we're really after is information. We're looking for someone. There was a man—an American—who might have come in here a week or so ago."

The diminutive shopkeeper adopted a puzzled look. Petrone's Past Fashionables was located on one of Milan's busiest streets, where tourists streamed in numbers that made an honest businessman salivate. To recall a single individual after several days was close to impossible.

"He's a bit over six feet tall," Espy went on. "Dark hair. Probably needed a shave and to have his clothes ironed." Espy paused, glancing around the store in a gesture meant to take in the whole of the intriguing chaotic mess of the place. "And he would have loved a place like this."

As she described Jack, she saw the proprietor's features slide in a different direction, as if he was trying to make a connection between the description and a memory and partially succeeding. She exchanged a look with Romero, who didn't speak Italian and so had only a vague idea of what was being discussed. When she returned her gaze to the man she could only presume was Petrone himself, she saw something that looked like distaste had joined the menagerie of other expressions.

"What was this gentleman's name?" he asked, and if Espy hadn't known better, she would have thought he had a name in mind.

"Jack Hawthorne," she said.

"Do you know where he is?"

Espy noticed a vein beginning to throb in the man's neck. She shook her head. "That's why we're here. We're looking for him and were hoping he'd been here."

Petrone's response was a dry spit that might have struck the ground near Espy's foot had there been anything to it.

"I guess that means he's seen Jack?" Romero remarked.

Espy ignored him.

"I swear to you," Petrone said. "If Hawthorne so much as steps one foot into my store, even with my money, I'll kill him." He spat again for emphasis.

Despite the vehement reaction of the shopkeeper, Espy couldn't keep a slight smile from finding its way to her lips. Even though Petrone wanted to kill him, the man's vitriol meant that Jack was alive. And knowing that half the people

Jack met ended up wanting to kill him made her less concerned about Petrone's threat than she might otherwise have been. After all, she'd watched more than one angry person level a firearm on him.

"Let me guess," she said. "He owes you money."

"He owes me *a lot* of money," Petrone corrected. "He borrowed a book. He was supposed to bring it back in a few days, but I haven't seen him since."

He shook his head and ran a hand through his dark hair, releasing a chuckle.

"I should have known," he said. "I loaned it to him because I knew him, but that's why I should have known better."

"How long have you known Jack?" Espy asked.

"Too long. At least ten years."

Espy nodded. "So, what was the book he 'borrowed'?"

Up until now, Espy was under the impression that the Italian viewed her as an ally—someone who could understand his anger against the man who'd deprived him of something of value, and probably not for the first time. Now she sensed something else in the pause before he responded.

"Who are you?" he finally said, ignoring her question about the book.

Espy moved deeper into the store, placed her hands on a glass countertop. Beneath the glass lay an assortment of rare and expensive items. The entire shop and its merchandise suggested that Petrone was not a man hung up on a single item's expense, which meant his anger at Jack had less to do with the value of the book than it did the principle of the thing.

"My name's Esperanza," she said. "I'm a friend of Jack's."

She turned away from the counter and aimed an apologetic smile at Petrone. "You won't hold that against me, will you?"

"I might say a prayer for you," Petrone said.

"Actually it's Jack who's in need of prayer. He's missing."

"Missing?"

"We think so, yes. The last time anyone saw him, he was boarding a plane for Libya. Before that, we know he was in Milan." She locked eyes with the Italian and shrugged. "Who knows? You might be the last person he talked to before he disappeared."

"I might?" Petrone asked, surprise on his face. He looked from Espy to Romero, who had not moved from his spot near the door.

"That's why we're here," Espy said. "If we can figure out what Jack was working on right before he went missing, it might help us find him."

Petrone was slow to reply, his expression appearing as if stuck between a willingness to help and a refusal to speak another word, followed by their expulsion from the shop.

"The way I see it," she said, "your helping us find Jack means that you stand a better chance of getting your book back."

"If he hasn't already lost it or sold it," Petrone said.

While Espy thought she knew Jack well enough to believe he wouldn't sell it, she could buy into the losing angle. She didn't have to put voice to that, though, as Petrone raised his hands in a gesture of surrender.

"I loaned him a book about Milan Cathedral," he said. "*The Tower of God*. It's a rare eighteenth-century history. *Very* rare. Only seven are known to exist."

"And you let him take it?"

"Sometimes he has a way of making you do things that you would not normally do," he said, his cheeks coloring.

"Do you know why he wanted it?"

"No," Petrone said. "Although he did seem more interested in the construction of the building than he did the history."

Espy took the information and rolled it around in her mind. She didn't know what to make of it, not yet anyway. "And he didn't tell you where he was going next?"

Petrone shook his head and then glanced from Espy to Romero and back. Reading his face, Espy couldn't tell if his anger had been replaced by concern for their mutual friend or a genuine desire to see Jack punished for the unreturned book.

"If you find him," Petrone said, "tell him if he comes into my store again, I'll kill him."

After she and Romero emerged into the evening air, she answered Romero's unspoken question. "Jack owes him money."

Romero uttered a grunt devoid of surprise and started down the sidewalk after his sister.

17

They had secured Templeton in the back room, and Jack couldn't help but ponder the similarities to his own confinement a few days before. He'd had nothing to do with Templeton's treatment, however. The men of the village had taken the initiative to take him into their custody the moment he began asking them questions about a lone American they might have discovered wandering in the desert. It hadn't taken Jack long to become something of a local celebrity and it seemed the villagers had something of a communal interest in protecting him.

Many of the men who had spoken with Jack earlier in the day had returned and they conversed in earnest tones while Jack simply watched, picking up some of what they said. Every once in a while Jack would see Nadia poke her head around the corner, glance over the men, fix Jack with a look just short of malevolence, and then leave. He did not begrudge her the thinly veiled animosity. He had entered her home and had possibly placed her and her family at risk.

Jack had shared with these men what little he knew of Martin Templeton and then left them to their deliberations. Someone had brought Jack his phone, recovered from the jeep, but when he tried it he couldn't get a signal, which, he supposed, was the reason none of the locals had cellphones. He suspected he would have to reach a more populated area before he would be able to contact anyone. That left him with few options, save for allowing these men to help him or taking the jeep Templeton had driven into the village and proceeding on to Raballah on his own.

The longer he listened, though, the more he began to wonder if driving off with the staff was even an option. Over the last few minutes, the tenor of the conversation around him had changed and he had only recently started to pick up on it, cued by a slow rise in the volume of the conversation that told him a disagreement was brewing. Concentrating, he tried to listen in, but it was more difficult to make sense of the Arabic with multiple simultaneous speakers than it was talking to a single person. Still, he picked up on key phrases, and when these began to arrange themselves in his brain, he understood that these men were starting to talk of taking the staff from him.

When that realization came to him, Khamel looked at him from across the table as if he'd known the precise moment when Jack would understand. The Tunisian said something to the other men and all conversation stopped, all eyes turning to the American. Silence settled over the room, broken a few moments later by what looked to be the oldest among them.

Staring at Jack, he said in a strong voice, "We believe Allah may have brought you here so that you could deliver his staff to us."

Jack had no good response to that. To these people, he was an infidel, unworthy to carry such a sacred object. He was only amazed that they hadn't taken it from him the moment they'd discovered it.

"For what reason?" he thought to ask.

"To protect it, of course," the elder said.

"From whom?"

"From whoever would see the power of the Staff of Allah abused."

Again, it wasn't a statement Jack could rightly argue with. His own experience had shown him the truth of it. Consequently he chose not to go down that path.

"No one's coming after it," Jack said, looking around at all the solemn faces.

"Except for the man who already has," one of the other elders said. "And who knows how many more."

"There aren't any more," Jack argued, though he knew it was a lie. Imolene was still out there somewhere—as well as whoever had hired the Egyptian to tie up loose ends. He decided to try another tack. "What if I was given the Staff of Allah for a reason?" he asked, resolving, as soon as the words left his mouth, to ask Khamel about that name. In his studies he hadn't come across it and wondered about its origin.

He saw that there were some with whom his reference to being God's instrument did not sit well, but the oldest offered a half smile.

"If that is true," he said, "how do you know that your

purpose was not fulfilled when you delivered the staff to those who could properly care for it?"

Rather than attempt to answer the question, Jack gave the elder a respectful nod, asked if he could be excused for a few minutes, then rose and left the room. He headed for the back room, where two men had been posted, each armed with an automatic weapon. For a moment, Jack wondered if they would allow him entrance, but as he approached the doorway they moved aside.

The lamp was low when he entered and saw Templeton sprawled on the bed. The Englishman sat up when Jack stepped into the room.

"Turnabout is fair play," Templeton said.

Jack didn't respond. Instead, after regarding the Englishman for a time, he settled himself in the room's only other piece of furniture, a much-abused wooden chair.

"It's time for some answers," he said.

After what seemed a long while, Templeton said, "In order to receive answers, you have to ask the right questions."

Jack took a deep breath and let it out explosively. "For starters, how about you telling me, once and for all, why you took me out of that cave. What possible reason did you have to take me prisoner and then drag me through two countries?"

"Aside from keeping Imolene from killing you?" Templeton asked.

"Aside from that, yes."

It was Templeton's turn to let out a deep sigh. "You're something of a mystery in certain circles, Dr. Hawthorne." When Jack didn't respond, he continued. "You had a promising career ahead of you, and then you threw it all away after what happened in Egypt. I understand, of course, that your brother's death must have been difficult to deal with, but from everything I've heard about you, you were one of the shining stars in our shared field."

"We don't have a shared field," Jack said, more sharply than he'd intended. "I don't know what you call what it is you do, but it sure isn't archaeology."

Even as he said it, he understood the hypocrisy of the statement. Over the last few years, the field he himself had practiced bore little similarity to what he'd learned at Cambridge and in legitimate work for years after that. Still, he'd never kidnapped anyone.

"But then after several years of teaching, you seem to be back doing what you're supposed to be doing, and I can't help but be curious as to the reason why," Templeton said, ignoring the insult.

Jack remained silent.

"And interestingly enough, your return comes on the heels of that incident in Australia we discussed the other evening. But one of the things we didn't discuss—one of the things I found most curious about the whole affair—was the number of esteemed archaeologists who seem to have lost their lives at about the same time. One of them in Australia, a Dr. James Winfield. Now, wasn't he a mentor of yours?"

Jack knew he was being baited, even if he didn't know the reason for it. He could feel the other man's probing questions do their work, a slow anger beginning to build. He knew, though, that he had to keep a level head.

"Of course, that was also about the time that Dr. Brown Billings was killed in Ethiopia, wasn't it?" Templeton pressed.

He gave Jack a sidelong glance.

"Wasn't Dr. Billings a colleague of yours as well? He and that other young woman who died?" He adopted a thoughtful look, as if considering the professional connections. Then he shrugged. "What was it the Ethiopian authorities said? That they walked into the middle of a gang altercation?"

"You of all people should know that archaeology can be a dangerous business," Jack said.

"I would think the more appropriate statement would be that knowing *you* can be a dangerous business."

At that point, the anger that Jack had worked to keep from manifesting could no longer be contained, although he restricted its appearance to his face, forcing his teeth together to keep from saying something that would only serve to validate whatever Templeton was working to prove. Along with the anger was a growing puzzlement at Templeton being able to throw out those names. Which meant he knew a great deal more about Jack than Jack knew about him. It hinted that, whatever else Templeton was, he and Jack seemed to have traveled in some of the same circles.

"I told you," Templeton said, again one step ahead of Jack's thoughts. "I took my degree at Oxford and your Dr. Winfield was a frequent guest lecturer. I was saddened to hear that he'd passed on."

The only thing that kept Jack from trying to hit Templeton was that the Englishman's words sounded sincere.

"I have to tell you, Dr. Hawthorne . . . I spent a great deal of time wondering about what happened to you three years ago."

"Why should you have any interest at all in me?"

That question did something Jack hadn't expected. It

briefly removed the smug smile from Templeton's face, and for just a few seconds he saw something else. Anger perhaps? However, the look was gone almost immediately.

"After you left Australia, and after word began to trickle in that a number of archaeologists had died within a short time frame, I found the whole thing too intriguing to forget. Because while you mentioned that archaeology is a dangerous business, in reality nothing could be further from the truth. It's an exceptionally safe line of work."

"Coincidence is a very real thing," Jack said.

"A belief in coincidence denotes a man who refuses to do the legwork necessary to make the connections," Templeton rebutted. "No, something had gone on in Australia—something that had made its mark in Ethiopia and who knows where else. Perhaps even Egypt."

Whatever Templeton's game, he had succeeded in putting Jack back on his heels, because much of what the man said was correct, even if lacking in particulars.

"Do you know when I made sense of it, Dr. Hawthorne?" Jack said nothing.

"The pieces started falling in place when I caught you trying to steal the Nehushtan from me," he said. "You see, Jack, what occurred to me when I saw you sitting on the cavern floor was that the two of us were fighting over the same thing—a priceless artifact with a rich tradition. In fact, you almost died for it."

"We all still might," Jack reminded him.

"Indeed. But that's all quite incidental to my theory."

"Which is?"

"That if a find like the Nehushtan—admittedly a glorious item—could put two decent men at each other's throats, then what kind of treasure would have pulled one archaeologist out of retirement and led three more to their deaths?"

The silence that settled over the room as the question hung in the air was something that Jack could nearly feel, and he was several seconds into it before he understood what Templeton had intimated. When it came to him, he felt the weariness of days of hard travel come over him.

"There's something remarkable out there, Dr. Hawthorne," Templeton added. "Something worth dying for. And apparently something worth killing for."

"So it's about a score," Jack said after a long while.

"Oh, I wouldn't say that," Templeton said, and the look in his eyes sent a chill down Jack's spine.

But any response he might have made to Templeton was cut off by the sounds of small-arms fire coming from outside. Popping up out of the chair, he started for the door.

"That would be the Israelis," Templeton said.

The remark caught Jack with his hand on the doorknob. He thought he'd misheard, because of all the things Templeton might have said in that moment, what Jack had heard seemed completely out of place. Releasing the doorknob, he turned back toward Templeton. Yet before he could say a word, the wall behind the Englishman's bed exploded inward and Jack had only an instant to see a large piece of cement hurtling toward him before everything went dark.

***

When Jack's eyes opened, he knew he hadn't been out long because the dust and debris from the blast hadn't yet settled.

With a groan he forced himself up and, holding himself steady on one knee, blinked until his vision cleared enough to allow him to see a gap in the wall large enough to walk through. Beyond the hole he saw tracers cutting through the darkness and a glow that had to come from something on fire.

As he pushed himself to his feet, he heard moaning from off to his left. He turned and saw Templeton lying on the floor near the opposite wall. The blast must have lifted him and tossed him through the air like a child's doll. Instinct caused him to take a step toward the injured man, but he overruled the impulse, theorizing that if he could make a noise at all, he wasn't badly injured.

Instead, Jack crossed the room until he was close enough to the hole that he could lean out, although he did so carefully, staying to the side and positioning himself so he could see a good portion of the village without clearing the cement wall. Despite the light from whatever was burning, it was difficult to see anything clearly. As he stood there, though, he began to see people resolve in the darkness, their movements punctuated by gunfire. What he didn't see was anyone paying any attention to the building he was in—a realization that urged him to action.

As he moved away from the wall, he realized he knew too little about local politics to understand who was attacking and why. But neither could he shake from his mind Templeton's mention of the Israelis. From what Jack could recall about the political situation in the larger region, an Israeli military presence in Libya didn't make any sense. Still, there were appropriate times to ponder such questions, and alone in a room with a newly formed window was definitely not that time.

Except, he had to remind himself, he wasn't alone.

The Englishman had stopped his moaning, and from where he stood Jack couldn't tell if the man was breathing. Jack had reached the door again and thought about leaving Templeton to whatever fate awaited him. It was what he would have done years ago; he would have walked out of the room, retrieved the staff if he could, and fled the village without a second thought. But then Jack wasn't the man he once was, even if his inner growth didn't seem to be happening fast enough for Espy.

Releasing a sigh, he turned away from the door and went to check on Templeton. A quick examination revealed a large discolored knot on the man's forehead. Jack winced in sympathy, put a hand on the Englishman's shoulder, and gave him a rough shake that pulled the man up from the depths. When Templeton's eyes fluttered open, Jack leaned in close.

"I'm getting out of here," he said. "Do you think you can walk on your own?"

To his credit, Templeton began to move immediately, and Jack put an arm under his shoulder and helped him to his feet. The Englishman caught sight of the large hole in the wall but did not linger, instead following Jack to the door.

When they entered the hallway, the two guards were gone, the house silent save for the continuing echo of gunfire. Jack proceeded to the front room, Templeton in tow, and found it empty. He turned to the wall against which he'd propped the staff, already knowing what he would find and thinking dark thoughts when his suspicion proved true. But pragmatism forced any brooding from his mind and he went to the table. Still lying there were his phone and the keys to the jeep. Then, without a glance at Templeton, he hurried to the front door, convinced that the sounds of conflict were growing louder.

Opening the door just enough to see out, he scanned the space in front of the cluster of buildings, spotting a sprawled form not far from the nearest home, as if the man had been cut down the moment he'd stepped outside. On the ground next to the unmoving villager Jack saw what looked like an assault rifle.

The body gave him pause, but Jack understood that he couldn't stay in the house. Whatever was happening around him, he knew his best chance of escaping it rested in getting to the jeep. He was outside an instant later, not caring if Templeton followed.

Jack ran to the villager's side and rolled the man over just enough to see the bloodstained hole in his chest. Jack released him and grabbed the assault rifle lying a few feet away. He didn't see any movement around him, but he disliked being in an open space and so took off running again, slipping into the narrow alley between two of the buildings. He looked back to take in the terrain: the well directly ahead and the line of structures on the other side.

By then, Templeton had caught up to Jack and was by his side in the alley.

"Where did you park?" he asked Templeton.

The Englishman shrugged. "We should be looking at it. I stopped in that open space past the well. That's where your friends and I made our acquaintance."

So the jeep had been moved.

As Jack pondered his next step, he caught sight of two figures stepping out into the village center on the other side of the well. They were dressed in black, head to toe, and with their faces covered. Each held a weapon, and Jack could pick out more ordnance on belts and vests. While there were no obvious markings on their clothes, Jack had no doubt that they were military. He pulled back deeper into the shadow of the alley and exchanged a look with Templeton, who appeared uncharacteristically grim. With a nod for Jack to follow, the Englishman turned and headed in the other direction. Both men moved to where the alley ended and surveyed the scene.

While the village center had been largely still, the area beyond the first line of buildings was awash with people and noise. As Jack took it in, he realized his original estimation of the village's size had been incorrect; it was in fact much larger. From his position he could make out more of the black-clad figures, perhaps a dozen, engaged in firefights with armed villagers. At first, Jack was surprised to see so many of the locals armed with such firepower. But then he remembered that this part of the world required a citizenry ready for any contingency.

"There's the jeep," Templeton said, pointing, and Jack followed the line of the man's index finger until he saw the much-abused vehicle. It was parked next to a house that was much larger than the others. Jack could see several still forms on the ground in the immediate vicinity. The problem was getting to it without being cut down. He took another long look at his surroundings.

"Nothing ventured," he said, and with the gun in his hands he stepped out into the open, aiming for the jeep. There was no way to tell if it was the darkness that covered their flight or if anyone who might have shot at them was

164

otherwise engaged, but they crossed the distance without incident, the keys jingling in Jack's pocket. As they neared their means of escape, though, he chanced a glance at the trio of dead men at the doorstep of the large home. It was just a passing glance and yet it was enough that a thought sprang up in his head.

When he veered off course and headed for the front door, he could feel more than hear Templeton's surprise. Jack didn't spend any time checking on the fallen men except to note that he'd sat at a table with at least two of them not long ago.

He entered the home with the gun ready, but the only thing that greeted him was silence. Templeton followed him in. Advancing past the front room, Jack continued down the hallway, seeing that the home had several more rooms than the one in which his hosts lived. Jack performed a quick check on each of the rooms, wishing for more time yet anxious to get away from there. When he reached the end of the hall, approaching the last room, its door ajar, he found what he'd hoped he wouldn't.

Going by the spray of blood on the back wall, the old man had been shot as he stood between the bed and the wall. Apparently he was then dragged to the center of the room. Before moving to him, Jack glanced around the room but suspected that if the men who had attacked the village were after the staff and had found it, they would no longer be fighting in the streets.

When he reached the elder's side, he almost jumped when the man opened his eyes. They were clouded and feverish, and Jack knew he would be gone in moments. The man looked up at Jack, a weak smile on his face. He reached for Jack's arm, wrapping thin fingers around his wrist. He looked as if he would speak, so Jack leaned in closer.

"The lights . . ." the old man whispered. It looked as if he would say more, but then his eyes closed. Jack placed a hand on the man's chest, felt it rising and falling but struggling to do so. He tried to rouse the man without success.

Seeing there was nothing more he could do, Jack stood.

"The lights—what did he mean by that?" Templeton asked.

Jack didn't reply, but he supposed it most likely meant nothing. Just the delirium of a dying man. Except that the look in the old man's eyes as he'd said it made Jack think there was some importance attached to it. As he pondered this—aware that he was playing a dangerous game with time—he looked up. It was then that he noticed the ceiling-mounted light fixture. It was simple, with a wide base and a trio of bulbs . . . and yet the light fixture tugged at something in the back of his mind.

"I hate to question the decisions of a man who could have left me for dead," Templeton said, "but I'm reasonably confident that remaining in this village is a death sentence."

Jack ignored Templeton while the image of the light kept tugging at his brain.

Finally it came to him. He shook his head and said, "The village doesn't have electricity."

He hurried into the front room to find a chair. When he returned, he set the chair beneath the light fixture. After reluctantly handing the gun to Templeton, he went about the work of figuring out how the thing was attached to the ceiling. It took a few minutes of pulling and twisting, but eventually he had the fixture off, the separation from the ceiling revealing no wires.

He handed the fixture to Templeton and then reached his hand into the hole, feeling the cool air above the ceiling. There seemed to be a good bit of space up there. Jack moved his hand around until he nudged something solid. He closed his hand around it and after a bit of finagling had the staff positioned so he could pull it from the hole. When he was finished and had climbed down from the chair, he saw the old man's eyes open again. Jack knelt down beside him. The elder's eyes moved from Jack to the Nehushtan.

"Perhaps Allah did choose you to keep it safe," the old man said, his voice throaty, fading.

Jack nodded solemnly.

"I'll certainly try," he said, but the elder had already passed.

When Jack and Templeton stepped outside, it seemed that the action had waned. What little of it Jack could hear seemed to have moved farther away. Thankful for good timing, Jack started for the jeep, the staff in one hand, the reclaimed gun in the other. Despite the circumstances, he found that his mood had improved and with that altered disposition he found himself harboring no more doubt of a successful escape from the besieged village. He put the staff in the jeep's open back and, leaning the gun between the seats, reached for the door handle.

He sensed the movement off to his left a second later—a figure in black stepping out of the shadows. Jack saw the man's gun rising even as he turned, as he tried to snatch up his own weapon that suddenly wasn't there anymore. He heard the shot, a deafening boom that seemed too near his left ear. He felt his body spasm but knew almost immediately that he hadn't been hit. He looked down to confirm the fact and then back up where, strangely, he saw the masked soldier swaying drunkenly.

As the man fell to the ground, gone before he finished his descent, Jack turned to see a shaking Martin Templeton. The Englishman was still holding the gun out, as if he would shoot again if the dead man twitched. He was breathing heavily, a wild look in his eyes.

18

"Our phones," Templeton said.

Jack, who had spent the last thirty minutes guiding the jeep north and away from the doomed village as fast as he was able, looked over at the other man, raising an eyebrow.

"That's how the Israelis found us," Templeton explained. "They tracked our phones."

Jack absorbed that and, eyes back on what was a road in name only, said, "So explain to me why Israelis attacked a Tunisian village in the middle of nowhere. And how you knew who they were." A pause. "If that's who they were."

"Because that's who hired me to recover the Nehushtan," Templeton said.

That pronouncement came just as the right front tire of the jeep dipped into a rut that had jumped out from the darkness into the jeep's path. The jostling sent their few possessions sliding around in the back, and Jack glanced over his shoulder to see that the staff was still secure. That done, he turned his attention back to the Englishman.

"Someone from Israel hired you to find the staff?"

Templeton shook his head. "When I said the Israelis, I meant the Israelis—as in the government. By my understanding, there are elements within their government who are engaged in a cultural mandate of sorts. I suppose you could call it a reclaiming of their history."

"You mean they're collecting things that speak to their past."

"Yes. That's my understanding," Templeton said. "And I would say that a staff supposedly used by Moses qualifies."

Jack turned silent for a moment. What Templeton had told him wasn't hard to accept. After all, hadn't the Egyptians been engaged in much the same thing over the last few decades? Reclaiming treasures plundered from them over the centuries? However, to the best of Jack's knowledge, they hadn't resorted to sending military units into other countries willing to slaughter people in order to get what they wanted.

"And they are trying to kill us because . . . ?" Jack asked.

"Why do the Israelis do anything they do?" Templeton said dismissively.

Jack aimed an irritated look in his direction.

"My guess is that once I took you prisoner, and once Imolene reported that to our employers, they decided I was not the sort of man they wanted on their payroll," Templeton said.

"But Imolene is?"

Templeton shrugged. "He does what he's asked, he does it well, and then he forgets. If I were the Israelis, I would probably choose him over me too."

"But why would they have to use outside resources in the first place? If you want to keep something quiet, the best way to go about it is by keeping it all in-house."

"I suspect that's exactly what they do," Templeton said. "At least as much as they're able. I'm sure they'd like to handle as many of these recovery operations by themselves as they can. But there are certain places in which the presence of an Israeli attracts too much attention."

"Like Libya."

"Like Libya," Templeton agreed.

"And yet they send an entire team into Tunisia."

"The village was likely remote enough for them to feel comfortable chancing a larger scale operation," Templeton said. "But you can be certain that none of the Israelis will have carried identification."

There didn't seem to be much to say after that, and both men lapsed into silence. Jack had a good deal to consider—chief among them, Martin Templeton. It seemed odd that the man who'd held him captive for days, the man who'd precipitated Jack's flight through the desert, was now sitting next to him as if none of it had happened. In truth, Jack wanted to do little else but find what passed for a police station in Raballah and drop the man off. The reality that agents from a foreign government were after them, however, changed things. After what Jack had witnessed in the village, he had no doubt that Templeton was telling the truth, and this being the case, he suspected that having the Englishman with him was necessary if he stood any chance of extricating himself from the situation. For at least a while longer he had to keep the man with him.

"I assume you can get in touch with whoever's paying you?" he asked.

Templeton's eyes were closed, but Jack knew he wasn't sleeping.

"I could. But the only good that would do would be to give away our location."

"Just cataloguing our assets," Jack said.

Templeton simply nodded, leaving Jack alone with his thoughts. And the longer he drove, the more he found those thoughts returning to the artifact, which had probably covered more ground in the past few days than it had for more than a thousand years. Despite everything he'd gone through, and everything he still might endure, he would not even consider the thought that it wasn't worth it.

There was something about recovering an artifact like the Nehushtan that superseded much of his other work. For even though he'd personally supervised the digs of more than a dozen ancient tombs, pulling an impressive number of priceless objects from them, and even though his experience with biblical relics, while minimal, was such that those who had devoted their entire careers to the field would have envied him had they known, Jack was so drawn to the mystery of the object that he could not begin to regret his circumstances.

"It's worth it," he said, not realizing he'd spoken the words aloud until Templeton responded.

"It's the story behind it," Templeton said. "Most of us heard the story when we were children. We could almost see Moses drive the staff into the ground, the Israelites crawling toward it in hopes of being healed." He paused and looked off into space, as if imagining the events he described. "It's such a visceral image. The dying pulling themselves across the ground or being carried by their loved ones, hoping to look upon a totem created at the instruction of God."

He glanced back at the artifact and let out a sigh.

"That's what separates this from just about anything else you could dig up," he went on. "When we went to Sunday school, we were fed stories of great deeds performed by people who were larger than life. This was already in our collective consciousness."

Jack nodded. It was as valid a summation as he could have come up with, and suddenly all he wanted was to hold it in his hands, to study the thing Templeton spoke of. Jack turned and looked at the bundle in the jeep's back.

Recognizing Jack's longing, the Englishman reached back to collect the staff. He unwrapped it and held it out, admiring it with an appreciation that might have equaled Jack's own. Glancing over while driving, Jack could look directly into the eyes of the serpent, aware of the fact that he was looking into the same jeweled eyes that, if the story was true, countless men and women had looked into in order to live.

Even as he thought it, he chided himself for his doubt. If past events had done nothing else, they had given him a unique perspective on the veracity of biblical claims—a perspective he suspected few people in the world could share. And as expected, he felt the twinge of guilt that often reared its head when he considered the gift he'd been given. Because while there had been no way to avoid accepting the faith his parents had taught him, since that time he and God had settled into an uneasy détente. And the things that kept him from considering the reason for the détente were the very things he feared losing in the process. His detachment, his irresponsibility, his beloved flippancy—they had defined him for so long that he didn't know what he'd do if he lost them. And he was convinced that's what would happen if he decided to practice what Espy called *spiritual maturity*.

"You believe it," Templeton said, breaking into Jack's thoughts.

"Believe what?" Jack asked.

"You can't look into the serpent's eyes like that and not believe the staff did what the Bible says it did."

Jack didn't answer right away. Instead, he shifted his eyes back to the staff, taking in the snake's body, the detail of each scale, following the coil around the staff. The longer he looked at it—a luxury afforded by flat terrain and no traffic—the more something about it bothered him, although that realization did not come to him right away. He simply found that his eyes kept returning to the serpent's tail.

"Yes, I believe it," Jack said, the response requiring no further elaboration.

Templeton carefully rewrapped the artifact and returned it to the back seat.

For some reason, Jack was irritated that Templeton had secured the staff, yet he didn't say anything. Still, he felt he'd been on the verge of figuring out something important and now whatever it was had suddenly fled.

He glanced down at the jeep's center console, at the cellphone sitting in the cup holder. He wondered if they were close enough to Raballah to get a signal.

"Remember, you're dealing with a government that is among the best in the world at clandestine operations,"

Templeton said, his eyes still closed. "They know your name. Which means they know your friends' names. And their phone numbers."

Jack knew Templeton was right and it bothered him that he hadn't thought of it—that he'd come close to making a huge mistake. If the Israelis were listening, then even using a public phone in Raballah would be a risk. They'd be monitoring Espy's calls, regardless of the incoming number. He was running out of options.

However, there was one thing Jack had in abundance: friends in odd places.

The farther north Jack drove, the more the road began to look like a road, with the requisite signs denoting routes and destinations, and when Jack hit the P19 he took it, removing Raballah from the playbook. If Templeton noticed the change, he didn't comment.

Two hours later, with Templeton legitimately asleep, they entered Medenine.

It had been years—prior to Jack beginning his teaching career at Evanston—since he'd been in the area, and on those previous occasions he remembered Medenine as a wonderfully eclectic place. He'd enjoyed touring the ghorfas, admiring the honeycomb structure of the ancient stone buildings that had served the people of the area for thousands of years. He hadn't the time to revisit those tourist spots, but in his present circumstances the town offered him something of significantly greater value.

As they headed north, hitting the first of the foothills that hinted at mountains farther on, the air had cooled. Before reaching the city proper, he pulled off the P19 and onto a narrower unmarked road that took them up a gradual rise, following the curve of the road until a cluster of buildings came into view—small homes set in loose confederation against the sprawl of the city only fifty feet below.

Templeton was awake now and regarded the place without speaking. When Jack pulled to a stop in front of a nondescript home amidst other nondescript homes, the Englishman exited with him. Jack, staff in hand, started up the incline to the front door, which opened before he reached it. A man in a worn jalabiya stood in the threshold, eyes that looked as tired as Jack's felt taking in the visitors. They touched Jack and moved off, but then returned and fixed on him. Jack offered a smile as recognition came to the Tunisian.

Being a wanderer by nature had bestowed on Jack a large and diverse collection of friends and acquaintances all over the world. Many of them he'd met only once. Yet he'd never met a man from whom he couldn't ask a favor, and Marwen Saidani was one such man.

In truth, Marwen was more Romero's friend than Jack's, though the last time he was there Jack had stayed up late with both men, telling tall tales and smoking good cigars.

Marwen seemed pleased to see him, yet his smile was tempered by the lateness of the hour and because Jack and Templeton appeared to have been dragged through the desert by a rampaging camel. Once inside, Jack assuaged the man's fears with broad strokes, telling him that all they needed was a place to spend the night—a request with which the Tunisian readily agreed.

After the exchange of a few more words, Jack was ushered into the back of the house, a dwelling larger and more modern than the last Tunisian home in which he'd stayed. A door on the left opened into a plain but clean room that Jack claimed as his own, closing the door behind him and leaving Templeton in his friend's care. The room had its own bathroom, and Jack spent a long while scrubbing away the grime of the last few days with water as hot as he could stand. When he'd finished, he collapsed onto the bed. Less than a minute later he was asleep, stretched out on a mattress about as giving as a boulder. In his present state, though, he could have been sleeping in a five-star hotel and would not have noticed the difference.

———

It had been the Israelis who had drawn Imolene to the small village, although he'd arrived when they were all but finished and he had remained out of sight as they left, disappearing into the night as quietly as they had undoubtedly descended on the place. He thought he'd been following the likely path taken by those he hunted, and seeing the lights from multiple fires over the flat terrain had validated that belief.

What bothered Imolene, however, was the possibility that his employers' insertion of a team without telling him suggested they were less than confident that he could handle the task given him. And if that was true, there was no guarantee they would not also come for him. He had known when he accepted the job that it was not without significant risk.

In the ruins of the village he had located a survivor able to tell him that Templeton and Hawthorne had escaped the carnage in a jeep, heading north. The Egyptian had spotted them before the American—who no longer seemed to be a prisoner—had taken the P19. Imolene had trailed them to Medenine, but had kept back, allowing the increasing city traffic to form a hedge between his truck and the jeep.

He wasn't unduly concerned about being spotted, as it would have been impossible for the men to know what sort of vehicle Imolene would be driving. Nonetheless, he also understood that the human body responded in odd ways to the feeling of eyes on it. While he stayed back, just keeping the jeep in his sight, he could avoid any chance of detection.

As they neared the city, the jeep slowed and Imolene, who had just started to close some of the distance for fear of losing them, slowed as well. Not long after that, his quarry left the P19 for a packed dirt road devoid of any other traffic.

Imolene slowed as he approached the turnoff, watching as the jeep disappeared around a curve. He drove past the dirt road but turned around a hundred meters farther down, heading back to where the jeep had left the P19 and following with only his running lights on, his way made visible by the help of the bright moon. Before long he passed the parked jeep and, nodding to himself, continued on.

Jack had been awake for a while, jolted to alertness by something he couldn't put his finger on. As a younger man he'd been a heavy sleeper, a skill born of necessity in a field where one slept in tents or was exposed to the elements in sleeping bags under the open sky, with other members of the team who kept different hours milling about. But for the last few years he'd slept lightly, perhaps because he'd lived those years suspecting someone would eventually show up to take his life. Tonight, though, he didn't know if the fact that he'd awakened was because of his personal circumstances or some external influence.

He lay still on the narrow bed, listening to the movements common to all houses. And he'd almost convinced himself that nothing was amiss when he heard a noise coming from beyond his door. A moment later the door opened, a form silhouetted in the doorframe.

Before Jack could cry out, he heard the distinctive click of a gun made ready. The form advanced into the room, closing the door. Even in the darkness he knew who it was.

"Why?" was all he said.

The room had no window and so, try as he might, he couldn't put features to Templeton's outline.

"Because I have a feeling that things are coming to an end," the man said. "I have no idea what that end will be, but I know it will rob me of what I want."

Jack didn't move. He had no idea what Templeton could see but guessed that the Englishman's vision was as limited as his own and he didn't want any sudden move on his part to make Templeton discharge his weapon.

"If it's a choice between me being dead or you taking the staff, believe me, you can have the staff," Jack said.

"You don't understand. It's never been about the Nehushtan." He paused, then added, "Don't get me wrong. I do want to walk out of here with it, but I think you know that's not what I'm talking about."

And in that moment, Jack did. Since the ordeal began,

he'd questioned why Templeton had thought it necessary to kidnap him. Logistically it had made no sense. If Jack's silence was what the man wanted, a bullet would have ensured that.

"Then tell me what it is you want, Martin."

"Answers," he replied.

The response brought a frown to Jack's face. "What are you talking about? What answers?"

"I had a brother," Templeton said. "A younger brother named Thomas. The sort of person who was never happy in one place. Always wanted to travel. So when he turned eighteen, he left home to see the world. Do you know where he went, Jack?"

"No. I have no idea where he went."

"He went to Australia. About five years ago."

When Jack heard that, he felt a shiver run down his spine. Although he couldn't know exactly what Templeton was about to say, he had an idea.

"For a long time Thomas couldn't find work. Finally he signed on with a company near Melbourne, working in security. . . ."

He paused for a moment. By now Jack was getting used to the dark and was able to make out the sour expression on the other man's face.

Templeton continued, "I never would have realized that corporate security was such a dangerous occupation."

"What happened to him?" Jack asked, despite himself.

"That's just the thing," Templeton said. "The Australian authorities couldn't really tell us. Just that he died in a house fire."

The more Templeton talked, the sicker Jack felt.

"What's interesting, Jack, is how you know a few of the other casualties of that fire."

And just like that, everything fell into place—the reason Templeton hadn't let him go. Of course, there was no telling the Englishman that his brother had broken into Jack's mentor's house and killed the older man and his wife, and that he would have killed Jack had he not defended himself. Hearing that would have no effect on Templeton. The answers the man wanted would not heal anything.

"What was in Australia that Thomas had to die for, Dr. Hawthorne?"

Even though Templeton couldn't see the gesture, Jack responded with a slight shake of his head. "Nothing, Martin. There was nothing in Australia—not worth dying for."

He knew that answer wouldn't suffice; and he knew that eventually Templeton would kill him for it.

But in that moment the door opened, light streaming in. After blinking a few times to clear his vision, Jack saw Marwen, who was pressing a gun against the back of Templeton's head.

Templeton's gun was still pointed at Jack, however, and given what he now knew about the man's motivation and seeing the fevered look in his eyes, Jack wondered if Templeton just might be foolish enough to pull the trigger. But then Templeton's face fell and he lowered the hand that held the gun. Marwen reached around and took the gun and then stepped to the side, motioning for Templeton to take a chair against the wall opposite the bed. Once Templeton was seated, Marwen turned to Jack.

"I think you need to exercise better care in choosing your friends," he said.

Jack rolled out of the bed, holding in a groan when his

sore muscles protested. "He's not my friend. In fact, up until about thirty-six hours ago he had me tied up."

The look of confusion on Marwen's face almost made Jack laugh, yet too much had happened within the last few days for levity to bubble to the surface.

"Thanks," he said to the Tunisian.

Marwen nodded. "I did not know this was happening until I reached your door. I was coming to wake you for something else."

Jack raised an eyebrow.

"A truck sits on the street just up the road," Marwen said. "And in that truck sits a man who is watching this house."

"Are you certain?" Jack asked, realizing as he said it that Marwen would not have awakened him if he had any doubt.

"He drove past once, perhaps an hour ago, with his lights out. He is back now and he is sitting, waiting, watching my home." At Jack's unasked follow-up, he said, "I know in the same way I knew you were here before your car stopped. Because I have eyes not my own to tell me things."

"Imolene," Templeton said.

Jack had almost forgotten about the man but now he found himself agreeing with him.

"Who is this Imolene?" Marwen asked.

"An Egyptian mercenary," Jack said. "The nasty kind."

Marwen absorbed that with another nod.

"I'm sorry, Marwen," Jack said. "I didn't mean to put you in danger."

The Tunisian shrugged Jack's concern away. "I have no fear. He is one man and there are at least six guns trained on him as we speak."

Jack smiled, but he also understood that the Egyptian's presence presented a problem. Jack had no doubt that the man would kill him in a heartbeat and so the logical thing for him to do would be to ask Marwen's associates to deal with him. But although Jack had killed in self-defense, arranging a man's murder was a different matter entirely. There was also the question of Martin Templeton. After tonight—after finally learning why the man had kept Jack around—there was no way the two of them could continue traveling together. There were too many things Jack had to work out for him to deal with that sort of distraction.

He pondered the double-edged dilemma, and when the answer came, he reveled in its simplicity.

"Can you find me a car?" he asked.

Marwen answered with a slow nod. "I should be able to."

"Anything will work," Jack said. "As long as it doesn't cost too much."

He saw Templeton's head raise, watching him.

"How about a broom?" Jack asked.

Ten minutes later, Marwen and Jack had marched Templeton to the front door. In the Englishman's hand was a broom, minus the sweeping end, wrapped in the fabric that had up until that point surrounded the staff.

"Just to show I'm not entirely without a heart," Jack said.

He gave the gun Templeton had taken from a dead villager back to him, Marwen keeping his own gun pointed on the man until he pocketed the weapon.

Templeton might have protested, but Jack made sure the man understood that he had no choice in the matter. So, without a word, the Englishman stepped out into the night.

A half hour passed while he kept his eyes on the house. In that time he saw no movement of any kind, no lights to indicate anyone was inside, although he couldn't see the dwelling well enough in the darkness to know if his inability to see any lights merely indicated the absence of windows on the side facing him.

While he waited, not a single car passed him. After another fifteen minutes, Imolene reached to the passenger seat for his knife, slipping it from its sheath. Lifting it to his eyes, he studied the Egyptian-made weapon in the moonlight. The falcon-shaped brass handle felt good in his hand, the curved blade polished so that it reflected what little light there was. He slid the knife back into the sheath and reached for the door handle.

As if on cue, the front door of the house he was watching opened. Imolene froze. While morning was not far off, the darkness was still almost total, which meant the man would not see him. Nor would he likely question the presence of another vehicle on the road. Imolene watched as the man who looked to be Templeton exited the house and walked toward the street, the artifact in his hand. The Egyptian waited for Hawthorne to walk out too, but no one else followed and the door closed. After placing the staff in the back seat, Templeton got in and drove off.

Perplexed, his hand still on the door handle, Imolene watched as the jeep disappeared down the road. He asked himself why Martin Templeton would drive off alone. And what had happened to Hawthorne? Imolene suspected that the Englishman had finally killed the American, though he couldn't be certain. What he was certain of was that he had a decision to make, and even as he realized that, he understood it was a simple one. The Israelis had hired Templeton and they wanted him dead. And Templeton had the artifact, which they also wanted.

Making his decision, Imolene set the knife back on the seat and drove off after Martin Templeton.

19

"Why else would he need a book that describes the construction of the cathedral?" Espy asked.

She'd hardly touched her breakfast. Seeing Romero close to finishing his plate, she caught him eyeing her own.

"Why indeed?" he asked, earning a glare from his sister.

"My guess is that Jack didn't have whatever it was he was going to sell to Sturdivant," Espy said. "I'm also betting that the book he borrowed had something in it that he was hoping would lead him to whatever he was looking for."

As she spoke, she watched Romero work on his sausage. She waited for his response. Romero seemed to be taking his time, chewed thoughtfully. After swallowing the last of the meat, he used his fork to gesture at her plate.

"Are you going to eat that?" he asked.

Despite knowing her longer than anyone alive, Romero consistently demonstrated an inability to anticipate when something he might say would push her buttons to the point that she would lash out. She felt one such eruption bubbling beneath the surface, but she headed it off by taking a deep breath. Even so, she would not give him the satisfaction of consuming even a morsel of her breakfast.

"Yes," she said matter-of-factly.

Romero nodded. "Anyway, I think it is obvious that Jack was hoping to use the book in order to uncover a clue to something," he said, his deep baritone projecting a calm over the table, as if realizing what he'd almost loosed. "I also think it is unlikely that we will be able to uncover what he was looking for unless we receive help from another source."

"You almost sound as if you think the book is a dead end."

"On the contrary," Romero said. "The book narrows our search down to one cathedral in a very large city. The problem is that the one cathedral is an exceptionally large structure, and without an additional clue, we might as well be canvassing all of Milan."

Esperanza considered that as she picked up her fork and poked around her plate, coming back with a small bite of crepe.

"You're right," she agreed as she chewed. "We have a very large cathedral. But that's not all we have." At Romero's questioning look she continued, "Whatever was in that cathedral led Jack to Libya. All we have to do is figure out the connection, and with each piece of information we get, we take another step toward finding Jack."

"So what do you suggest we do next?"

"The first thing we need to do is check in with Duckey. For all we know, he's found something that could help us on our end."

"In which case he would have called us," Romero said.

"Maybe," Espy said. "But it's not going to do us any harm to check in. After that . . . ?" She shrugged. "I think we need to find someone around here who can help us dig up any sort of connection between Milan Cathedral and Libya."

Romero nodded, taking on a thoughtful look. "There is a man I used to do business with years ago. He lived in Vigevano, about thirty miles southwest of Milan. His name is Carelli. Filippo Carelli. He knew a great deal about the history of the region. I had him appraise a few Lombard pieces."

"Did Jack know him?" Espy asked.

Romero frowned. "I don't believe so. I didn't meet him until I was already well established in my store. And I've never met him in person."

"So we're going to drive thirty miles on the off chance a man you've never met may know something about a connection between Milan Cathedral and Libya?"

"It is worth a try, yes." Romero paused and added, "If he still lives in Vigevano. And if I'm remembering his name correctly." He gave his sister a smile and a wink.

"Well, at least it's something," she said.

The deep-green rolling hills through which they drove paid gradual deference to the revelation of the ancient city, which Espy watched come into view as they crested a hill in the Porsche Romero had insisted on renting for the day, despite her objections. She'd acquiesced only when she won the concession that she would handle the outbound drive.

Not long after entering the city proper, Romero pointed and she pulled off the SS494 and onto Via Podgora, on their way to Corso Argentina. Espy suspected that was the simplest portion of the directions her brother had jotted down and that once they began to head south on Corso Argentina, it was anyone's guess if they would arrive where they were supposed to.

However, less than ten minutes later, she had, under his direction, guided the sleek sports car through a series of turns on streets with no signs, around a few sharp curves that seemed built for the Porsche, and onto a narrow street lined with small homes that had shared walls and courtyards hidden behind tall metal gates.

She found a spot to park a few houses down from the one they wanted. Soon they were walking up the sidewalk to meet Filippo Bramante—a name Romero had finally remembered after they had spent more than an hour searching for a Carelli in the phone directory. Romero had explained that Carelli was the name of an art dealer in Madrid with whom he was acquainted. Bramante answered on the second knock.

He was a short man and older than Espy was anticipating, somewhere in his early seventies. But despite his age, she could tell right away that he carried himself like a much younger man. He greeted the visitors with a warm smile.

"It's a pleasure to finally meet you," he said to Romero. Then he turned to Espy. "And you must be Dr. Esperanza Habilla. Your brother's told me a great deal about you." Eyes dancing, he reached for Espy's hand. Acquiescing to the culture—and because she immediately liked the man—she

190

leaned down so that he could greet her with a kiss on her cheek.

Stepping away from the door, he ushered them into his home, the trio passing through a short hallway and into a living room that looked larger than the size of the home would have allowed. The size of the house, though, held less interest for Espy than the fact that it was decorated in a fashion she recognized as opulent. She looked toward her brother, who was better suited to appreciate a number of items he might have sold from his own shop if given the opportunity.

Bramante saw them taking in the room and its many objects. "Appraising items for others often gives me first choice of a number of exceptional pieces," he explained. Saying it seemed to stir a memory, because his eyes narrowed and he turned to scan a portion of the room until he found what he was looking for. "Do you see that Incan death mask on the shelf?" he asked, pointing.

To Espy, the piece looked much like the other masks she'd seen in Romero's store. She saw her brother walk past their host, crossing to the shelf to get a better look.

"I sent this to you so that you could appraise it," Romero said, turning to face the Italian.

"And I did," Bramante said. "Fairly. Once I'd shipped it back to you, I had a friend in London purchase it and then she sent it on to me." Telling them this little story seemed to tickle the old appraiser, and although what the man had done was unethical, Espy felt a smile ready to show itself. "So tell me," he said. "What brings you to Vigevano?"

He gestured for them to sit and began to sit as well, but

then jumped up again. "Where are my manners? Can I get you some tea?" He was starting off toward the kitchen when she and Romero called him back, declining the tea.

"We're here because we need your expertise," Esperanza said. She went on to explain the riddle they were hoping Bramante could help them solve.

The Italian didn't interrupt as she laid out what was needed. Even after she'd stopped speaking, Bramante continued to ponder what had been shared, his eyes on the marble tile that ran through the house.

After what seemed a long time, the old man said to his guests, "You must understand, I'm no expert. Most of my work involves setting values on the usual sort of thing—things procured from places that people have studied extensively. I can give you the auction estimate or insurance replacement value. But this . . . ?" He shook his head and released a small laugh. "I don't know," he finished.

Esperanza leaned forward, close enough that she could have placed her hand on Bramante's knee. And judging by the Italian's reaction, that was precisely what he thought she would do. Instead, she gave the man one of those smiles that had failed on Sturdivant.

"My brother told me that you know more about Italian history—especially northern Italian history—than just about anyone alive," she said, smiling. "And my brother wouldn't lie to me."

Espy's vote of confidence seemed to breathe new life into the older man. He sat up straighter; then a few seconds later he nodded.

"I'm not saying I can't help you," he said. "It's just that

these days I don't spend enough time in the history books for something to immediately come to mind."

Espy remained undaunted, her warm smile assuring Bramante that he knew something of great value to them, whether he recognized it or not. And under that kind but demanding gaze, the Italian appeared ready to move heaven and earth.

"Milan Cathedral . . ." he mused. "While the cathedral itself is dated to 1386, there has been related construction on the site since the early fifth century, when the Lombards were at their most powerful."

"From what I understand, it took almost six hundred years to finish," Espy said.

"Right," Bramante said. "And during that time, Milan came under a number of influences, which you can see immortalized in the cathedral. It's a remarkable mixture of styles, although a good portion of it was constructed under a Gothic aesthetic."

Espy considered the six hundred years during which the Milan Cathedral had come into being, attempting to process the logistics involved in completing such a monumental task. Over six centuries, she thought it improbable that succeeding architects held fast to the same vision. How many generations took their turns toiling to build the magnificent edifice, the largest church in Italy? She suspected laborers had traveled to and from Milan continuously. And with that traffic Espy hoped that a north African connection might not be difficult to find. Rather, pinpointing the right one would be the real challenge.

"Were all of the architects Italian?" Romero asked, on the same track as Esperanza.

"Not at all," Bramante answered. "The cathedral's Gothic beginnings were due to French influence, but at different times the project was headed by Italians, Englishmen, a German, and a Greek. And I'm certain I'm missing a few." He chuckled, adding, "But the national influences were by no means pure. It is said that even when the French architects were laying out the plans, Chaucer was busy sketching a design for the nave, and there are some who believe that at least part of his plan was adopted."

"Do you know of any northern Africans who were involved?"

Bramante, lips pursed, disappeared back into thought. When he emerged just moments later, he said, "To the best of my knowledge, none of the architects assigned to the project had a connection to northern Africa. I could be wrong of course, but I do not believe I am. Also . . ."

Espy nodded. "Also what . . . ?" she pressed.

"Also, the men who did the majority of the work would have come from the regions immediately surrounding Milan. There were undoubtedly some who came from longer distances, but during the period the cathedral was constructed, a number of similar projects were taking place all over Europe. One would not have had to travel far to find work at a building site. And even if laborers from northern Africa had made it this far north, these would have been people intent on trying to support their families, not building riddles into cathedrals."

"Anything else come to mind that might help us?" Espy asked.

"Perhaps," Bramante said. "It was my mention of Chaucer

that makes me think of it. In a project of this size, one has to consider who has the potential to do something such as you're suggesting. Because what you've laid out involves someone deeply involved in the construction and with the resources necessary to carry it out. Means and opportunity, as it were."

Espy pondered that for a moment. "I think you're onto something there. Since we're using that language, we also need to consider motive."

"Absolutely, Unfortunately, that's the variable most difficult to qualify. But even without knowing a motive, we can still narrow down our suspect list."

"A list that will include anyone assigned to oversee a small portion of the cathedral," Romero said. "Small enough that ensuring all but a few people remained unaware of his deviation from the approved plan—and that it would stay undetected."

"An artisan," Bramante said. "Of which there were many who worked on the cathedral, although I think we are safe in restricting our sample to those who worked on the project prior to 1510. After that, much of the work involved finishing and cosmetic touches."

Esperanza leaned back in her chair and released a sigh. "That still gives us more than a hundred years to sift through."

"A task that might be easier than you think," Bramante said.

Without waiting for a reply, he rose and left the room, returning less than a minute later carrying an enormous leather-bound book. Sitting, he placed the book on his lap and opened it to the index.

"I maintain a variety of resources that help me with challenging appraisals," he said as he scanned the index. "This monstrosity of a book is the most exhaustive I've ever found that lists artists dating all the way back to the seventh century, as well as biographies, notable works, and, important in this case, countries of origin."

He opened the book somewhere in the middle and began flipping through the pages. Espy and Romero remained silent as he landed on a page and began reading it. He flipped one more page and then, with a satisfied smile, beckoned his guests to step over to his chair and take a look for themselves.

"There have been a number of artists of varying types who came from the area we now call Libya," he said. "You have to remember that at one time northern Africa was home to a number of Greek colonies, and much of what they brought with them in terms of sculpture, painting, and construction techniques remained long after the colonies disappeared."

As Espy looked over the Italian's shoulder, she saw a list of perhaps thirty names, a quick scan telling her that she was not familiar with all of them. However, she suspected that by reviewing the birth and death data next to each, they could begin to narrow the list down a bit.

"Our first step is to find out which of these would have been alive during the time period we identified," Bramante said. "Then, if we're lucky, there will be some mention of one of them having paid Milan a visit."

Esperanza understood that it was a big *if*. She also understood that if they failed to find a name on the list that could be tied to the cathedral, they would be back to square one. She felt herself sinking into a darker mood and it took her a few minutes to identify the cause. When she and Romero had decided to drive to Vigevano, she'd been hoping that Bramante would provide them with some magical piece of information that would tie things together for them. She'd forgotten the hard work necessary to make the connections.

With that in mind, she shrugged off her disappointment and joined Bramante and Romero in poring over the list.

20

The sheer size of Milan Cathedral was enough to make even someone as travel-seasoned as Espy pause in a spot from which she could view it in its entirety. In her lifetime Espy had witnessed some truly remarkable sights. This was different, however. Standing with her brother and staring up in awe at the majestic cathedral, it did something to her—made her wonder at the human spirit, the creativity and persistence it took to raise up something so grand. She suspected her brother felt the same way, though he'd spent the last half hour distracted, complaining about his empty stomach.

As if to lend credence to that thought, Romero shuffled on feet that had to be as tired as Espy's own and said, "As much as I admire your on-again, off-again beau—and this remarkable building—I have to warn you that I have only a certain amount of reserve to expend before I abandon the entire enterprise and go hunting for the rarest piece of red meat in the area."

There was nothing exaggerated about the statement; Espy knew her brother well enough to understand that when presented with a task, he would work for hours without complaint. Yet when his circumstances called for aimless wandering, his stomach often held sway.

"We have a good idea about what we're looking for," Espy said. "I think you can hold out for another half hour."

The look on her brother's face suggested otherwise, but she knew he would acquiesce, if only to keep his sister from punching him. And as much as he might grumble, he wouldn't abandon a friend.

Once they'd stepped into the building, it hit Espy that if she wasn't careful she could lose her focus. They were there for a specific reason—to study a small portion of the massive cathedral. But everywhere she turned, she saw something she wanted to learn more about—something she could spend hours studying. Without the specter of Jack's disappearance hanging over her, she would have been content exploring every corner of the building. And so it was with a sigh that she shook off the lure of leisurely study and set her sights on what they'd come there for.

Leaving the entryway, they entered the nave, where in less than two steps, Esperanza's resolve to stay on point faltered. The nave rose up more than 140 feet, the cupola decorated with so many statues—saints, church fathers, mythical beings—that Espy felt as if a crowd of mute but attentive witnesses surrounded her. Romero, knowing his sister well, put his hand on her elbow and guided her forward. She looked up at her brother and saw that he wasn't immune to the masterwork that surrounded them. His eyes moved over everything, his trade granting him an understanding and appreciation for details that the average tourist would not notice.

The nave was filled with people, and Espy and Romero had to weave their way down one of the aisles toward the altar, Espy trailing her hand along the pews as she walked. Before they reached the altar, they passed a large two-tiered marble dais—a platform in the empty space between pew and altar that looked ready to act as a base for something large such as a statue, although the position of the dais made it an odd place to set anything large, as doing so would obscure the view of the altar. Espy paused for a few moments to study the dais, with its stones adorned with a variety of symbols, most of which Espy did not recognize. However, as much as she would have enjoyed spending time around the platform and hazarding guesses as to its use, she knew it wasn't the reason they'd come.

When they reached the front, Espy paused because, while no service was in progress, a few people were kneeling in front of the altar, heads bowed in prayer. And while what Espy and Romero had come to see required them to ascend the steps, she couldn't help feeling that doing so would be an intrusion on their private moments.

"If they wanted privacy, they could pray in their homes," Romero said in a stage whisper.

Espy considered that and, with a shrug, stepped around a woman well into her rosary.

Standing near the altar with her brother, Espy spotted the choir stalls she'd noticed when they'd first entered the sanctuary. Now that she was closer to them, she found herself surprised that, if they were right, the information they needed was somehow linked with the simplest structures in a building of beautiful, intricately detailed artwork.

The wooden stalls had been constructed on two levels, with the first level running in a semicircle around the back of the raised platform. The second level was separated into two elevated sections akin to theater boxes. From Espy's perspective, the stalls possessed a simple beauty; she could see the intricate carvings along the rails and seams, but other than those, the lines were straightforward and clean.

"They hardly seem the place in which to implant a clue," Romero said, echoing her thoughts.

"There may be nothing here," Espy said, "but there was only one artist from northern Africa in the records and this is what he worked on."

Romero looked unconvinced, yet with the absence of another plan he kept silent.

They'd spent more than an hour sitting with Bramante, going through his book, and regardless of how many different searches they'd performed on the text, they kept returning to a single name. And after they'd finished their review of the book, Romero had used Bramante's computer to validate the findings. But while the Internet search opened up the door to a few additional candidates, none of them seemed as good a fit as al-Idrisi.

According to the construction logs—documents that spanned hundreds of years and were compiled with varying degrees of detail—the choir stalls had been added in the early seventeenth century, with the charge of design and construction falling to an artisan carpenter named Francesco Brambilla. However, rather than assign the stalls a strict European identity, the man had involved an African carpenter in both the design and construction phases.

To even Espy's unpracticed eye, Muhammad al-Idrisi's cultural identity had been formed by both the region's old yet fading Greek presence as well as the influx of Islamic influence. This could be seen in every detail, from the gentle arc of the handrails and the intricate latticework to the denser base that would have looked crudely hand-carved if one did not notice the complete uniformity of its entire span.

Esperanza began her study of the first level of stalls to her left, looking at both the flat facing surface and the more detailed portions that gave it life. From the corner of her eye, she saw Romero do the same, starting from the right. Espy's experience with this sort of thing was limited; she'd proven helpful in the hunt for Elisha's bones years before, but that was because, ultimately, the most important element of that search had been a language puzzle, which was her province. She doubted she would get that lucky again. It was why she held out the greatest hope in her brother, who while not as accustomed to the practice of archaeology as their missing friend, had a good deal more experience with the process than she.

She took her time walking along the stall, her hands running over certain places, bending so she could get closer to review something of interest. But as she walked, and as she saw Romero making similar progress, she could not find anything that stood out as something other than adornment.

Fifteen minutes later, they met in the middle and shared a look that communicated their disappointment.

"The other side?" Romero asked.

Espy nodded and they separated again, each finding the small opening near their respective walls that allowed them access to the place in which the choir would stand. With less light on that side, Espy found it more difficult to study the stalls and had to rely more on her hands. As she moved along, slower than she had with the front, she caught the occasional glimpse of her brother disappearing from view, then popping up at some distance farther down.

On the choir side, a wooden footrail ran the length of the stalls. While Espy was impressed that she could not find a seam in the entire run of the rail, neither could she find any mark or symbol on its surface.

"There's still the second level," Romero said when they'd finished their search.

"Unless we've missed it," Espy said, acknowledging the fact that the person most suited to conduct the search was the person who was relying on them.

"There's also the distinct possibility that we're wrong," Romero said. "That our conjecture regarding a Libyan connection being found in this building—and that the only north African artisan on the project somehow fashioned a message into his work—could be completely without merit."

"It certainly sounds ludicrous to *me*," Espy said.

"But what other choice do we have?" Romero finished for her.

With that, the two found the narrow stairs that led up to the second level, this time choosing to stay together. When Espy arrived at the top, she moved to the wall and looked out over the nave, the whole of it stretched out before her. Some of the people sitting in the pews, or walking about taking pictures of the sculptures, frescoes, and stained-glass windows, were looking in her direction, making her wonder if she and Romero had crossed some line no one had shared with them. With that in mind, she stepped away from the wall and set to work.

In backing away, she noticed that the panels of the stall contained a level of detail and design missing from their counterparts below. Romero noticed it too, and lowered his large frame to a knee so he could lean in and get a closer look.

"I don't know what these are, but there's an Arab look to them," Espy said, pointing to a symbol formed of an outer box, an inset triangle, a box within that, and an interior circle. The only thing that made it seem more than a progression of geometric shapes was the decorative edges of the outer box.

Romero grunted. "It's not Arabic. It's an old European symbol for alchemy." He pointed to the edges of the outer box. "This looks similar to an Arab technique common to Muslim craftsmen of the time period."

Espy absorbed that and was about to ask a follow-up question when she saw her brother frown.

"What's that?" he asked, pointing to something blue along the edge of the outer box.

Espy followed the line of his finger and saw what he meant. It was just a small amount of color, hardly noticeable. She traced the edge of the box with her finger, and when she pulled it back, her fingertip was blue. Puzzled, she rubbed together her finger and thumb, then watched as the powdery substance spread.

She stared at her discolored fingers for several seconds, brow furrowed. When the answer came, a smile replaced the former expression. Turning to Romero, she held her finger up for investigation.

"It's powder," she said. Her smile grew wider. "Jack was here; he took an etching."

Romero reached for her hand, using his own larger finger to wipe a portion of the blue powder from Espy's. Then he turned his attention to the stall panel, his eyes tracking downward. He pointed to a short trail of the same powder on the floor.

"I'd say we're on the right track," he said.

Esperanza felt her excitement level growing, yet she tempered it by realizing that neither she nor her brother understood the significance of the symbol.

"I suggest we study the rest of the panels," Romero said. "I don't think that this by itself will take us where we need to go."

With no further prompting, Espy backed away from the find and continued on, this time keeping an eye out for any telltale marks left by Jack's etching chalk. However, in studying the rest of the panels, she didn't find anything that stood out. The rest of the ornamentation, excepting the alchemy symbol, looked solely decorative, forming a semicircle with what appeared to be a bisected flower at the midpoint of the handrail. Romero thought so as well, and as he and Espy took a break to sit against the wall, the stall paneling across from them seemed content to retain its secrets.

"There has to be more than that," Espy said.

Romero nodded his agreement. "Perhaps it's in the loft we haven't yet searched."

"Perhaps." Although . . . while she lacked Jack's, and to a

lesser extent Romero's, experience with this sort of thing, she thought that finds like the one they'd made often followed a definite pattern. Which meant they would find another symbol—perhaps even the same one—in the other loft. Assuming that was true, she tried to envision what they could do with the information. How could they take two different symbols and learn something meaningful from them?

"That can't be all of it," she said. "Symbols are one thing, but what about instructions about how to use them?"

"Maybe Jack already had those," Romero suggested.

Espy supposed that made as much sense as anything else, and she released a resigned sigh and lapsed into silence. After a few moments, though, she heard footfalls on the steps to their left. Neither sibling moved as a head came into view—an older woman with a camera, followed by a younger woman who bore a family resemblance to the first woman. Catching sight of Esperanza and Romero sitting against the wall, both sets of eyes turned in her direction, the woman stopped before reaching the top of the steps, a startled, almost guilty expression on her face—as if she, rather than the Venezuelans, had been caught hiding in the choir loft.

"Excuse me," she finally said and, grabbing the younger woman by her elbow, disappeared back down the stairs.

"Well, now she has a story to tell when she gets back home," Romero said.

Espy didn't answer but found that the incident had left a smile on her face. As she turned back to the panels that had tantalized but ultimately disappointed her, her spirits were higher. She decided to enjoy the moment, to appreciate the fact that she was in another part of the world, in one of the most extraordinary buildings she'd ever seen, and had stumbled onto a clue left by an artisan almost four hundred years ago. When considered in those terms, she was rather pleased with their progress. Too, the last choir loft still remained to be searched and might yield something they could use.

She was about to suggest that to Romero when something about the design on the panels struck her in a way it hadn't before they'd been interrupted. At first she couldn't figure out what it was about the semicircle design that bothered her and she tried examining it from afar piece by piece. When that yielded nothing, she changed her focus, trying to take in all of it at once. How long she remained like that, absorbing the panels as a single unit, she didn't know, except that when she emerged from it, when what had been pressing itself upon her suddenly clicked and she snapped to alertness, she found her brother watching her.

Rather than saying anything, Espy rose and walked over to the loft wall, placing her hands on the rail and peering down at the lower level of the cathedral, toward the dais that had so intrigued her earlier. After committing its shape and basic features to memory, she moved back and studied the panel walls. She did this twice more, and by that time Romero had reclaimed his feet, though he knew better than to interrupt.

When she'd satisfied herself that she was on the right track, she turned her attention to Romero.

"It's a representation of the dais in front of the altar," she said, pointing at the outline. "While al-Idrisi didn't reproduce the pictures from each of the stones, you can see where he identified the edges."

She watched as Romero studied the panels with new eyes, and then as he performed the same back and forth dance she'd done.

"Okay, I'll grant you that," he said. "Now, what does it mean?"

"I don't know. But it can't be coincidence that the alchemy symbol sits right in the middle of one of the stone block segments."

Espy went back to the alchemy symbol, knowing she would have to return to the dais to see if the stone represented on the panel held the same symbol. Letting her fingers trace the lines of the outer box, she was surprised when a word popped into her head, coming as if from nowhere. And as she considered the word, she was even more surprised by the fact that it was neither Spanish nor English.

"You've got to be kidding," she said.

"What is it?" Romero asked, but Espy shushed him.

Pulling back her hand, she looked at the ornate outline in a new light, working to separate the words from the unnecessary line that gave it the appearance of trim. It took some time; after all, the language had been extinct for hundreds of years. But after some trial and error, she was convinced she had it.

"It's Gafat," she said.

Romero looked at the panel and then back at his sister.

"I've asked you not to curse at me in foreign languages," he said.

"It's a language that went extinct in the mid-seventeenth century," Espy said. "About forty years after al-Idrisi carved this." At Romero's incredulous look, she shrugged and explained, "It's a Semitic language, so the basic structure isn't hard to identify if you know what you're looking for."

"What does it say, then?" Romero asked, sounding unconvinced.

Espy turned to the panel and used her finger to point out the message. "Two parts; two steps."

He frowned. "And that means . . . ?"

"I have no idea," she admitted. "But I'm going to head over to the other loft and see what I can find."

Less than ten minutes later, they had another symbol, different from the first, and even Romero was unable to provide it with a meaning. The words around this symbol, though, were the same as those around the first. Having exhausted their well of ideas, they descended the narrow stairs and headed straight to the dais, where they were pleased to discover that the symbols on the stall panels matched the positions of their marble cousins. They studied the dais for a long while, trying to determine how to use the information but came up with nothing. Espy, seeing a priest walking up the far aisle, hurried to corral him.

"Excuse me," she said in Italian. "Could I ask you a few questions about the dais over there?"

The priest smiled and followed her over to where Romero waited.

"Can you tell me about these symbols?" she asked.

She had hardly finished the question before the priest began to answer, causing Espy to believe that hers was not the first inquiry into the nature of the designs.

"In each of the smaller naves, you will see sarcophagi for some of the duomo's prominent saints," he said. "This monument was installed after the last interment—that of Archbishop da Intimiano. The symbols you see here are also found on the sarcophagi."

Espy nodded. "And is each symbol on each sarcophagus? Or is each combination of symbols unique to the deceased?"

"While several of the symbols are used on more than one of the tombs, the combinations are all unique," he said. "But to the best of my knowledge, the symbols do not represent anything beyond the whims of those who designed them."

"Thank you," she said. "I appreciate the information."

They waited for the priest to leave before speaking again.

"We treat it as a road map," Romero said. "My guess is that only one of the tombs will have both symbols."

The layout of the cathedral made for quick work, and they found the sarcophagus they were looking for on the third try. To be thorough, they examined the fourth and last tomb as well to be sure the one they'd selected was indeed the only one with both symbols in the stone.

As they moved around the tomb of the Archbishop Ottone Visconti, the two symbols assigned an unobtrusive spot on the lid at the position where Romero suspected the man's feet to be, they worked to determine what the symbols and their positions meant—and if the other tomb markings and adornments were tied together. But with no point of reference, nothing to give them direction, they foundered.

"There are several symbols along this side of the lid and lower, along the containment vessel here," Romero said, gesturing. He pointed at one in particular. "This one is on Intimiano's tomb but in a different spot."

"So position is a clue," Espy said.

Romero nodded, but slowly, as if his thoughts had suddenly gone somewhere else. As Espy watched, Romero retrieved his phone and began to scan through the pictures he'd taken of the symbols around the dais. When he'd cycled through them, he frowned.

"This one here," he said, pointing at a symbol on the side of the tomb. "This one does not appear on the dais."

"Are you sure?"

Romero didn't answer. Instead, he muttered, "I need a pen." He pulled the cathedral guide from his pocket. While Espy looked among her belongings for a pen, Romero unfolded the guide until he found a panel with white space. Taking the pen from Espy, he quickly drew one of the symbols and then, after studying the sarcophagus for a moment, he drew the second symbol directly over the first. When he finished, he held the paper out for Espy's inspection.

The result of Romero's efforts was a near-perfect representation of the symbol that was not on the dais.

"I knew there was a reason I brought you along," Espy said.

She knelt down and began to trace along the outer edge of the new symbol. A moment later, she looked up.

"It's not Gafat," she said. "It's Latin. Two words. The first is—I'm not sure I'm reading this right—*Nehushtan*? The second is easier: *Cyrene*."

"Cyrene is the name of a Greek settlement. I've sold pottery recovered from the ruins there." He shook his head and aimed a wry smile at Espy. "It's in Libya."

The smile the two shared was one of satisfaction, but floating along the edges of that feeling was the ugly fact that knowing Jack had gone to Libya was not the revelation they'd hoped for. However, there was still the promise of the second word.

"Any idea what *Nehushtan* means?"

Romero could only respond with a shake of his head.

"Give me a minute," he said, pulling his phone out again. It took what seemed a long while to Espy before Romero could establish an Internet connection and find any information about what they'd uncovered. When he did, he released a low whistle. "I know now what Jack's searching for. And why Sturdivant wouldn't tell us even after I threatened to fly there and present a convincing argument."

He handed his phone over to Espy, who brought it close so she could read the small screen.

"You're kidding . . ."

"I never knew the name for it," Romero said.

"You're kidding," Espy repeated.

"I think we've covered that," he said, reaching for the phone. "According to legend, it had the power to heal snakebites."

"I remember," Espy said. "I was the one who always paid attention in Sunday school."

Romero chuckled but the laughter faded quickly. "Does your boyfriend ever do anything that doesn't have quite so dramatic a flair?"

Esperanza knew that the question was meant to be light-hearted, but it had a sobering effect. Now that she knew what Jack was after, she felt an iciness grip her insides. There were simply too many similarities to the last time Jack had gone after a biblical artifact. And since she couldn't reach him, she couldn't help but imagine a number of horrible possibilities.

Her brother didn't have to rely on their familial relationship to understand that his normally strong sister was falling into a dark place, and he did the only thing a brother could do. He reached out and drew her into a hug that all but enveloped her. When a few moments later he released his embrace, tears were trailing down her cheeks.

Yet her eyes held a smile. Stepping back from Romero, she nodded her thanks and wiped her face with the back of her hand.

"So what now?" she asked.

"We study," he said. "We build on what your friend Duckey is doing in Al Bayda and we figure out what happened to Jack once he reached the ruins."

"Okay," she said. "But I think we need to be prepared to accept that Jack had to know more than he learned here. Or what he learned here provided him with a specific plan of action we know nothing about right now."

Romero nodded and turned to leave.

Espy absorbed her own words, considering the difficulties posed by their imperfect understanding of Jack's profession. Then, as she pondered that, something occurred to her. "What about the Gafat text?"

Romero turned back around. "What about it?"

"It wasn't necessary to use the text to find this symbol," she said. "So why put it there?"

He shrugged. "What did it say?"

"Two parts; two steps."

Espy went to the tomb, stopping in front of the symbol they'd just discovered. Using that one as a starting point, she found the symbol two spaces to the right. It was a representation of one of the symbols on the dais and was absent of any writing around its outer edge. She tried again, this time moving left, and landed on a symbol she was reasonably certain she'd not yet seen. It was surrounded with the markings of the dead language.

It took her longer than it had with the Latin, but when she looked up at Romero, her face was flushed.

"It says *Cyme*," she said.

"Are you sure it doesn't say *Cyrene*?" Romero asked.

"It's Cyme," she repeated.

"Alright, Cyme it is. So what does it mean?"

Espy stood and stepped back from the sarcophagus, wiping her hands on her pant legs. "Two parts; two steps."

She and Romero pondered the mystery for a while as tourists shuffled around them, some of them coming near to take pictures of the tomb, oblivious to what it had just revealed to the Venezuelans.

"Doesn't the Bible say that Hezekiah destroyed this pole?" Romero asked.

"Supposedly people were praying to it and so he had it destroyed," Espy affirmed. "But if Jack is looking for it, and if the effort that went into these clues is any indication, I'd say that Hezekiah wasn't successful in destroying it."

"Unless . . . he didn't destroy it completely. What if he broke it, perhaps in two pieces?"

"Two parts; two steps," Espy said, excitement in her voice.

"Two parts; two steps," Romero agreed.

Espy's eyes widened.

"Jack wouldn't have known." At Romero's questioning

look she explained, "He wouldn't have seen the Gafat. He wouldn't have known there was a second symbol."

"And so even if he finds it, he will have only found a portion of it."

"If he's in any position to find it," Espy said quietly.

Romero had no response for that, and Espy, despite what they'd accomplished, felt her mood darken.

21

As Duckey mounted the single flight of narrow wooden steps to his room, he tried to think of a time when he felt wearier than he did at that moment and found himself hard-pressed to do so. Waking up that morning, he'd followed a few more leads, but after nothing panned out he'd caught a cab to the Al Bayda university district and had spent much of the afternoon questioning students about things to see and do in and around the city—especially those things that might require a motorbike to reach. He'd reasoned that, regardless of nationality, college students were adventurous compared to most other demographic groups. Too, they would be plugged in to their surroundings; they could narrow Duckey's search quicker than he could ever hope to accomplish on his own.

The jury was still out on whether his stroll around campus had been an efficient use of time. The students he'd talked with had given him a great deal of information, though he had to parse all of it against what he knew of Jack. He hoped, once he could think about things in the morning with a clearer head, he could make a connection worth investigating.

His room was at the end of a dark hallway, and while it wasn't the Ritz, the bed was large and comfortable. Once inside, he dropped onto the bed with a grunt, removed his shoes, and leaned back against the headboard to relax a little. A cigar and a scotch would have helped him achieve that state, but on his side of the closed door was a sign in Arabic that he didn't have to be able to read to know that it warned him against lighting up on the premises. The picture of a cigarette with a red X through it transcended all difficulties with the written word. As far as the scotch, Libya was a dry country, and Duckey had no interest in getting dragged off to a Libyan prison by the country's version of Eliot Ness.

Even so, it felt good to lie down and allow the strain of the day to slide away. Before allowing himself to drift off, however, he decided to discharge one last duty and then call it a night. Fishing his phone from his pocket, he found Espy's number and dialed. When he brought the phone to his ear, he didn't hear the customary sounds his phone made when attempting to make the connection. He pulled the phone from his ear and looked at the display, surprised to see that he was in a dead zone with not even the hint of a bar to offer encouragement.

He hadn't used the phone at all that day, except to check the time, and so he didn't know if the lack of a signal was common to Al Bayda or just his hotel room. Regardless, his legs ached at the thought of heading out into the street to try to get a signal. Instead, he set the phone on the nightstand and reached for the room phone—a canary-yellow rotary phone, something he hadn't seen in over a decade.

218

While spinning the dial for the last in a long series of digits, he chose not to think about how much the call would cost him.

"Hello . . . ?"

"Esperanza, it's me—Duckey."

"I tried to call you a few minutes ago," she said, and what struck Duckey was how good it was to hear her voice, which he thought strange considering he'd never met the woman.

"I'm in my hotel room and it looks like I can't get cell service here."

"You found the one hotel in Tripoli without cell service?"

"Nope. I found the only hotel in *Al Bayda* without service," he corrected.

"Al Bayda?"

Duckey explained the interview with the Alamo clerk that had resulted in an abbreviated stay in the Libyan capital, then gave an overview of what he'd found out since arriving in Al Bayda—an update truncated by his having not learned as much as he'd hoped by now.

As he spoke, he sensed an impatient energy coming from the other end of the line—even with the high level of static coming through an old rotary phone in a cheap hotel in an African city. Consequently, when he finished and Espy jumped in without a pause, he was neither surprised nor offended that his efforts had been summarily glossed over.

"I know what he's looking for," she said with obvious triumph.

"Come again?"

"I know why Jack went to Libya. I know what he was going to sell to Sturdivant."

Throughout Espy's pronouncement her voice grew louder,

and Duckey noticed how the excitement brought out the Spanish flavor in her English. He pulled the phone away from his ear, only returning it when he felt that doing so would not burst his eardrum.

It occurred to him then that his immediate reaction to the news wasn't what he would have expected. Of course there was a level of pleasure at hearing the news, but Duckey also recognized a small amount of disappointment—envy, perhaps, that Esperanza and her brother had accomplished a good deal more than he had.

"Don't worry," Espy said. "From what I can tell, at least a portion of the staff is in Libya—near Al Bayda, in fact—which makes you our man on the ground now."

"The staff?"

"That's what he's after," Espy said. "He was looking for a staff mentioned in the Bible. It's called the Nehushtan."

"Never heard of it."

"Didn't your parents take you to Sunday school?"

"They didn't serve Bloody Marys in church," Duckey said.

"A shame," she said. "Well, the Nehushtan was a pole with a brass snake on it. According to the Bible, Moses made it to heal people of bites from a plague of snakes God sent them."

Duckey was well aware that the abbreviated account Espy had just provided was likely leaving out crucial details— things that might have made the whole thing sound much less absurd.

"Let's back up a minute," he said. "God sent snakes to kill people and then changed his mind. But instead of just taking the snakes away, he has someone construct a snake totem to heal the people from snakebites?"

"That's right," Espy said, though her answer was slow in coming.

"Never mind the fact that while Moses—or his smithy—spent however many hours it took to make this fake snake, the real ones kept slithering around and biting people?"

"I suppose, yes . . ."

"Then there's the fact that one of God's biggest commandments—from what I remember, it was something he felt pretty strongly about—was that the Israelites weren't supposed to make any idols. But then he tells them to put a snake on a pole, have people pray to it, and voilà!"

"I don't think they actually prayed to it," Espy said, and yet Duckey's questions had taken the confidence from her voice.

Duckey blew out a deep breath, his exasperation all theater. "I guess it has to be true. I don't think you can make stuff like that up."

The silence that greeted him was one he couldn't qualify. And as it dragged on, he began to wonder if Espy had taken genuine offense at his irreverence. He was about to issue a mild *mea culpa* when she responded.

"It's amazing how much you sound like Jack," she said.

"Completely uncalled for," Duckey said, imagining the smile on Espy's face.

"I'm not afraid to pull out the big guns if you're going to get feisty with me," she warned.

"Point taken. Now, where were we?"

"We were in Libya, where it seems there's a biblical artifact waiting to be discovered."

"A brass snake pole," Duckey said.

"A brass snake pole," she agreed.

Duckey nodded to himself. "So Jack finds a clue in Milan that leads him to Al Bayda, Libya, and after he gets here, he just disappears?"

"No one just disappears, Duckey."

"Normally I'd agree with you. But this is Jack we're talking about. I wouldn't put anything past him."

Espy had to chuckle at that.

"Haven't you and Jack been down this road before? A few years ago, the two of you went after a biblical artifact and it almost got you killed."

"Apples to oranges," Espy said. "For one thing, I don't know of any super secret organization that would kill to keep the Nehushtan from being discovered."

"If there was a super secret organization, you probably wouldn't know about it," he reminded her.

"Another difference," she went on, ignoring him, "is that I'm not with him this time."

Both were valid points, and Duckey wondered if the years spent in higher education had simply left him soft. Before he'd retired, he wouldn't have balked at a dangerous assignment. Of course the difference was that Jack was his friend and was the one in harm's way.

"So what now?" he asked.

"It's up to you," Espy said. "We've confirmed the reason Jack went to Libya. Now you have to figure out what happened after he got there—if he even made it to Cyrene."

"How did we get from Al Bayda to Cyrene?"

Espy explained and Duckey stayed silent as she did so. He learned about the Greek ruins near the city he was in, and about the potential second piece of the staff that might be somewhere else entirely.

"You couldn't make this complicated?" Duckey asked.

Ignoring the comment, Espy said, "Romero and I are on our way. I'll call you when we reach Tripoli."

"You're not going to this other place, what did you call it? Cyme?"

"We thought about it, but this is about finding Jack, not hunting for treasure."

Up to now, Duckey had been twirling the phone cord while he talked with Espy. He saw the phone beginning to slide across the table. Releasing the cord, he watched as it unraveled between the table and the bed on which he sat. When the cord stopped unwinding, he leaned toward the table to push the phone back. It was from that position that he saw the small wire protruding from beneath it.

The instant he saw it, he froze. Then, after taking a short time to consider the implications of that one wire, he straightened and, with no change in the tone of his voice, exchanged a few parting pleasantries with Espy before ending the call. When he heard a dial tone, he used his finger to depress the cradle sensor. Setting the handset on his lap, he used his free hand to retrieve the TV remote control from the table, placing it across the cradle so he could remove his hand without reengaging the dial tone. That done, he picked up the handset and studied the mouthpiece.

As he peered through the holes, he saw nothing, so he unscrewed the cap, noticing it came apart a bit easier than one on a phone that old should have. When the cap came off, he didn't have to rely on his Company training to see the small chip-like thing that shouldn't have been there. After a snort of irritation, he set the partially dismantled handset on the table.

So they were bugging his calls. It made him wonder about the dead spot—if perhaps the Libyans were using some kind of dampening technology to kill the signal to his cellphone. Anyone could buy one online. For while the range wasn't wide, it was effective for a room the size of Duckey's.

He rose from the bed and walked over to the window, looking down at the street that ran in front of the hotel. The sun had long since disappeared, but he could see well enough to spot three cars parked across from the hotel. One was an old Dodge Caravan and he ignored that. The other two, though, were possibles. One was a dark sedan that he hadn't remembered seeing there when he'd returned to his hotel; the other was a decade-old SUV with tinted windows. His gut told him there were men in both, despite the fact that their assigning multiple agents to keep an eye on a middle-aged retired spy—who was only in the country to look for a friend—seemed like overkill.

He ran a hand through his hair, allowed the curtain to fall back into place, and walked back to the bed. What concerned him more than the agents parked out front was that they'd heard his call with Espy in its entirety. But even as he thought about it, he wondered what they would make of it. It would have been clear to anyone listening that the mission Duckey was on had nothing to do with the American government. Still, when it came to international politics, there was no way of telling how the Libyans would react. For all Duckey knew, they might assume the whole conversation was encoded and Duckey had passed crucial information to other agents.

Depending on the type and sensitivity of their equipment, they might have figured out that Duckey had discovered their bug. With that in mind, he returned to the curtain to see if he could spot any movement. Whether it was the fact that he'd looked out the window twice in the last few minutes or that he was right and they'd picked up on his tampering with the surveillance equipment, he saw the door of the dark sedan open.

The man who stepped out was wearing dark pants and a white shirt. No coat and no tie, as would have been standard CIA dress code. Yet even in the dim lighting, Duckey picked up on the sense of authority the man gave off.

Then the doors of the SUV opened, and two men, both looking like the one who'd exited the sedan, joined the first man. Together the trio crossed the street, heading for the hotel.

Duckey stood frozen for as long as it took for his dormant training to kick in. Hurrying toward the foot of the bed, he grabbed his suitcase, thankful he hadn't unpacked anything, and then moved to the door. Once in the hallway, he paused and looked toward the steps leading down to what passed for a lobby but knew he wouldn't make it down before the agents stepped into the hotel. To his right was the fire exit, with the large, boxy sensor attached to the release, but then Duckey saw the cut wires sticking out from the bottom of the box and guessed the door hadn't been used for its intended purpose in a long while.

He pushed on the release, hoping he wasn't wrong about

the door alarm and hearing the sounds of footsteps on the stairs behind him. The door opened with only a slight creak. Once in the stairwell, Duckey held the door handle as it closed, helping it to shut quietly.

He rushed down the single flight of stairs, his suitcase thumping against his knee. At the bottom was a small vestibule. He ran through it, pushed open the metal door leading outside. Stepping into an alley, Duckey stopped and took stock of his surroundings. The alley was empty, but the only way out led to the street where the sedan and SUV were parked. And he had no idea if other men had stayed behind and were waiting in the vehicles.

Still, he had no other choice. Sticking close to the wall of the hotel, he walked toward the street, slowing as he neared. Peering around the corner of the building, he saw the sedan and SUV, finding the vehicles unmoved. Because the vehicles' windows were tinted, he couldn't see if anyone had been left behind. Before stepping out onto the sidewalk, he took a half dozen steps back, then strode forward, giving the air of a man with every right to be walking out of a dead-end alley. Heading away from the parked cars, he resisted the urge to look behind him. He also avoided making the first left but instead proceeded through the intersection along with a few other pedestrians.

Only when he'd made it to the other side and had reclaimed the sidewalk did be begin to feel as if he'd gotten away cleanly, and he kept that feeling for as long as it took him to reach the next intersection. There, as he began making the turn that would take him out of sight, he chanced the glance he'd avoided earlier.

The sedan had pulled away from the curb and was passing

through the first intersection, and although it wasn't traveling at an excessive speed, Duckey's gut told him they were on to him. He quickly disappeared around a corner, hoping that he was wrong. Once around the corner, he cast his eyes about for somewhere to go, someplace he could slip into and get off the street. The first thing he saw that looked promising was a block away. Behind him, he heard the sedan round the corner, its tires squealing on the pavement, removing any doubt that they'd seen him.

Duckey took off in a run. He heard the revving of an engine close behind him. Pushing himself harder, he tried to ignore the fact that his lungs felt as if they might burst. Then he heard the loud screech of brakes and cringed against the sensation of metal on flesh that he knew was coming. Except that the blow never came. When he looked back, he saw that the dark sedan had barely missed a truck that had lumbered by from the other direction.

The near-accident bought him the time he needed, and a few steps later he reached a retail establishment that he saw was a cellular-phone store. He swung open the door and stepped in as quickly as he could. He didn't know if the agents behind him could have seen him enter with the obstacle of the truck.

As he looked around, he was glad to see there were other customers, which meant the one clerk on duty was too busy to do more than nod at him. Duckey moved toward a wall display of phones, searching for a back exit and finding one in a far corner of the store. That done, he turned so he could keep an eye on the street while not completely giving up on the ruse of considering a new phone.

It felt as if a long time had passed as he stood there, occasionally reaching for a phone and pretending to test some of its features. When he was on his fourth phone, Duckey was beginning to think that maybe he'd gotten away with it. He was about to set the phone back on the shelf when he saw the dark sedan come to a stop in front of the store.

Feeling a fresh rush of adrenaline, Duckey put the phone back and started for the rear exit, heading toward the sales counter, where the clerk was still busy with a customer. The clerk paid Duckey no notice until he saw the American pass by the counter. He called out something in Arabic that Duckey couldn't translate on the fly. Duckey ignored him and pushed through the door, emerging in an open space that looked as if it served as both warehouse and break room.

He ran by a folding table and some metal shelves and in another few strides he'd reached the rear exit. As he pushed open the door, he couldn't help but feel as if his entire escape attempt had been a series of door openings—as if, were he only to pick the right door, he would be home free. However, when he stepped through the newest door choice and into the sunlight, the blur of a man's fist accelerating toward his face told Duckey that he'd picked the wrong one.

Although the blow caught him by surprise, exceptional reflexes allowed him to turn his head a few inches before impact, which meant that the man's fist caught him in the cheek rather than flush on his nose. Even so, the pain was stunning and it was all that Duckey could do to keep his feet under him. But the ex-CIA agent was no stranger to a good fight, even if it had been a while since he'd had the opportunity to test his skills.

Forcing the stars away, Duckey raised his arm to block a second punch. Using his assailant's momentum against him, he sent the Libyan into the wall. Duckey then initiated a series of kidney punches until the Libyan, in an effort at self-preservation, pulled away and moved along the wall, trying to get out of reach of Duckey's large fists.

The American was not about to let his attacker off that easy, so he followed him. When he'd closed the distance, the other man delivered an elbow to Duckey's midsection that, despite the American's size and experience, took him to a knee—which meant he was unprepared when the Libyan agent used the same elbow to catch the nose Duckey had tried to protect at the outset.

Things went black for a while—how long, Duckey didn't know—but when he came to, he was on his back and the Libyan was readying to deliver a kick that would have broken a few of Duckey's ribs. As the man pulled his foot back, Duckey rolled into it, catching the kick before it could gain momentum. He pulled the agent to the ground. In a close quarters fight with a much smaller man, Duckey was in his element, pulling himself on top of him and delivering a series of brutal punches meant to end things before they escalated any further.

In seconds, the Libyan had stopped moving, and Duckey, after making sure he wouldn't come to too quickly, straightened and tried to catch his breath. Except that he knew there were more of them, likely in the store behind him, ready to step out of the back door at any moment. And were those men to see what the American had done to one of their own, Duckey doubted they would bring him in intact.

With that in mind, he ran his hands over the unconscious man's pockets, pulling out his wallet, phone, and a gun. Duckey took the first two without question, if for no other reason than to obtain information about the men who were after him. The gun, though, gave him pause. Because of his former profession, Duckey had used his share of firearms, and had taken a few lives in the process. Consequently, the feel of the gun in his hand was familiar; he could have slipped it into his pocket with ease.

Yet the fact that his current job—the one he practiced when he wasn't hopping around the globe in search of a lost friend—was of the genteel variety gave him pause about returning to something he thought he'd left behind. What helped him make up his mind was that he was woefully short on resources. And there were men after him who most likely had the same type of weapon as the unconscious man, and they wouldn't hesitate to use them.

Duckey pushed himself to his feet and slipped the wallet, phone, and gun into his pockets. Then he disappeared into the crowded city.

22

Once again, Jack found himself waiting. He'd woken up in his friend's house on the outskirts of a Tunisian town, every muscle in his body hurting and no way to contact anyone without giving away his position to a government with an array of agents at their disposal who'd like nothing more than to hunt him down and kill him. He'd spent the morning in Medenine, feeling relatively secure surrounded by Marwen's allies. The Tunisian had assured him that no one would get into or out of their community without him knowing. Jack was grateful for his friend's help and knew that, for the moment at least, his best course was to stay put.

He had rid himself of Imolene and Templeton, he seemed to have temporarily deterred the Israelis, and so far he'd avoided bringing danger to his friends. The problem was that he couldn't stay in Marwen's home forever. And when he left, there was no way to know what might happen. Of one thing he was certain: Marwen would do what he could to facilitate Jack's flight from the country, even if that meant using less than legal channels to secure that exit. Marwen wasn't a well-connected man—he was but a simple trader—yet he knew enough of the right people to pull some strings that would help his American friend.

As Jack waited, he thought of Templeton. It wasn't until he'd sent the man on his way, when he'd begun to feel some measure of safety within the walls of Marwen's home, that he could consider what the Englishman had told him. Of all the things that had happened in Australia those years ago, the one he most tried to forget was what happened in the home of James Winfield. In one evening he'd lost a man who meant almost as much to him as had his father, and he'd been forced to kill two men. One of those men was the brother of Martin Templeton. It seemed the man had spent significant time and effort trying to uncover what really happened that night, only to be stymied by the Australian government. He'd only been certain of one thing, and that was that Jack was involved. Then fate went and dropped Jack right into his lap. It made Jack wonder what would have happened had he decided not to search for the Nehushtan. If he and Templeton had never crossed paths, would the Englishman have eventually come looking for him?

As he pondered this, Marwen returned from wherever he'd gone earlier that morning, leaving Jack to entertain himself for a few hours. He wasn't long in the room before he picked up on Jack's mood, though he didn't know what had prompted it. He did, however, have a remedy. From a coat pocket, the Tunisian produced two cigars, offering one of them to his guest.

Jack smiled. "Thanks. Very kind of you."

"Think nothing of it," Marwen said, taking a seat next to Jack.

Neither man said a word as the cigars were clipped, lit, and savored. Some minutes later, Marwen cleared his throat.

"I hope you will forgive a curious old man," he said, "but I took a look at the thing you have brought into my home."

Jack used his cigar to wave off the apology. "I wouldn't have expected otherwise."

"Is it . . . ?"

Jack nodded. "It is."

Marwen released a low whistle.

Jack knew that at one time, Romero had done business with the man and that such business had involved items that had passed through Romero's shop. He knew that their history went back a long way, which meant he could trust Marwen with the knowledge that he had a priceless biblical artifact in his possession.

"I had wondered what sort of treasure is worth the danger in which you find yourself, and now I see."

Marwen's thoughts mirrored Jack's own, which reminded him that he was still not out of that danger.

"So what will you do now?" the Tunisian asked, reading Jack's expression.

"Not sure," Jack admitted. "Normally I'd call someone who could give me a hand—either a friend or maybe even the embassy."

"But your friends' phones will be monitored," Marwen said. "As for the embassy—"

"They might be reluctant to assist an American citizen

attempting to smuggle an artifact out of the country," Jack interrupted.

"Yes."

"Technically I didn't even find it in Tunisia, so I think the smuggling part is already done."

"Nevertheless, I do not think your embassy would care to split those hairs."

Jack was certain that what Marwen said was true. They were the reasons he hadn't found the nearest police station and marched in and told them what was going on. Because doing so would mean having to give up the artifact. He understood that the thing hobbled him, that refusing to divest himself of it meant limiting his options. But until all his other choices were taken from him, he would *not* be giving it up.

"What made you think it had not been destroyed?" Marwen asked.

"You're referring to Hezekiah," Jack said, to which the Tunisian responded with a nod.

"I am not as versed in biblical history as I am sure you are," Marwen said, "but I distinctly remember reading about how he had the thing destroyed so that the people would not worship it."

Jack couldn't speak to that part of the story as much as he might have liked. "I don't know," he admitted. "I was only able to track it back to about 200 AD. Before that, there's no record at all. At least none that I could find."

Marwen thought about that as he took a long pull on his cigar.

"But what made you begin looking for it in the first place?" he asked. "If the Bible says it was destroyed, why search for it?"

It was a question Jack would have been happy leaving un-answered, because to tell the truth meant admitting to dumb luck—a commodity with which he was intimately familiar. Giving Marwen the answer he wanted meant telling him that he'd been searching for something else entirely and that only the accidental reading of the wrong book—he'd reached for a different tome and hadn't realized he'd grabbed the wrong one—had set him on the Nehushtan's path.

"Let's just say that sometimes archaeology involves being open to opportunities when they present themselves," he said.

Marwen fixed him with a look that told the American he knew obfuscation when he saw it, but he let it pass—a gesture that Jack was grateful for.

"I can get you a car," Marwen said. "Or I can arrange transport anywhere you wish. There are several towns much larger than Medenine that would offer you the opportunity to leave the country. You could likely purchase transport out in either Gabès or Shkira, although I would recommend Sfax. It's larger. And I have friends in the shipping industry."

The thought of being packed up in a box and shipped somewhere made Jack smile, until he wondered if that was so far from the truth of his situation. Once again he lamented his inability to call someone like Duckey, who would have the whole thing figured out for him within an hour. Even talk-ing with Romero or Espy would have been helpful, if only to improve his mood.

As he thought of Espy, he couldn't help wondering what she'd done once he missed his flight to Caracas. If he were Espy, he knew what he would do: nothing. Jack knew that his years of being unable to keep a schedule, of eschewing the appearance of permanence, and in all other ways avoiding responsibility had left him in a position in which he could have probably gone missing for a month without anyone noticing.

On most days he would have found a thought like that amusing. At the moment, though, as he thought of how far away he was from Espy—in a relationship sense as well as in physical proximity—he found his mood growing even darker. For quite a while he'd known that she was dissatisfied with what he'd offered her. And she had every right to be, considering what they'd gone through together. He'd even suspected that she was coming close to ending things.

Had someone said that to him only a week ago, he would have returned with some flippant response, some statement filled with bravado. Now, as he sat in his friend's house in Tunisia, he felt completely different—about everything.

He missed her greatly. He only hoped he would get the opportunity to let her know.

———

The real problem, as Duckey saw it, was trying to hide in a city where he stuck out like a sore thumb.

He'd spent the night in an Al Bayda hotel several blocks away from the one he'd run from and had exhausted a good portion of his cash to secure the room. He could not chance using a credit card, knowing that, even though the domestic surveillance infrastructure in the country was woefully behind compared to the technology and tactics employed by his own government, it would not take them long to track his credit card use. They would have been at the door of his hotel before he'd finished brushing his teeth.

And so he'd paid in cash, said little, and slept in his clothes, and when he awoke the next morning, it had been with the understanding that the quality of his sleep had left something to be desired. With the sun rising enough for him to see the street, he slid the shade aside and watched for several minutes, looking for any car that passed more than once, or a parked vehicle that looked as if it didn't belong. But he saw nothing out of place and decided to take a shower.

Since the hotel didn't see the need to supply a private shower, Duckey padded down the hall and entered the communal bathroom, grateful that the shower area had been separated into stalls. He washed quickly and dried himself as best he could with a clean shirt. After getting dressed and brushing his teeth, he regarded himself in the mirror. A few days' worth of stubble begged for a razor, but it occurred to him that the face on his passport was clean-shaven and the facial hair might make him harder to identify if one did not look too closely.

Accepting that as a possibility, Duckey left the razor untouched and headed back to his room. Once there, he repacked the few things he'd removed from his bag and then sat down to plan his next move.

His primary focus had to be in getting out of the country. Had the Libyan authorities detained him at the airport, he would have undergone a few hours of questioning before they put him on a plane back to the States. The fact that he'd made it into the country, and that he'd successfully avoided a team meant to bring him in—or worse—meant that things would not go as pleasantly were he to allow himself to be picked up. In his experience, there would be no demands made on his government; he would simply be detained and questioned, and then either imprisoned or killed. His wife would never know what had happened to him. Indeed, aside from some unverifiable information that might make its way through clandestine channels to the ears of Duckey's former associates, he would simply disappear.

The prospect did not frighten him; he'd long ago come to grips with the idea of losing his life in the field, and of the CIA's need for plausible deniability. However, having been out of that line of work for a long time, he'd dismissed the idea that it might still come to pass.

As he considered the events of the last few days—events that had left him virtually stranded in Africa, with the forces of a small but vicious intelligence agency after him—he couldn't help thinking about Jack. His friend had always taken pleasure in vexing him, and were he to know the straits to which his disappearance had consigned Duckey, he had no doubt that Jack would be sporting a grin.

He couldn't think in those terms without also thinking of his wife, Stephanie. She would be expecting his call. Duckey hadn't been married while he worked for the Company; he'd spent far too much time in the field to even consider the possibility. It wasn't until he'd left government service and taken up vocational residence at Evanston that he'd considered his romantic future in anything but a transitory light.

He never took a trip without checking in with her, and even with the time difference between Libya and North Carolina that made connecting with her a challenge, he knew she was waiting for him to call. Long ago, he and Stephanie had come to an agreement that whenever he found himself away from home, he'd call her when he retired for the evening. In this case, that meant she would be expecting to hear from him somewhere between five and eight o'clock eastern standard time. When she hadn't, she would have called him. And the fact that he couldn't take that call—couldn't even turn his phone on—left him with a feeling of guilt he hadn't experienced in a long while.

The Libyan government knew who he was; they had access to all his records the moment he entered the country. Consequently, while it was possible they had his cell number, they most certainly were tapping his home phone. Accepting a call from Stephanie meant giving away his location, which was something he was not prepared to do. At least not at the moment.

It was the same reason he couldn't immediately call Esperanza. When he'd called her from the hotel, he had turned over her number to the Libyans. And that meant not only would her calls be monitored, her arrival in Tripoli would also be tracked. Considering these issues in the light of day helped him set his agenda—a list that, as he added items to it, grew considerably.

Pulling out his wallet, he saw that he had less than one hundred dinars and three American dollars—a paltry sum considering what he had to do.

After gathering his few belongings, Duckey did a sweep of the room to make certain he wasn't leaving anything, then walked out the door. In the lobby, he asked the man at the desk for the locations of the nearest coffee shops and banks.

Once the Libyan gave him the information, Duckey asked him for a few sheets of paper, sliding a couple of dinars across the desk.

Stepping outside, he took a few moments to scan the area for the same things he'd watched for from his room. He saw nothing suspicious and so started off toward what he determined to be the second nearest coffee shop, situated across the street from the third nearest bank. The selling point of both of these establishments was that, of all the coffee shops and banks mentioned, these were the ones situated closest to each other.

It took about five minutes before he reached Ben Arous, a well-traveled street that bisected Monastir and Msah. Duckey located the coffee shop in short order. Dodging the people who filled the sidewalks, Duckey reached the establishment and followed a pair of young women inside. The line moved quickly, and after parting with a bit more of his meager resources, he had a steaming cup of coffee and a table at which to drink it.

Thus situated, he pulled a pen from his pocket and arranged the paper on the table. He retrieved his phone and pressed the power button, his eyes finding the clock on the wall and noting the time. It was 7:42 and he guessed he had less than ten minutes.

When the phone powered up, he drilled down into his contacts list and began to transfer a selection of numbers to the paper as quickly as he could. Of the more than forty entries in the phone, he transcribed five and was in the process of committing the last one to paper even as he dialed one of them.

Esperanza picked up on the second ring.

"I don't have much time," he said. "So I just need you to listen. Your phone has been compromised so this is the last call you'll receive from this number. Do you understand?"

It took a moment for Espy to process what he'd said, but when the gravity of Duckey's voice hit her, she acknowledged her understanding.

"Don't come to Libya," Duckey said. "They'll have tracked your identities through your phone records and you'll never make it through customs."

"Who—?" Espy started to ask, but Duckey cut her off.

"You and your brother need to either stay where you are or go investigate the other place we discussed. I'll be in contact as soon as I can." He looked up at the clock. 7:43. "Don't call this number again."

He hung up and was dialing another number before the clock had ticked over again. He knew how early it was back home and that Stephanie would be sleeping, but she answered on the second ring, sounding remarkably alert.

"You're late," she said, and while Duckey could hear the affection in her voice, it also held a hint of worry. He thought that appropriate, however, considering the hour he was calling.

"Steph, I need you to listen to me. Before I say anything else, I want you to know that I'm okay and I'll be home as soon as I can, alright?"

"Okay," she said, intuiting that it was important to Duckey that she give some sort of acknowledgment.

"I don't have much time." He glanced at the clock—7:45. "There's something happening over here that's going to require me to stop using this phone. So this is the last call you're going to get from this number."

As he said the words, as he weighed each one against the ticking of the clock, he felt a sick feeling building in his stomach.

"I understand," she said, and Duckey could hear a quiver in her voice.

"That's my girl," he assured her, but that was all the encouragement he could spare. "As soon as we hang up, I want you to call the guy I used to play tennis with. Tell him where I am and that I could use some help. Got it?"

He wouldn't share the name of his old boss with anyone who was listening and had to trust Stephanie to make the connection. And because of the roundabout way in which Duckey had made the request, she probably also understood that their call was being monitored.

"I'll call him," she promised.

"I'm sorry I can't explain, Steph," he said as he rose from the table, gathered his papers, and headed for the door, "but I'll fill you in when I get back. And then we'll have a good laugh over it."

After telling her he loved her, Duckey ended the call. He left the coffee shop and crossed the street on his way to the bank. Reaching the ATM outside the bank, he pulled two credit cards from his wallet and took a cash advance on each. When he was finished, he felt a lot better about the condition of his wallet.

He looked at the clock on his phone—7:49.

Turning away from the ATM, he watched the cars passing by on Ben Arous. Seeing nothing promising, he started off again, heading toward Msah and continuing to scan the traffic as he walked. He held the phone in his hand, his thumb on the power button. Before long, he spotted what he was looking for.

As the pickup drew closer, Duckey moved his thumb away from the button, leaving the power on. Then, as the pickup drove past, its speed hindered by the traffic, Duckey tossed the phone into the back of the truck, where it landed among a stack of cement bags. He watched long enough to make sure the driver hadn't seen the disposal, and then he went on his way.

23

Esperanza pounded on Romero's door, knowing that her brother slept deeply. And with all the walking they'd done since arriving in Milan, it might take a thunderclap delivered by the Almighty himself to awaken him. It was almost noon and she had been up for hours, even getting in a workout in the hotel gym. Although their flight to Tripoli wasn't scheduled for departure until almost four in the afternoon, she knew Romero was liable to awaken with just enough time to shower and get to the airport.

She pounded again, this time calling his name through the door, and was soon rewarded by sounds from the other side: a fumbling with the lock, the door opening. Romero looked as if she'd awakened him while it was still dark and not with the sun nearing its zenith.

Seeing the stern look on his sister's face, he shook off the vestiges of sleep, moved aside, and allowed her to enter. As he closed the door behind them, Espy related her call from

Duckey, her words coming so quickly that they clipped each other on the way out. As the phone call had been brief, it didn't take her long to complete the telling.

His initial response was a wide yawn, despite the gravity of the news, but when he was done he adopted the expression that told her he was giving the news its due consideration.

"So we head to Cyme," he said with a shrug.

At that, Espy's eyes widened.

"You're talking about abandoning Duckey," she said.

"Not at all. I'm talking about doing what a former operative for the CIA has suggested we do." Before Espy could reply he went on. "What do you propose? That we fly into Tripoli and find ourselves detained, as he said? Or perhaps engage in a surreptitious border crossing? What then? If he's no longer using his phone, how do we contact him?"

Of course, Espy knew all of that, but sometimes she needed someone like Romero to push her in the right direction. She understood that, while they shared the same blood, she ran hotter. Given some time to think things through, however, she generally avoided making choices based solely on her level of passion. That alone had been what had kept her from killing Jack when he'd walked back into her life three years ago. That and the fervent religious belief she had accepted not long before Jack's coming. That was why she needed her brother now—to help her make the right decision instead of the passionate one.

"You're right," she admitted. "I just don't like leaving him to fend for himself."

"Of the three of us, Jim Duckett is best suited to be put in such a position," Romero reminded her. "In fact, my guess is that he will call on some of the same resources that made him an asset to you and Jack in the past."

Espy was forced to admit that Romero was right. But she didn't have to like it.

"Alright," she said. "Change of plans. We go to Cyme."

"Wherever that is," Romero remarked, and Espy knew that he was considering how many more appointments he would have to cancel the longer their adventure continued.

As he placed the phone back in its cradle, Boufayed found himself wondering if he had done something that would occasion his continued rise within the organization or if the information he had provided to the undersecretary would bring about the end of his career. What he decided was that great things were not accomplished without equally great risk.

Rising from his desk in the office he'd taken upon his arrival in Al Bayda, he walked to the window and looked down on the street below. The view paled in comparison to the one from his own office window, but he also knew that somewhere on those streets, there was a man who stood to make up for what he'd lost with the death of the German historian. Because, in Boufayed's mind, there was no way these two events could not be connected.

Admittedly the information they'd gleaned from the American's phone call had been minimal and the incompetence of those who had planted the bug had tipped the man to the fact that he was under surveillance. Because of that, the prospects of uncovering additional information about the artifact were slim, especially now that he had gone to ground.

That was the reason for Boufayed's call to the undersecretary—to inform him that an American agent was wandering the streets of one of Libya's largest cities, that he had switched to paper currency and cut off all contact. In his decades playing the game, Boufayed knew what James Duckett would do. He would not run; rather, he would find a hole and settle in until the pressure eased. Only then would he attempt to leave. And Boufayed knew that an agent of the CIA could dig in deep, and could wait a very long time.

There were only two courses of action available to him. First, he would spread a net, hoping the American would make a mistake. And then he would watch the borders with greater care. Duckett would eventually require help, and that help would come from outside.

Boufayed returned to his desk, but rather than turning his attention to the report he'd been reading, he reached for the Christian Bible he'd had one of his aides bring him that morning. He was not a religious man but did appreciate much of the philosophy espoused in the book, as well as in the Koran more widely read among his countrymen. Too, in the culture in which he lived, it was beneficial—even necessary—to have more than a passing familiarity with the Scriptures. He opened it to the portion he'd bookmarked and reread the story in its entirety. An abbreviated account, it did not provide much detail, yet enough was there to paint a vivid picture in Boufayed's mind.

It was the sort of account that lent credence to the possibility that the event had happened, if not in the book's final form, then in some fashion—before the mysticism espoused by a primitive people had added to it the fantastic elements that made for good fiction.

Despite his failure to believe in the account as it was written, Boufayed saw no reason to discount the possibility that the staff itself existed. The presence of a CIA agent in his country, and the hint that an archaeologist had gone missing in the hunt for the object convinced him that ignoring the prospect of its reality was not an option.

To recover an object of antiquity in his own country, regardless of the religion to which the item belonged, would provide Boufayed with a groundswell of support that, if he were to move in the right manner and at the right time, would greatly increase his political capital.

Then there were the Israelis, who apparently wanted the artifact badly enough that they'd risked sending in Mossad agents to recover it. The thought of claiming the staff before they could succeed in what could only be an alliance with the Americans was something Boufayed could not pass up.

Something like the staff was a rare opportunity to achieve something extraordinary. So as far as he was concerned, the American could stay in his hole for as long as he wanted. Because Boufayed would be there waiting for him whenever he chose to emerge.

The car worked its way through the thick traffic that clogged the streets of Milan, a mass of disparate parts made up of cars, buses, mopeds, and anything else with wheels, combining to form a single organism. The car became part of that organism and then, after a few miles, separated from it, pulling up in front of the cathedral. A man emerged from the car and walked quickly toward the massive church, entering the duomo without so much as a glance at the architecture. Once he was inside, another man joined him. They greeted each other in Hebrew before switching to Italian.

"Where are they?" the first man asked.

"They're staying at the Carlton Baglioni and have not yet left."

The first man nodded and then turned his attention to the altar area.

"It's this way," said the other, gesturing for him to follow.

When they reached the dais, the first man gave it a quick perusal but did not stop. Instead, he allowed the other to lead him to the sarcophagus.

"You are certain they discovered something here?" He reached out and felt the smooth stone of the tomb, sending his fingers over the lines cut into the lid and the interment chamber.

"I sent pictures to our experts and they believe they may have discovered something, although they are not certain."

This was received with a nod.

"I took the liberty of conducting a background check once they checked in to their hotel," the second man said. "The woman is Dr. Esperanza Habilla. A foreign language expert with the University of Caracas. The man with her is Romero Habilla, an antiquities dealer."

The first man raised an eyebrow. "Habilla . . . are they married?"

"Brother and sister."

"Interesting."

After regarding the tomb for a few moments longer, he pulled his hand back, smiling at an elderly couple who had approached, camera at the ready. As he stepped out of their way, the other man gestured him aside.

"Why are we interested in them?" he asked.

"Because Jack Hawthorne used to teach with a man named James Duckett, who also happens to be a former CIA agent. And as Duckett is now in Libya, and as he called this Esperanza Habilla last night, we can only assume that the circle of this enterprise has grown to include them."

The other absorbed that and gave a nod.

"There is something else," he continued. "It seems that Hawthorne was also in Milan recently. In fact, his flight to Tripoli originated here."

The first man frowned.

"The involvement of the Americans complicates things," he said after a time.

"It always does." A pause. "Perhaps we should have hired Dr. Hawthorne to begin with."

"Ours is not to make such decisions."

"So, what now?"

"We wait to see what the analysts say. And we wait to see what the Habillas do next." He cast his eyes over the sarcophagus again, as if searching for something, then turned on his heel and left.

24

As Imolene drove, he all but ignored the man in the seat next to him—a man who hadn't spoken a word for several hours, not even to complain about the mild injuries the Egyptian had inflicted upon him. Not long after leaving the Medenine suburbs in pursuit of Templeton, the Englishman had surprised him by pulling the jeep to the side of the road, exiting, and then standing there until Imolene pulled in behind him. At that point, as Imolene watched in amazement, Templeton had reached into the back seat, picked up the staff, and removed the wrappings, revealing a broom handle. That done, Templeton had tossed the thing to the ground and strode to Imolene's truck, opening the passenger door and sliding in. The only thing that had kept the Egyptian from killing him in that moment had been the utter absurdity of it all. That hadn't stopped him, though, from making sure the other man was keenly aware of his displeasure.

Templeton had told him about the danger that would present itself if he returned to where Hawthorne had holed up, and so Imolene had been forced to choose a different course of action. Templeton, meanwhile, hoped to buy his life by helping to retrieve the artifact from the American. As Imolene headed north toward Gfat, he pondered what sort of help that might be. Still, Templeton had spent a good deal of time with the American and could have insights Imolene did not have.

He pondered his circumstances. Not every job turned out precisely as he'd planned it; it was the outcome that mattered, rather than the process by which one achieved that outcome. If he succeeded in recovering the staff, and if he was able to dispatch Templeton and Hawthorne to the Israelis' satisfaction, perhaps then he would see his current business arrangement come to an amicable end. He wouldn't fool himself into thinking he would ever work for them again, but if he could end the relationship with his skin intact, he would count it a win.

His musing was interrupted by the ringing of his phone. Recognizing the number, his first thought was that some higher power had orchestrated it. He answered.

"There has been a change in plans" came the familiar voice.

Imolene kept his silence, waiting for the man to continue.

"You will catch the next flight to Istanbul," the Israeli said. "Once you arrive, I will contact you again."

Imolene understood that acceptance of any directives given him was the best choice. However, leaving northern Africa for Turkey was a significant enough change in the parameters of his employ that he felt the need to ask, "While I'm pleased to do as you ask, would you tell me why my presence in Turkey is needed?"

"It's needed because you have lost what we are paying you to recover, and because there is the potential that you may yet redeem yourself."

There was nothing in the Israeli's tone to indicate the words were personal or were a threat of any kind. Rather, the statement told Imolene that this was nothing more than an expedient business arrangement—one the Israelis could end when, and in whatever manner, they chose. It was one of the reasons he didn't mention his knowledge of their foray into Tunisia. Admitting to that sort of information would have made his position even less tenable.

With that in mind, he decided to tell them of the recent turn of events, with Templeton expressing special interest at the mention of his name. When Imolene had finished, there was a calculating silence on the other end of the line.

"Bring him to Istanbul," the man said.

Imolene pondered that—how he would get through the airport a man who would have no desire to do so.

"Tell Mr. Templeton that accompanying you to Turkey is the only hope he has of living once this mess you've caused is over."

Imolene acknowledged his understanding. After ending the call, he turned to Templeton and gave the man a smile, although it was absent of any kindness.

Duckey removed the gloves, now covered in black dye, and tossed them into the trash can next to the sink, then turned his attention back to the mirror. He tried to review his work, despite the crack that ran through the center of it. He thought the black hair made him look younger, especially with the touch-up of the thin beard that had begun to show the gray spots. The difference between the man who looked back at him in the mirror and the picture in his passport was significant enough now that few people would make the connection at first glance. When one threw in the added effects of sleep deprivation and stress, which had caused dark circles to form under his eyes, the transformation was even more remarkable.

He grabbed a handful of paper towels and dabbed at a few spots on his temple and next to his ears, where ash-colored water was gathering to form a run down to his neck. He watched for a while longer, towels at the ready, but didn't see any additional runs.

Sending the towels after the gloves, Duckey removed his clothes and changed into a pair of old jeans and a long, flowing white shirt—both of which he'd purchased at a thrift store. As Duckey had walked the streets of Al Bayda over the last few days, he'd noticed that more than half the people he saw wore jeans. The long and baggy shirts were common as well. Duckey had marveled at the variety of colors and patterns of the shirts, though he'd opted for white so as to draw as little attention as possible.

Once dressed, he donned the Yankees cap he'd received in trade from a teenager in exchange for his lighter. Duckey had tried to offer the kid money, but the boy had held out for the lighter. When he finished, he gave himself one more review and found himself chuckling—wondering if even his wife would recognize him if he came up to her in a crowd and stood at her side.

Satisfied, he gathered his clothes, stuffed them into the thrift-store bag, hoisted the bag that had made the trip from the States with him, and exited the restroom. As he walked past the counter, the man who had allowed Duckey the use of the café bathroom did a double take at the man who'd gone in as an American and come out as some indistinguishable ethnicity. Duckey kept his eyes forward and exited onto the street, where he entered the flow of foot traffic and remained there until he reached his next objective.

Entering the cellular store—the same one through which he'd negotiated his escape the previous evening—he purchased two disposable phones, paid to add extra minutes, and paid the added fee to have them activated at the point of sale. Minutes later, he walked out, almost a hundred dinars lighter.

He walked for fifteen minutes, surrounding himself with people whenever possible and keeping his head down when he didn't have the assistance of a crowd. As he'd given thought to where he should go, he decided that his first order of business was to get out of Khansaa. He thought the Libyans would concentrate their search in that neighborhood, which created an incentive for him to find a hole somewhere they wouldn't expect—which was why he was headed toward Andulus. As the heart of Al Bayda's legislative district, with homes that rivaled a decent suburb back in the States, Andulus would have seemed to harbor few places in which an unsavory element such as he could have disappeared. But Duckey had reviewed his map carefully, comparing it against what he remembered from his cab ride into the city, and had decided that it would do just fine.

When he entered the neighborhood, he adjusted his posture, straightening his back and raising his head. If someone belonged in a good neighborhood such as this one, they acted like it. Using the same techniques in Andulus that he'd used in Khansaa to maintain his anonymity wasn't an option.

Picking a road that took him along the eastern edge of the district, Duckey walked with purpose but still avoided eye contact with anyone he passed. After several minutes, he entered a part of the neighborhood that looked a lot like the section of Khansaa where he'd run into trouble, and he began to search for a place into which he could disappear. He found it two blocks farther down, in the form of a hotel that looked much like the one Duckey had occupied the night before. Entering, he paid for a room for one night, appreciating that the man who took his money and gave him the key didn't look up, not even once.

His room was on the second floor. Duckey ascended the stairs, slipped the key into the lock, and retreated into his temporary sanctuary. After he closed the door and threw the dead bolt, he gave the room a once-over. While it left a lot to be desired, he thought it would do.

He tossed his bags onto the bed, then went to the window and looked down on the street but didn't spot anything worrisome. Leaving the window, he checked the entire room as a precaution, despite that there was no way anyone would have known he'd selected this hotel.

Satisfied, Duckey pulled one of the phones from his pocket and dialed one of the numbers he'd copied from the phone he discarded. Tom kept the number unlisted, which meant he would answer even if he didn't recognize the number.

"Hello?"

"Tom, it's Jim," Duckey said.

"Where are you and what do you need?" Tom asked.

"I take it you heard from Stephanie?"

"Probably thirty seconds after she hung up with you."

"How is she?"

"How do you think she is? She's scared and angry. And for your sake, I hope she focuses on the scared part when she sees you."

Despite the circumstances, Duckey couldn't help but smile, the short conversation already making him feel better about his prospects.

"Tell me what's going on," his old boss said, who was still the CIA unit chief.

After a long sigh, Duckey did just that, filling in as many of the details as he could. Throughout the telling, Tom Fitzpatrick remained silent, listening. When Duckey finished, the other man allowed the silence to stretch out as he considered what his former agent had told him. When he broke that silence, he did so with the familiar manner Duckey remembered from the old days.

"I assume you've found a spot where you can hole up?" Fitzpatrick asked.

"I have," Duckey affirmed. "Cash only. Disposable phone. Regional clothing."

Fitzpatrick grunted his approval. "I don't have anyone in the area. Maybe one local guy, but no one I'd trust with an extraction. How long do you think you're good for?"

"I'm good for however long you need me to be."

"Alright, because I'm not sure how long it's going to take to arrange everything."

"Understood." Even though Duckey's situation was on the precarious side, he felt a sense of ease come over him.

"Jim," Fitzpatrick said, and it was clear by the tone that he didn't share Duckey's feeling that this was just a walk in the park, "Just so you know, I had our side check the records. Customs in Tripoli has no record you went through."

While the news served to dampen Duckey's mood, he couldn't say that it surprised him. The only reason they wouldn't have a record of him entering the country was because they didn't expect him to leave.

"Thanks, Tom," he said.

"I'll be in touch," Fitzpatrick said and then he was gone.

Duckey held the phone to his ear for several seconds after the call ended. When he finally lowered it, he set it on the nightstand, retrieved the TV remote, and settled in to wait for his next call.

It had happened while Jack was outside, enjoying a walk through the quiet community. Marwen had left again, giving Jack the run of the place and assuring the American he could walk the grounds secure in the safety of the small hamlet. It was early afternoon and he'd walked down to the street and then across it where the sloping ground gave him a postcard-worthy view of the ancient city. How long he stood there he couldn't have said, but he knew that at some point the tension he'd been feeling eased. He even forgot that there were eyes watching him, ostensibly for his safety. Nonetheless, it was disconcerting.

He watched the unfolding of life in the city, his vantage point giving him the metaphorical historian's view, as if he could see its past and its future along with the present. That was one of the chief reasons he spent so much time in this part of the world, from northern Africa to the Middle East and on through some of the ancient places in Europe. It was to feel a connection to a history that eluded him, even as he uncovered many of its secrets. Looking out on a city like Medenine, he couldn't help but wonder that civilization had run through its paces in this spot for thousands of years. When Christ walked the earth, the city below him was thriving.

Reminding himself of that helped put things in perspective. It allowed him to think about the treasures he found, the artifacts he discovered as they would have been in the times that saw them created or used. Thinking of the Nehushtan not as a mystical staff hidden in a north African cave but as an icon of hope for a beleaguered people was sobering. He could imagine the hasty crafting of it, and he admired the beauty of it more because of the attention to detail that went into it—despite the urgency of its need. And he could picture the scene of its only other biblical reference: its destruction at the hands of a king intent on appeasing God, who had turned his back on the nation.

Jack frowned, remembering that that part wasn't true. The Nehushtan hadn't been destroyed; he had proof of that in the house behind him. And that made for a tricky question. As a believer, he'd come to accept that large portions of the Bible he had once thought of as fables were in fact the accurate account of historical events. His own experience was sufficient to make that case. However, he didn't know where he came down on the question of the Bible's complete accuracy. He'd read enough of it to have his doubts about what Espy had called inerrancy, which Jack thought was just a religious label that meant the whole thing had been thoroughly fact-checked by the king of all editors.

From what little Jack had ascertained in researching the matter, he'd come to the conclusion that most theologians supported inerrancy for the principal reason that a failure to do so raised a number of difficult questions. Chief among them was that if the Bible wasn't accurate in every detail, how could the reader be tasked with identifying what was true and what was not? It was a question well beyond Jack's ability to answer.

To Jack, it seemed that truth was in how one looked at something—that perhaps approaching something in the Bible from a different point of view provided one with something that was true in one sense, yet perhaps not entirely accurate from a more rigid interpretation.

He had pondered all of this while city life progressed below him, and he had just decided to head back up to the house when something that had been nagging at his mind for a while suddenly swam up to the surface. When he latched onto it, he broke into as much of a run as his sore knee would allow.

Reaching the house, he burst through the door and found the Nehushtan in the main living area, once again leaning against a corner, as seemed to be its lot since Jack had liberated it from the cave. As he had used the original cloths to wrap a broomstick, he removed the bed sheet that now protected the artifact. He held it up to the light, turning it around so that the eyes faced away, so he could see the back of the serpent.

When he saw what he was looking for, he broke into a grin.

"It's all a matter of one's perspective," he said to himself.

Releasing a tired but happy sigh, he set the staff back in its corner and went to gather up his belongings.

25

Jack could have made the call from Marwen's home, but his presence had already put the man in enough danger, regardless of the Tunisian's protests to the contrary. So he'd borrowed a car and driven to Sfax, into a city center of clean-lined white buildings and stone streets that made much of the city look like an angled chessboard.

As he drove, Jack had the feeling of being in any coastal city on the other side of the Mediterranean, with the palm trees, open layout, and the lights that came on outside the restaurants, clubs, and shops that made up the city's nightlife. It didn't take him long to find a place that looked as good as any in which to pull over.

One of the benefits of making a call like the one he was about to attempt while in a populated area was that if it didn't go as well as he hoped, he had some time to find a place to hide. Too, he assumed that the people whose work he witnessed in the decimated village just two scant days ago would be less inclined to conduct the same sort of operation in a thriving metropolis.

With the car parked, Jack exited and indulged in a long stretch before pulling Templeton's phone from his pocket. Neither his nor the Englishman's phones had been switched on since the moment Templeton determined that the Israelis were tracking them, and he knew that pressing the power button was a gamble now.

He looked at the phone for a few seconds as people walked by, singles and groups of various ages and ethnicities. Then he shrugged and turned the thing on. He went to the menu and, while there was no way to tie a listed number to Templeton's former employers, he guessed that the number called most over the last several weeks would be the one.

It rang twice before it was picked up.

"This must be Dr. Hawthorne," a voice on the other end said.

Jack was surprised at that but then supposed he shouldn't have been. The Israelis might well have known that the pair was no longer traveling together and that Jack had taken the man's phone.

"And you are?"

"Someone who wants what you found in the cave" was the answer. Jack didn't know an Israeli accent from a Jordanian one, but he guessed the former.

"And yet you've not once asked nicely," Jack said. "It's all angry Egyptian giants and covert teams."

There was a pause from the other end.

"We acknowledge that things have gotten a bit out of hand," the Israeli said. "But the quickest way to end all this unpleasantness is to bring us the staff."

"You'll forgive me for not being as assured by that as I might be," Jack said.

He was enjoying himself, despite the fact that he was ticking off someone who worked for a government that had shown no qualms about killing those that got in their way. But when the Israeli responded, his voice didn't harbor any animosity.

"You must understand, Dr. Hawthorne, that when we send our people in to retrieve something important to us, it can be exceptionally dangerous. We have lost a number of men and women."

That might have been the one thing he could have said that would make Jack feel anything other than cool resolve.

"I'm sorry," he said.

"And so when we send in other people to do something we are not able to do, and when the ones we send appear to betray us, there can be a heavy-handed response."

Jack wasn't sure he bought that, but in the end he didn't suppose it mattered. "I want to make a deal."

"What sort of deal?"

"A trade. The Nehushtan for my life and the lives of my friends."

Jack was sure that this representative of the Israeli government, or at least a faction within that government, had been expecting such an offer, which made the long pause before his replying seem contrived.

"Agreed. Tell me where you are and I will send someone to you."

Jack was smiling before the man finished. "Do you read the Torah?"

"Of course."

"Then you know that Hezekiah was to have destroyed the Nehushtan."

"Obviously that did not happen."

As Jack talked, the sea of people passing in front of him had increased.

"I'm telling you that it did happen," he said. "Just not in the way we're made to think when we read the story. We have this vision of him destroying it completely—burning the staff, melting down the serpent. But what if the word *destroy* meant something else?"

"What are you getting at, Dr. Hawthorne?"

"The Nehushtan is in two pieces. I have one of those pieces." He could hear the man's breathing through the phone—the sound of exasperation.

"Why should I believe you?"

Jack had been expecting that question. "Give me a minute." Pulling the phone away from his ear, he opened the car door and removed just enough of the bed sheet to see the tail. He snapped a photo and sent the image along. "You'll be getting a picture soon. I want you to notice the tail."

He waited for what seemed a long while for the Israeli to speak.

"I see it," the man said.

"Good. Then you'll notice the very end—the way it looks like there's something missing?"

After several seconds, his adversary said, "I will send you a team. They will support you as you search for the missing piece."

"That's not how this is going to work," Jack said. "Instead, I'm going to the airport tomorrow, where there will

268

be a voucher waiting for me and an exemption to transport antiquities. I'll use that voucher to fly wherever I want. I'll find the missing piece and then I'll turn both pieces over to you. After which we'll part ways and never see each other again."

He understood that he didn't hold many cards. If the Israelis really wanted the staff, and if they were unwilling to trust him, they could come for him, claim the artifact, and then expend whatever resources were necessary in order to find the missing piece. After all, Jack was confident he could find it if given the time and resources. He had to think a well-funded government research unit could do the same.

"And if we refuse?"

"Then I destroy it," Jack said.

"You would not do that," the Israeli replied, but Jack heard the question in the statement.

"If it's a choice between a biblical artifact and the lives of my friends, I wouldn't think twice about it."

He ended the call without waiting for a response. Then, for good measure, he powered the phone down.

He stood on the busy street, pondering what he'd just done. He was taking a huge chance, but most end games were not without risk. The real risk would come if he did find the second piece, and if he failed to turn the pieces over to the Israelis. They had killed people just to add something to their collection. As far as he was concerned, that made them unworthy to have it. Making the deal bought him a ticket out of the country. More important, it got him someplace in the Western world, where he stood a chance of finding a way out of the mess he was in—and perhaps keeping the artifact in the process.

With that in mind, he got back into the car, relocating so that if they had tracked Templeton's phone, he wouldn't be there when they arrived. After that, he had another call to make, a call he'd wanted to make for days.

———

"Hello?" said the most beautiful voice he'd ever heard in his life, with an understandably hesitant inflection.

"Have you missed me?" Jack asked.

Perhaps two seconds passed before it clicked for Esperanza, and Jack had to pull the phone away from his ear to survive the scream.

"It's nice to talk to you too," he said.

And then Espy had the floor, talking in that rapid-fire way that only she could do, regardless of the language. Jack couldn't follow all of it but understood a number of the key words, as well as the general sentiment.

"Wait a minute," he said when she took a breath. "One question at a time."

Jack spent the next couple of minutes sharing the events of the last week in broad strokes with Espy, and while Jack's story required more than a little suspension of disbelief, the benefit of the things they'd been through over the years was that there were few things that could happen to either of them that the other wouldn't in the end believe.

When he'd finished, Espy chuckled. For Jack, hearing her laughter through the phone was the best thing to happen to him in a long time. And as he extended that thought, he realized that this also included the discovery of the staff.

It was a revelation that surprised and pleased him at the same time.

"Do you think things like this happen to normal couples?" she asked.

"I wouldn't know," he said with a laugh that mirrored hers.

"So where are you now?"

"Sfax. A coastal city on the other side of the Mediterranean."

"And you have the Nehushtan."

He knew how Espy would view that. Once again he'd put his life in danger to procure something he thought was valuable. Inadvertently he'd also put the lives of her and her brother in danger, though he didn't expect her to know that. What he wasn't prepared for, though, was the somber tone in her voice.

"There's a lot going on that you don't know about," she said, and then she proceeded to share with him everything that had been done on his behalf. When she'd finished, Jack was dumbfounded.

"You got Duckey to go to Libya?" was all he could think to say.

"Jack, he's in trouble."

Jack ran a hand through his hair, considering all that Espy had told him.

"Have you called his wife?" he asked.

Espy admitted that she hadn't.

"As soon as I get off the phone with you, I'll call her and see if he's checked in." He shook his head and added, "Duckey knows what he's doing. He'll get himself out of whatever he's gotten himself into."

He said it because he had to, and Espy understood that, but Jack couldn't help but feel tremendous guilt that, once again, his actions had caused harm to people he cared about. And in light of what Espy had just shared with him, the staff had lost some of its draw.

He was about to offer additional encouragement when Espy, a note of panic in her voice, spoke first.

"Jack, he said my phone was compromised."

"He what?"

"I'm sorry, Jack. With all the excitement I forgot. They've probably heard everything."

"Who has?"

"I don't know."

Jack blew out a breath. "Okay, I'm going to hang up and call Stephanie. Then I'll find a way to call your brother's phone. It'll be from a different number."

Seconds later, the phone was off and Jack was left wondering how a single phone call could turn a man's world on its head.

It took three tries before he remembered Romero's number, and the Venezuelan answered on the first ring.

"You've alternately upset my sister and made her extremely happy, so I am undecided regarding whether I should injure you or hug you when I see you next," Romero said.

"I've had a few of your hugs," Jack said, "and I think you could go either way and it wouldn't matter too much."

He knew that if he was in Romero's presence at that moment, the man would have wrapped him in an embrace that would have squeezed the air from his lungs.

"It's good to hear from you, my friend," Romero said.

"Same here," Jack said.

He paused as someone passed behind him. Jack had convinced the lobby desk clerk of a hotel he wasn't staying at to let him use the desk phone. He'd told the man that he couldn't get a dial tone on the phone in his room, and while he felt bad about the lie—which he hoped indicated spiritual growth of some kind—he reasoned that it was for the greater good.

"I'm in a bad spot here so I have to be quick," Jack said.

"Understood," Romero returned.

"I spoke with Duckey's wife and she told me in a roundabout way that an old friend of his at the Company is going to pull him out of Libya."

"That's good news," Romero said. "Can I take it from his bride's circumspectness that she believes her phone is also being monitored?"

"I think that's a valid assumption."

Out of the corner of his eye, Jack saw the desk clerk growing impatient. He would know the call was long distance, and good customer service only went so far.

"That's why I think we need to listen to him and not try to find him ourselves. He's right—we'd get picked up the minute we got off the plane."

"So what do we do in lieu of that?" Romero asked.

"That's the million dollar question," Jack said and he heard Romero snort in response.

"Esperanza said you won't leave Tunisia without the staff

and that you have brokered some deal to make that happen. And if you do not mind my being frank, I think that cheapens what has been done on your behalf."

It wasn't the comment that struck Jack so much as the man who'd made it. In years past, Romero had accompanied him on many an outing, and while danger hadn't become an element in Jack's work until the last few years, the Venezuelan had always possessed a sense of adventure that made him the equal to any challenge. He wondered, as he considered his response, if Romero's stance indicated that he too was entering a more mature phase.

The clerk was looking at him again—a more pointed look now. Jack ignored him.

"I understand what you're saying," he said. "But even you have to admit that this isn't just a treasure hunt anymore. I've seen men killed for this thing and now we have someone tapping our phones and sending Duckey on the run. Are you going to tell me that you just want to walk away without seeing this through?"

While pleading his case, he'd turned away from the clerk to avoid seeing the man's dour expression. But when he turned back, he saw that the look on the Tunisian's face had changed. He seemed to be hanging on Jack's every word.

"Except that you are ready to risk your life for something that is not even whole," Romero said.

"What . . . ? How did you know the staff was separated into pieces?"

"Surely Espy told you about Cyme."

Confused, Jack said, "I'm not following. What about Cyme?"

274

He heard fumbling on the other side of the line and the next voice he heard was Espy's.

"There are two pieces," she said.

"I know," Jack said. "It's missing part of its tail."

"The other piece is in Cyme."

Jack paused. "That, I didn't know," he finally said.

"Which is what you get when you decide to travel without a linguist," she chided.

"Believe me. If I have the opportunity to make a choice like that again, I'll think it through a little better. Now, do you want to explain?"

Espy did, beginning with their discovery of the Gafat text around the symbols and the subsequent discovery of the second destination. By the time she finished, Jack felt thrilled for the discovery and irritated that he hadn't made it himself.

"Al-Idrisi was a crafty one," he said with admiration. "I never would have known about the location of the second piece." At the clerk's puzzled look, he put a hand over the phone and said, "Al-Idrisi hid one of the symbols we need in order to find the second part of the staff, using a language that no one's spoken in hundreds of years. But an associate of mine just so happens to speak practically every language known to man, so she was able to figure it out. Are you with me?"

The clerk nodded to indicate he was on board, but judging by his expression Jack thought he was just saving face.

"Good. Try to keep up," Jack said before turning his attention back to Espy. "So we head to Cyme," he said, and despite the fact that he thought she shared his enthusiasm, her silence suggested she wasn't ready to head to Turkey just yet.

"What about Duckey?" she asked.

It was a legitimate question—probably the only question she could have asked that stood a chance of derailing the train.

"I'll tell you the same thing I told your brother. There's no way any of us are getting into Libya—at least not quickly. Yeah, we could probably sneak in across the border, but what would we do after we got there?"

"I don't know," Espy admitted. "But it just doesn't feel right to look for the second piece of the staff when we don't know what's happened to him."

Jack didn't begrudge her those feelings, because he shared them. Duckey was a close friend, and the thought of anything happening to him because of something Jack had done sickened him. He'd watched friends die before and would give anything to never have something like it happen again. Yet he knew there was nothing he could do to help the man. The CIA had sent help and the U.S. government was in a significantly better position from which to render aid. Too, the thought that kept coming to his mind was that finding the rest of the staff would put an end to all of it.

He shared this with Espy, the only person in the world who could understand, because she'd lived through so much with him.

"Alright," she said after Jack had given her time to consider. "How are you going to get to Turkey? I know you said you've worked something out, but they're not going to let you take a rare artifact out of the country."

"Don't worry, I've got it covered. I'll find some way of

getting into Turkey. Why don't you and your brother go and I'll call you when I get to Istanbul."

He could sense Espy's hesitation.

"Are you sure?"

"Absolutely. I'll meet you in Istanbul within two days."

He knew there was no certainty he could offer her, and Espy was strong enough not to require any. What was becoming clear to Jack—and it was something that should have been clear to him long ago—was that she required him. And he was starting to remember that it was a shared need.

"I'm sorry," he said softly.

"For what?" she asked, although she needn't have.

"For walking away again."

She could have told him that he hadn't done that—that they were still together these three years later. But it wouldn't have been the truth and both of them knew it.

"I love you," he said, meaning every word.

"I'll see you in Istanbul," she replied quietly and then the line went dead.

Jack stood holding the phone to his ear for a long while. When he finally came back from where he'd been, he turned to hang up the phone and found the desk clerk waiting with expectation.

"She said she'd see me in Istanbul," Jack said.

He couldn't tell if that answer satisfied the man. He didn't even know if it satisfied *him*.

He left it at that, offering the clerk a tired smile and walking away.

When Boufayed walked into the room, he was already in a poor mood, having made no gains in locating the hidden American agent. He'd taken his frustration out on those around him and he could see that knowledge on the face of the technician who turned in his direction.

He was less familiar with the Al Bayda office than he was with the one in Tripoli, but he could see that the technical analysis unit was almost as advanced as the one in the capital. Even in Tripoli, though, he rarely visited this room, even if he appreciated the information it provided. He knew that the hum of the servers, the clicks of multiple fingers dancing over keyboards, and the playback of recorded conversations were a music of sorts that, when worked over by those with the proper skill set, produced a symphony. Simply put, he had too much to do to spend time observing the accumulation and analysis of raw data—data that would make it to his desk at some point if the men and women studying it determined it was worth his review.

At present, the data that had come in—that continued to come in—was worth the personal touch.

The room he entered was sealed off from the rest of the floor, and the entire ten-meter length of the far wall was lined with flat-screen monitors. Below the monitors ran a large table with keyboards spaced evenly along its length. In front of each keyboard sat a technician, wearing headphones and watching the screen in front of them with clinical interest. Some of them looked back as Boufayed entered, but only one gestured for him to approach.

Boufayed stood behind the technician, watching the dark image on the screen. He could see a bed, and someone beneath the blankets, although it was too dark in the room for Boufayed to tell much more than that. After watching for a time and seeing no movement, not even the rise and fall of a blanket to tell him that the man was breathing, he addressed the technician.

"Let me hear the call," he said.

The technician's hands flew over the keys and the image on the monitor changed. The room was lighter and he could see a man sitting at a desk near the wall opposite the camera. He could see only the man's back.

Freezing the image, the tech handed back his headphones and, once Boufayed was ready, set the scene in motion. Boufayed listened to the entire exchange, though he could only hear one side of the conversation. As much as they'd tried to procure the technology that would allow them to crack the security protocols used on the phones the Americans issued to their agents, they had been unsuccessful. And for calls such as the one he was watching and listening in on, the people who worked in this office were tasked with filling in the part of the conversation that went unheard.

As Boufayed listened a second time, he tried to forget about what he'd been told by his analyst. But willful ignorance was a difficult skill to master. Still, even with his attempts to prejudice what he'd heard, he found himself agreeing with the analyst's assessment.

He returned the headphones to the technician.

"It's not much," the young man said, "but there are a few phrases that make me believe he's about to try to help someone get out of the country."

Boufayed nodded. He'd heard the tells as well. Again, he

279

thought his analyst was correct: an extraction attempt was in the works and he could think of no one who needed that service more than a missing CIA agent.

What gave him pause, however, was the conversation he'd heard between Esperanza Habilla and a man named Jack. He assumed he was the missing archaeologist who'd been referenced in other calls. Boufayed was still amazed that she'd spoken so freely on a phone that she should have suspected was no longer useful for private conversations. Her slip had been a boon to the Libyan, for it had provided information he would never have been able to get otherwise. It almost convinced him to suspend the hunt for Jim Duckett. He wondered how much more he could hope to learn from the man, and what that information would cost him in resources. More often than not, though, good information was worth considerably more than the cost to obtain it.

Even so, the decision to use the new information to apprehend Jim Duckett was not an easy one. The man who appeared on the monitor, the picture having switched back to a real-time feed, had cost them a great deal of time and money, which had been spent toward the development of a surveillance system that could track his every move. It wasn't often that an intelligence agency had the opportunity to monitor the movements of another nation's agent working in the field. One did not make the decision to burn that resource without good reason.

What tipped the scales for Boufayed was Agent Robert Ingersoll, whose handlers felt that Jim Duckett was worth the risk to Ingersoll's painstakingly cultivated placement. If they valued Duckett that highly, how could he not?

"He will have to make contact with Duckett in order to arrange the extraction," Boufayed said.

"Of course, sir," said the technician, but he was speaking to Boufayed's retreating back.

26

"You have no idea how much I appreciate this, Tom."

Tom Fitzpatrick broke into a laugh, which told Duckey that, on the contrary, the man did know how much Duckey appreciated it, and that a recompense of some sort had been factored into the assistance. Once the laughter subsided, he said, "As soon as they get you in, you and I are due for a long talk. Checking someone's records is one thing, Jim. Using the Company's resources to smuggle you out of Libya is another thing entirely."

"I understand," Duckey said.

"You know I'm always willing to help out," Fitzpatrick said. "But whatever it is you've got yourself mixed up in has you asking for more resources than you ever did when working for me. I can't keep doing this without someone asking questions."

"And I'll have the answers to each and every one of those questions as soon as I can shake your hand," Duckey promised.

"Fair enough."

After Duckey ended the call, he turned his attention to the street, waiting for the signal from whomever Fitzpatrick had sent. He wore the headphones he'd picked up in the cab that had stopped at the corner early that morning, and that he'd ridden around the block in once before returning to his room.

In Duckey's mind, the operation had already taken too long. In his day, he would have been in and out in less than sixty seconds. He was a firm believer that no amount of planning, checking and rechecking could take the place of rapid deployment and a precision extraction. Still, he knew it wasn't his game anymore; things had changed and he could only sit back now and let younger men do what they'd been trained to do.

His hand drifted to the gun on the table—the other item left for him in the cab. It would be untraceable, the serial number filed away. Tom had broken several rules in getting it to him, and Duckey knew he owed his friend for that too.

Less than two minutes after he'd finished with Fitzpatrick, Duckey saw a white Ford Taurus roll up, parking a few buildings away in a spot near the truck with the flat tire. According to the company name and information on the door panel, the car belonged to a local flower shop. Yet he couldn't see past the tinted windows to confirm that. That need was removed from him, though, when his phone rang.

"We're ready" was the simple message, spoken in perfect English.

"On my way," Duckey replied.

Letting the curtain fall back into place, Duckey rose and headed for the stairs, which he was forced to take at normal speed regardless of how much he wanted to reach the flower-shop car, as every step nearly sent him tripping over his dress. He wondered if the full Muslim wraps were now standard Company procedure or if Tom was just having fun with him. Even if the latter was true, he suspected he deserved it for what he was putting his friend through.

When he stepped outside, he saw that two of the car's occupants had exited. They weren't quite heading in his direction but were approaching circumspectly, a technique that allowed them to scan the area for threats while also leaving the exit point of their cargo a mystery until the last moment.

Though both men were dressed like locals, Duckey could see the telltale sign of a cord running from one of the men's ears to somewhere inside his jacket. Shaking his head, Duckey resolved to give these two a little advice about the art of remaining invisible. Of course he would wait until they'd ferried him somewhere a bit friendlier before doing so.

Duckey started for the Taurus, navigating his way through the people passing in both directions, although he was having a hard time seeing through the small space between the top of his nose and his eyebrows. He had no idea how the women here wore these things. And to make matters worse, he was sweating badly.

The car wasn't far away, but in the short distance he'd traveled he found that he was drawing a number of looks from the locals. He kept his head down, eyes forward, and resisted the urge to adjust his dress where it was riding up. Most passersby seemed willing to give the very large, per-spiring Muslim woman a wide berth and he was at least grateful for that.

He glanced at the agents, who apparently having seen that all was going according to plan, turned and headed back to the car. Duckey frowned beneath his veil at the break in procedure.

It was when the agents reached the car that Duckey—still some distance away—first felt it. He couldn't quite pinpoint what it was he was picking up on, only that it didn't feel right. In his former career, he'd become convinced that the truly good agents were those who learned to listen to their instincts, and then to act on them. And it seemed to him that the men who'd come to collect him were not paying close enough attention to their surroundings.

He never heard the car coming. One moment there was nothing and in the next a dark sedan had passed him and come to a stop in front of the Taurus, startling the agents who were about to get inside the car. The doors of the sedan flew open and Libyan agents piled out—three of them, their guns drawn. As Duckey watched, it became clear that at least one part of the training the younger generation hadn't missed was the part about setting down their weapons when faced with a stronger opposing force.

The Libyans hadn't spotted him. He'd frozen on the sidewalk, but that alone didn't give him away. Most of the people who had been passing by when the sedan came racing up had also stopped to watch what was happening.

Duckey continued to watch as the men Tom had sent were thrown against the Taurus and roughly frisked, and he knew he was watching his best chance of getting out of the city—out of the country—disappear. And that made him angry.

Gathering up the folds of his dress, Duckey stalked forward. The crowd of bystanders across the street began to notice him. When he reached the center of the action, one of the Libyans looked over and, seeing a woman in full robes, looked away again. Then, a moment later, something must have registered because he looked back—just in time to meet Duckey's fist with his nose. He went down like a bag of cement, and when the other Libyans saw what had happened— seeing a Muslim woman with a clenched fist standing over their downed colleague—they hesitated. That was all that Duckey needed.

He bull-rushed the nearest one, releasing a decidedly unfeminine roar as he drove him into the side panel of the sedan. Before the Libyan could slip to the ground, Duckey released him and turned his attention to the remaining Libyan agent. Duckey hadn't been quite quick enough; the Libyan had his gun out and trained on him. But his hand was trembling.

Duckey reached out and wrapped his strong fingers around the man's hand, pushing the gun down and to the side and then using his other hand to bring the Libyan in close, until the man's nose was an inch away from Duckey's own. He looked into the man's eyes and saw nothing but raw fear. Then the gun fell to the street and the Libyan pulled himself loose, turned and ran away.

When it was over, the people gathered along the sidewalk began clapping. Breathless, Duckey acknowledged the crowd's applause with a nod of his head, his smile hidden by the veil. He went to the men who'd been sent to take him someplace safe. They both looked dumbfounded.

Duckey clapped one on the shoulder. "That's how it's done,

boys," he said, then slipped into the car, making sure to gather up his dress before shutting the door.

───

When Boufayed reflected back on the events of the last week, he could see various points at which he could have made different choices. With so many avenues that might have benefited from his focus, there was no need for him to show more than a passing interest in a German historian, or decide to dive into the presence of a retired CIA operative in Al Bayda. He could have selected from an almost endless supply of cases and worked any of them to satisfactory results. But he'd selected the cases he had—or perhaps they had selected him—and now he had to either benefit or suffer from them.

He'd reassigned the agents who had failed in their attempt to bring Duckett in. While Boufayed was alive, they would see nothing but desk duty. What made things worse was that the failure had sent two other agents into the wind; all of them were either at the embassy or had found another means of flight from the country. All that was left for him was to report his failure to the undersecretary, who was unlikely to punish Boufayed but who would realign his ever-changing hierarchy of senior agents.

He had almost resolved to dial the phone when one of the agents who still remained in his favor entered the office. Boufayed made a motion for the man to sit.

"What do you have?" he asked, nodding at the paper the man held.

"Information about the place Jim Duckett mentioned

on his phone call to his associate in Milan," the man said. "Cyme. It is the ruins of a Greek city in Turkey. We have reviewed the available literature and there is no reason to think that it holds anything of value."

Boufayed processed that information while the agent sat in silence. Boufayed knew the man well, knew that he would have performed his due diligence. However, what Boufayed understood was something that one could seldom gain through research. Rather, a man needed to see a number of years spreading out behind him in order to see that there were things one could not prove in order to believe.

"We are going to Turkey," he said in his usual abbreviated style.

He could see the order take his man by surprise, but he recovered quickly. Rather than ask questions, he rose and exited the room, on his way to carry out Boufayed's directive.

After he was gone, Boufayed wondered why it was that men, even when they knew what they were doing was a foolish thing, continued to do that thing. He, of course, knew the answer to that. It was because all that a man needed was a single occasion when the performance of his action did not produce a foolish result. A single such instance could carry a man for a long while. Great accomplishment was not without great risk.

He sat at his borrowed desk and pondered that.

***

Jack stepped off the plane and into what might have been the busiest airport terminal he'd ever seen. He'd never had occasion to fly into Istanbul, despite the many times he'd passed through the city. As he walked through the concourse, he took it all in, enjoying it in a way that only someone who truly loved to travel could do.

As near as Jack could tell, he was only fifty or so miles away from the second piece of the staff, which pleased him beyond measure. He wondered if the Israeli agents on the plane felt it too—the end of the quest approaching. He hadn't noticed anyone on the plane, at least not anyone he recognized as someone assigned to keep an eye on him, but he would have bet a great deal of money that there was more than one.

He had already passed through customs, armed with the paper that told anyone who cared that he was allowed to carry the long serpent pole around with him. Once he finished there, he passed through the regular security checkpoint, and when he stepped past the part of the walkway where he could no longer turn back without facing the wrath of the security staff, Jack saw a flurry of movement and then something flew at him with enough force to cause him to nearly drop his carryon. By the time he processed what had happened, he'd already instinctively wrapped his arms around Espy. He was the first to let go, although she wasn't quite ready and held on for a while longer. When she finally pulled back, Jack found himself pulled into another embrace, one of a more bone-crushing variety.

"It's good to see you, my friend!" Romero said.

Jack reached over and squeezed Romero's forearm, but his eyes didn't leave Espy.

Neither of them spoke for a long while as Jack simply took in the sight of her. There was much he'd learned over the past few weeks, and he and Espy were due for a long talk to cover all of it. But an airport terminal in Turkey was not the proper place for that discussion.

"Thanks," he said—a simple word but one vested with much meaning and he knew she would understand.

When he glanced at Romero, he saw the man's eyes on the thing in Jack's hand. As he'd been carrying the thing around with him for what seemed far too long, he extended it to his friend. Romero took it gingerly and, after glancing around, pulled the bed sheet back. He didn't regard it long—perhaps twenty seconds—but when he had replaced the makeshift wrapping and held the item out to Jack, he wore a satisfied smile.

"Was it worth it?" Romero asked him.

Jack drew in a deep breath, his eyes moving to Esperanza.

"If you'd asked me that a few weeks ago," he said, "I may have said yes. Now . . . I'm not so sure."

Seeing her emerge from the terminal, Imolene's first thought centered on her beauty. He usually insulated himself from such considerations and suspected that it was a testament to the woman that she could make him lose focus on what he had to do.

The Egyptian watched her brother—a man as large as he was—set their bags next to the rental car. With them was Hawthorne, and Imolene's eyes narrowed at the sight of the man. The Israelis had called him only an hour ago to tell him that Hawthorne would likely join the Habillas in Tripoli. The

American held the staff as casually as if it were a piece of luggage, and the man's demeanor—and the fact that he'd eluded Imolene thus far—angered the Egyptian. He kept the anger in check, though, understanding that he would have time to work out his issues with the American once they reached the ruins. After loading their bags in the trunk, the trio got into the car and it pulled away. Imolene let it get a few car lengths ahead before he told the driver of his cab to follow.

In the seat next to him sat Templeton, who still had said very little. Indeed, the man seemed to have lost his spirit entirely, and nowhere was that more evident than in his apparent unwillingness to attempt an escape. It had been in his mind since Medenine that the only reason Templeton had given up, had thrown his lot in with the man hunting him, was because he'd had little choice. Hawthorne had thrown him to the wolves and his only hope of survival rested in turning the wolf. Once they'd reached the airport, however, there had been ample opportunity for the Englishman to simply walk away, knowing that there was little Imolene could do to him in such a crowded place. And once they'd reached Istanbul, the chances to flee had increased exponentially. It left Imolene wondering if Templeton had something in mind that was hidden from Imolene, or if perhaps the Englishman had lost his senses.

It was something he didn't have time to consider at present, he told himself—although he had no doubt that the proper moment would come.

27

The fifty miles from the airport to Cyme passed too quickly for Jack's liking, which was as good an indicator as any that something was wrong with him. Under normal circumstances he would have been chafing at the bit to reach the ruins, to begin the process of searching for the missing piece of the staff. But as the car Romero had rented chewed through one mile after another, it was all Jack could do not to ask him to slow down.

He'd slipped into the back seat with Espy and had taken her hand in his almost the moment he sat down and neither of them had let go. Romero didn't seem to mind that he was alone in the front and left his sister and his friend to whatever discussion he imagined they needed to have.

"I'm sorry," Jack said after a long silence.

She'd been watching out the window, but after he said it she turned her attention to him.

"That's something I've heard a lot of from you over the years," she said.

"But this time I mean it," he said, and for once there was nothing in the way he said it to leave any doubt as to its truth.

She studied his face for a while, as if searching for something. "Do you know why I went to Milan?"

"You already told me. I went missing and you came searching for me."

She was shaking her head before he finished. "Why would I have been searching for you? You go missing all the time. I probably wouldn't have started worrying until you were three weeks late."

While Jack could appreciate that, it also puzzled him.

"I went to Milan to tell you we're through," Espy said, no humor in her voice. "I was going to meet you at the museum when you showed up to sell the staff to Sturdivant, and I was going to tell you I didn't want to see you again."

Hearing that, Jack found himself at a loss for words, but what really struck him was that he didn't feel any of his normal defenses rising. Perhaps it was because he knew she was right—that she'd said nothing he did not deserve.

"And I wouldn't have blamed you for it." It was an admission that she must not have been expecting because her eyebrows rose. "I've spent a good portion of my life digging up things that people have lost, thrown away, or considered valuable enough to place in pottery and surround with gold. And the one thing I'm starting to realize is that sometimes what you pull out of ancient trash piles is the priceless stuff, while the things people tried their best to preserve wind up being sold on eBay for ten bucks."

"I have no idea what that means," she said.

"It means he's finally starting to realize that you're worth a lot more than the old musty things he pulls out of the ground," Romero said over his shoulder.

Jack nodded in agreement. He wasn't sure if the back seat of a rental car in Istanbul was the proper place for such a talk, but he was willing to try. Yet before he could continue, his phone rang. Releasing Espy's hand, he fumbled around in his coat pocket and pulled it out. When he saw the number, he broke into a grin.

"Hey, Ducks," he said.

Duckey said, "If you decide to go after Noah's ark next year, you're on your own. I've had it."

"Duly noted."

"They made me wear a dress."

The mental picture Jack formed from that statement made him shudder. "Was it your color?" he asked. Hearing Duckey laugh pleased Jack more than he could say. "I'm sorry I didn't call you. I spoke to Stephanie this morning, and she didn't know anything so I figured you were still working things out."

"I was," Duckey said. "In fact, I still am."

"What's that supposed to mean?"

"It means I'm not about to let you have all the fun. Look behind you."

Incredulous, Jack turned and saw Duckey waving in the car behind them.

"You're kidding," he said.

"My flight landed right after yours. I saw you in the terminal, but you slipped out before I could get to you."

"You want us to stop?"

"Why? We're just about there."

Jack swung back around and looked ahead and saw that Duckey was right.

———

"How old are they?" Espy asked.

"No one knows for certain, but there are records dating back to the fifth century BC," Jack said.

He held the staff, still in its wrappings, and with it began to walk around the ruins. Like many ancient cities, much of it had been reduced to rubble—so much so that the only standing structures were a single wall from the temple to Isis, a pair of freestanding pillars, and a wall from a building of indeterminate use. Jack had read about Cyme but had never visited, something he regretted now that he needed the information.

"What are we looking for?" Romero asked. He'd appeared at Jack's side and, hands on hips, looked every bit the expert ready to dig in.

"Your guess is as good as mine," Jack said. "But we've proven that this thing hasn't gone untouched for thousands of years. It's seen the light of day a few times or else Espy wouldn't have found the Gafat text in Milan."

"So we're looking for a structure that's still standing," Romero reasoned.

"I'd say that's a good bet."

They separated, with Romeo heading toward the neglected temple and Duckey in the direction of the lone wall.

Espy tugged at Jack's arm. "That leaves the pillars for us."

As they started toward them, Jack found himself reaching for Espy's hand. But she moved it out of reach.

"There's time for that later," she said, a hint of a smile in her voice. "Right now we have work to do."

The four of them worked beneath the sun for more than an hour, scouring every inch of every piece of stone that rose more than two feet above the ground. Jack and Espy were on their third round of studying the second pillar when they were joined by Romero, who wiped the sweat from his brow with his sleeve.

"I have touched every inch of that accursed wall," he grumbled. "There's nothing there."

"I'm in agreement with him," Duckey said as he walked up.

"Well, I can't be in agreement with him too, because that would mean we came all this way for nothing," Jack said.

"Which is a distinct possibility," Romero added.

Espy, who had been studying the pillar from the other side, came out from behind it, brushing the dust from her pants. She gave Jack an apologetic look and shook her head.

"In my opinion, these pillars are the only place where someone could hide a relic while still retaining a marker for its eventual recovery," Romero said.

"That's my thought too," Jack said. "But I'm at a loss."

He glanced over at Duckey and then back at Romero, who was also wiping the dust from his hands. Jack watched as the fine particles went up and scattered with the breeze. When he turned back to Espy, she had an odd expression on her face. She looked at her hands.

"Espy?" Jack asked.

She reacted as if Jack had startled her.

"'You will crawl on your belly and you will eat dust all the days of your life,'" she said.

297

"Excuse me?" Jack said.

"It's from Genesis," Espy said. "The curse God placed on the serpent that tempted Eve."

"And what's it mean?"

Instead of answering, Espy went to her knees in front of one of the pillars and began to dig, removing dirt from around the pillar down to a few inches below the surface. Not entirely understanding what she was up to—although in looking at Romero, who appeared to be tracking with his sister—Jack began to do the same around the next pillar.

"What are we looking for?" he asked.

"A snake hole," Espy replied.

A half hour later, they found it after digging out a foot of earth. The hole was small and would likely have gone unnoticed except for the fact that it was a perfect circle.

Jack stepped into the ditch they'd dug and lowered himself until he was on his side. He peered into the hole but saw only darkness.

"I don't see anything," he said.

Espy took a turn looking and came to the same conclusion.

"That's impossible," Duckey said. "It has to be here."

"Nothing has to be anywhere," Jack said. "Even if it was here at one time, there's nothing that says someone couldn't have beat us to it."

"In my store I sell a number of totems," Romero said. "Much smaller than these, of course, but similar in proportion." He paused and regarded the inscrutable hole. "Some of the totems contain primitive pressure locks. Places where one would insert a crude key—either a rock in a certain shape, or later, one made of metal." He lapsed into silence, continuing to stare down at the hole, as if he expected a snake to emerge at any time.

"But we don't have a key," Duckey said.

"I think we do," Romero said.

And then Jack understood what Romero meant. Stepping out of the ditch, he hurried to the staff and unwrapped it, then held it up for examination. The top of the staff was too wide, as was the base. He looked closely at the serpent's truncated tail.

He hurried back to the pillar and, taking a knee, angled the staff so that he could slide the snake's tail into the hole. A few inches of the staff disappeared into the stone before Jack felt resistance. He slowed but kept pushing, and through the staff he thought he felt something click. Before pulling it out, he shared a look with Espy, who returned with a wide smile.

Pulling the staff free, he stood and presented the holy relic for inspection. The tail had added a good seven inches to its length and it was difficult to find the seam. However, the large stone at the tip of the tail made a review of seams a secondary concern.

"What is that?" Jack asked.

"A ruby," Romero said. "A very large one."

The two old friends shared a look, and Jack shifted his attention to take in Espy as well, who beamed with the same thrill of discovery. He was turning to congratulate the last member of their party when he heard a gunshot, followed by the disintegration of the pillar six inches to his right.

Jack had been shot at enough in his life for his response to be instinctual. He crouched down, making himself half his normal size, and then ran, grabbing Espy's hand and dragging her along in his flight, dropping the Nehushtan in the process. Chancing a glance over his shoulder, he saw at least four men emerging from the cover of the trees that provided a border for the ruins.

He saw that Romero was also running, heading for the wall he had spent hours exploring. That left Duckey who, as Jack watched, pulled a gun and began firing on the attackers.

"Libyans!" Duckey shouted.

The attackers scattered, and even with the difficult task of running while looking over his shoulder, Jack thought he saw two of the men carrying a third between them.

Jack and Espy had almost reached cover where several large trees would offer some protection, yet as he closed to within a few steps of the nearest tree a shape suddenly loomed before him. At first, Jack couldn't process the man's identity, but then he realized that was only because the prospect of the man turning up in the ruins of a Greek city in Turkey was something he'd never considered.

Jack couldn't halt his momentum before Imolene raised a giant fist and sent it sailing toward Jack's nose.

28

Jack huddled behind a tree, blood streaming from his nose, fighting to keep from passing out from the blow delivered by the Egyptian. From his position he surveyed the field, tried to see where everyone had wound up after the gunplay. The only person he saw was Romero, who waved in Jack's direction—a gesture the American returned.

Jack tried to process everything that had just happened. He'd lost Espy to the Egyptian and had no idea where he'd taken her, though he suspected they would not have gone far. His abduction of Espy seemed strange, because Jack was certain he would have been the man's target.

Because he'd lost his bearings in the scramble, he took a moment now to consider where everyone had been standing, hopefully to provide him with a better understanding of the direction they'd all scattered to. He suspected the Libyans had retreated behind the temple, the only structure large enough to hide four men. Where Imolene and Espy could have gone, he didn't know exactly, but he thought the copse of trees at almost ninety degrees from his own location was as good a spot as any.

That left Duckey, and he suspected his friend could remain unseen better than any of them. In fact, he was a bit concerned for what Duckey might do to the Libyans.

By the time Jack had a clearer picture of his surroundings, silence had reclaimed the ruins. Aside from Romero, he felt as if he were the only person around for miles. He gestured to Romero to get his attention, and the Venezuelan returned with a shrug of the shoulders.

Almost forgotten, the Nehushtan rested on the ground in front of the pillar. Despite the fact that Jack would have left the artifact in an instant if it meant securing the lives of his friends, he couldn't keep his eyes from drifting to it. Earlier he'd suggested to Espy that the lure of discovery—the fulfillment that came from finding something extraordinary—was something that one, if not outgrew, at least learned to relegate to its proper place. At the time, what he'd told her had been the truth. Now, however, he recognized the stirrings of that thing inside him that superseded all else; it was something that lived by its own meter, lying dormant yet on occasion rushing to take control of him when he least expected it. While he'd carried the staff, priceless but incomplete, it had lacked much of the intangible quality that activated that covetous part of his soul. But with the promise of its wholeness within reach, he found it creeping in, ready to lay claim to his reason.

Twenty yards away from Jack, Romero hunkered behind a wall. He fired a fierce look in Jack's direction, as if intuiting his friend's thoughts.

Jack gave an acknowledging nod, even though Romero's admonition did little to dampen his desire to go after the artifact. He had no time to act on that desire, though, because a thickly accented voice called out, "You will come out or we will kill all of you." The words echoed amid the ruins. It was one of the Libyans.

Jack looked around, trying to determine where the voice had come from. He thought he'd been correct in placing them behind the temple of Isis. He didn't respond, nor did any of the others. Then Jack caught sight of the angry expression on Romero's face that suggested he was considering doing something foolish.

"You are heavily outgunned," the Libyan went on. "Your only hope of surviving is to step out and throw down your weapons." The conviction in his voice was such that Jack didn't doubt the man's willingness to make good on the threat.

"You're speaking as if the rest of us are working together," Jack finally called back. "Some of us aren't really concerned with anyone else."

Romero looked surprised by Jack's words, but Jack quickly motioned for him to remain quiet.

There was a long pause as the men who'd hunted for Duckey in Africa talked it out among themselves. When they responded, Jack couldn't fault their logic.

"Then I suggest that those of you who care for anyone else in the group—that you come out now. As for the rest, I'm sure we can come to some other arrangement."

Jack wasn't sure how to reply to that. Romero aimed a silent question in his direction; Jack answered with a shrug.

If these men were indeed part of the Libyan intelligence establishment, that meant they were professionals. They would kill everyone in an instant if doing so would help them meet their objective. But Jack also understood that if he went out there, he would be sacrificing his life but with no guarantee of saving anyone.

As he opened his mouth to speak, his words were cut off by a gunshot. Before Jack could react, several more reports echoed off the rocks.

Fearing that his friends were in harm's way, he took a single step before a frantic wave from Romero caught his attention. When he was certain he had Jack's eye, Romero pointed toward the temple. Imolene was emerging from the structure with Espy firmly in his grasp.

"Where's the staff?" Imolene shouted. He moved forward, pushing Espy in front of him. "If you do not turn over the artifact to me at once, I will kill this woman!" He raised his gun to Espy's temple.

"Wait!" Jack walked out from behind the tree, his experience with Imolene assuring him that the Egyptian was within a second of ending Espy's life. At the same moment, Romero burst into the open, ready to rush the man who held his sister.

"Where is it?" Imolene demanded.

"I don't know," Jack said. "Once the shooting started, I dropped it."

He made a pretense of looking around, surprised that Imolene couldn't see it. But all the commotion had kicked up a great deal of dust.

"Then you will find it," Imolene said.

"Listen, it's around here somewhere. And when we find it, you can have it. Now let her go, and take me instead."

Jack exchanged a look with Romero and saw that his friend had the same thought, except that while Jack was willing to trade his life for Espy's, Romero appeared ready to charge the man. Which would force the Egyptian to turn his attention to Romero and in turn allow Espy to escape. Jack knew they were both poor plans, yet he felt they were running out of options.

Then, out of the corner of his eye, he saw Duckey step out from behind the freestanding wall, leading with his gun. And from where Imolene stood, he couldn't see him.

Even as Duckey approached, though, Martin Templeton came out from the cover of the trees. Without hesitating, he walked up behind Imolene, raised a gun, and pulled the trigger.

For the first time since he'd met Templeton, Jack was convinced the man would shoot him if need be. His fevered expression revealed just how much he'd allowed his passion for the holy relic to consume him. His striking down Imolene had just confirmed the truth of that.

"I'm leaving with it, Jack," Templeton said, breathing hard.

"How did you get here, Martin?" Jack pointed to Imolene's lifeless body. "With him?"

The Englishman released a harsh laugh. "You abandon me to him and then you question why I might have joined him?"

"No one's questioning anything," Jack said, holding his hands up by his shoulders. He could see over Templeton's shoulder; Duckey hadn't budged.

Jack stepped forward and saw Templeton's hand flinch. Very slowly he crossed to where he'd dropped the staff. He bent to retrieve it, all the while anticipating the shot. But after a second look at Templeton, and after using his head to gesture toward the bed sheet, he walked the few yards and gathered it up. He made his way back and then quickly and carefully wrapped the staff. When finished, he approached Templeton but stopped several feet away, placing the staff on the ground between them. He then retreated, backing up to where Espy and Romero waited. Without looking at her, Jack reached for Espy's hand.

Templeton watched the trio for several seconds, and during that time Jack saw the sane part of the man begin to surface, although only for a moment—until desire swallowed it up again. With the gun still trained on them, the Englishman stepped up to the staff and lifted it from the ground. Once he had it in his possession, he held it aloft.

As he did so, Jack felt a sick feeling building in his stomach. The look Templeton aimed at the staff was almost frightening in its intensity. It lasted only a short while before he lowered the artifact and turned his attention to Jack, who wondered why Duckey hadn't made his move yet.

"I want to know what happened to my brother," Templeton said.

It was in that moment Jack understood that none of this was about the staff. Templeton was fixated on the artifact but only as a substitute for something else—something he considered more valuable.

He wanted answers.

"What happened in Australia is between me and God," Jack said, realizing how absurd that sounded but knowing that few people in the world had as tangible an example as he. He gave Espy's hand a squeeze and then slipped away from her, getting her and Romero out of the line of fire. "You have what you came here for," he said. "You're walking away with a once-in-a-lifetime find. Isn't that enough, Martin?"

"Normally, yes," he said. "But not today."

"Tell him, Jack," Espy said quietly.

He and Espy—and the few friends who knew—had made a pact to keep the events of those days to themselves. But Jack was no martyr; he wouldn't take the secret to his grave. He knew as well that Templeton wouldn't fall for a lie. He wouldn't even ask why the man needed to know. When Jack had lost his own brother, when an accident in a dig in Egypt had killed him, Jack would have given anything to have answers for all his questions. Only now, many years later, did he know that the kinds of answers Martin was seeking would be of no help. He also knew that Templeton would not come to that place for a long while.

He began recounting for Templeton how he'd come to kill the Englishman's brother.

Yet as he was speaking, Imolene stirred behind Templeton—the twitch of a hand at first, then a fluttering of the eyes. Jack didn't notice until Imolene raised his hand and by then it was too late.

Templeton staggered beneath the force of the shot. Even

then, Jack didn't think the man comprehended what had just happened. It wasn't until his legs began to give out, causing him to sink to the ground, that understanding seemed to dawn.

Then Jack heard a second shot that sounded as if it came from much farther away—the high whine of a sniper rifle.

The bullet found its target in Imolene's neck, and the Egyptian's eyes closed for the last time.

Startled, Jack glanced around for the sniper, but no one was visible beyond Romero, Duckey, and Espy. Jack rushed to Templeton, helping him to ease down. He removed the gun from the man's hand and tossed it away.

Romero meanwhile moved to Imolene's body, reached down and extricated the gun from the large Egyptian's hand.

Looking down at Templeton, Jack saw the man's mouth move but no words came out.

"Don't try to talk," he said.

Espy came to Templeton's side, her hand going to the man's wrist. "His pulse is weak." She took Templeton's hand, holding it between both of her own.

Jack nodded as he considered what to do. Seeing the blood that had already pooled beneath the Englishman, he knew there was little that could be done.

A small smile touched Templeton's lips and he turned his head toward Jack, trying to speak again, but Jack couldn't make out what he was trying to say. It was only on the third attempt that he understood the man was asking to hold the staff one last time.

Rising, Jack went to retrieve it. He returned to Templeton

and placed the serpent staff in his hands. He thought that the Englishman released a sigh, but he couldn't be certain. As Jack watched, Templeton used his remaining strength to shift the position of the staff until he was looking directly into the serpent's face. He seemed content as he stared into its eyes—an unblinking stare that made it look as if an invisible line had been drawn taut between snake and man.

Jack couldn't recall when he first noticed the ruby on the snake's tail begin to glow, but by the time he noticed he suspected it had been growing brighter for some time. Espy saw it too, her eyes widening, and the two of them— who had, together, experienced the full revelation of God's power in the most tangible of ways—watched as that same power was poured out over Martin Templeton. The ruby continued to brighten, and along with it Jack began to hear a buzzing noise that seemed to come from within the staff itself.

Romero had drawn closer, along with Duckey, who was limping. There was a trail of blood running down his pant leg.

When the buzzing sound reached a crescendo, the air around Templeton grew brighter. Jack wasn't sure if it was a result of the ruby that now was almost white, or if something else was at work. And then just as it had occurred, it disappeared with an equal abruptness. One moment the staff was glowing and buzzing, and in the next it was as if someone had flipped a switch.

Jack hadn't realized he'd been holding his breath until the need for air impressed itself upon him. As he began to breathe again, he saw Templeton's eyelids flutter.

Jack rose and left him to his private moment, corralling

Romero and Duckey as he moved away. Although his friends followed him, they couldn't help looking behind them, as if trying to process what they'd just seen. Jack couldn't blame them; it had taken him a long time to deal with it the first time too.

After putting what he thought was sufficient distance between themselves and Templeton, who was still in Espy's care, Jack turned back to take in the scene. Which was why he was the first one to see the men who emerged from the tree line, advancing on the group.

Duckey saw them next, and Jack took his cues from the expert, who didn't move or raise his gun.

The black-clad men paused when they reached Templeton and Espy. Jack, despite a hiss from Duckey, started toward them. He saw a single gun shifted in his direction, but he kept his hands out and stayed on course. Reaching Espy—who was still on her knees, looking up at the apparitions who'd materialized as if out of nowhere—Jack took her by the hand and helped her to her feet. Once she was at his side, he turned to the Israelis.

"It's yours," he said. "Both pieces."

One of the Israelis shifted his gun to his other hand and then bent down to take the staff. When he straightened, he brought it close to his face, and Jack saw him looking at the now-dormant ruby in the tail.

Less than a minute later, the Israelis were gone, which Jack suspected was their silent way of fulfilling their part of the bargain.

In the aftermath of the events at Cyme, all those involved resolved to keep their silence. At first, Jack had struggled with the decision, understanding that with spilling the blood of several men in a country not one's own, there existed a certain obligation to disclose the matter to the local authorities. But if past experience had taught him anything, it was that turning himself over to a potentially unsympathetic police force was not a thing readily done. Had extraordinary circumstances not served to spring Jack and Espy from their incarceration in Australia, they could both still be languishing in prison cells.

Consequently, while they waited at the hospital for Duckey, who was having the Libyan's bullet removed from his leg, they'd agreed to a blanket silence. Of course that silence had been tested when the police showed up at the hospital after having been called by the treating physician. They'd explained the incident away, though, and finally the police had left, if somewhat dissatisfied.

There were still some details to be worked out. Among them was how to get Duckey back to the States without a passport. Jack hoped that Duckey's CIA friends could spring for one last favor. If not, they'd have to work something out themselves.

Duckey had been in surgery half an hour when Espy— who'd been pacing the waiting room nonstop—finally came and sat in the chair next to Jack.

"It must have killed you to let them take it," she said.

Jack shook his head. "Not as much as you might think."

"But it was worth an absolute fortune," she reminded him.

"Point taken." Then, after giving it more thought, he added, "In the grand scheme of things, it's not that important."

"You can't be serious. You let a priceless biblical artifact get away and you don't think it's a big deal?"

Jack shrugged and leaned back in the uncomfortable plastic chair. "You've seen one holy relic, you've seen them all."

Espy opened her mouth but nothing came out. Then after seeing Jack aim a mischievous smile at her, she couldn't help but mirror it.

Which Jack liked because he didn't want to think too much about it. Despite his seeming indifference, it had been difficult to watch the staff walk off with someone else. But he remembered the feeling that had come over him in the ruins: the desire, the need that had made him want to run out and reclaim the Nehushtan. What had washed over him seemed to invalidate everything he'd told Espy on the way—that there were things more valuable than priceless artifacts. It was something he'd have to continue to ponder, perhaps for a long while.

Whether Espy could follow his progression of thought or not, she didn't pursue it and the two lapsed into a comfortable silence, one that Espy broke some minutes later.

"Do you think they'll misuse it?"

Jack sighed. He'd asked himself the same question.

"I think there are things that were meant to serve whatever purposes God wanted them to serve. And if they disappear after serving that purpose, who are we to make that call?" he said, not even sure he meant it. All he knew for sure was that when he'd handed over the staff, exchanging it for something much more valuable, it had felt right.

That line of thinking prompted him to think about something else that felt right. In truth, it had felt right for a long time. Reaching over the armrest, he took Espy's hand in his.

"I love you too," she said before he could say a word.

"I'll see you in Istanbul," he said, which meant the same thing.

Acknowledgments

As always, many thanks go to everyone at Bethany House for their hard work and support—Dave Long, Luke Hinrichs, Noelle Buss, Jim Hart, Debra Larsen, and many others.

Thanks to my agent, Les Stobbe.

And special thanks to everyone who enjoyed Jack's past adventures enough to want to see them continue.

Don Hoesel, the acclaimed author of *Elisha's Bones*, *Hunter's Moon*, and *The Alarmists*, lives in Spring Hill, Tennessee, with his wife and two children. Don holds a bachelor's degree in mass communication from Taylor University.

More Page-Turning Action from Don Hoesel

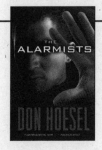